THE REAPER'S DAUGHTER

KM RANDALL

DMP

Dragon Moon Press

PRINT ISBN 978-1-988256-23-8
EPUB ISBN 978-1-988256-24-5
Library of Congress Control Number: 2015906859

Cover Design by Shari J. Ryan
Edited by Bethany Root

This is a work of fiction. Names, characters, places, brands, media, and incidents are either the product of the author's imagination or are used fictitiously. Any resemblance to similarly named places or to persons living or deceased is unintentional.

For my husband, Ron ...

For believing in this concept when I first told you about it, for the nights you go to bed alone while I write, for all your hard work. I love you for every light bulb of inspiration. And more.

Before us great Death stands
Our fate held close within [her] quiet hands

—RAINER MARIA RILKE

PROLOGUE

Present

THE ROLLING GREEN of her eyes was dimming fast, losing color and life to the quick click of time that beat out her days and nights, a perpetual circle that was now fading to a close. Light brown hair that had been recently styled into looping curls was limp against the black pillowcase—a metaphor for her wilted spirit, I mused, thinking offhandedly how proud my English professor would be at my thoughtful use of language.

I sighed. I didn't want to be here.

When her eyes met mine, I knew she saw me for who I really was—*what* I really was. She reached out an eager hand to take mine. I didn't want anything to do with it. But it wasn't because her fingers were slick with blood, deep crimson dripping down her arm and fingernails from where she'd so precisely placed a razor blade to her vein and dug deep, thinking she'd be free of her pain. It was because her face reflected back to me all the times I'd felt I'd been given a shitty deal. Current situation: case in point.

"Hi," she whispered, her once pink lips fading with every pump of her life, which was idly dripping away from her to the plush white carpet below. I could smell the newness of it, the fresh aroma of a recently laid floor. *That's going to be a bitch to get clean.*

I looked around her bedroom, at the dance trophies and pictures of smiling friends, and wondered why.

Why me?

"Blake ..." Hearing my mother's warning tone, I looked over at her where she stood in the shadows, overseeing my tutelage.

"Why can't we just call an ambulance? It's not too late. They could save her," I whispered fiercely, staring at the girl's hand stretched out to me as if I were her savior and not her end. "We should save—"

"It's not for us to decide, you know that. We are only here to bring souls over, not save their mortal lives. Take her, she wants to go."

"And will she still feel the same when she's looking down at her body?" I asked, not even bothering to check my mother's expression when she didn't answer. Suicide wasn't a peaceful death. It was pain—that much I knew.

I choked back the tears that wanted to rise in my eyes for this girl, for me ... I turned to her once more and leaned down, brushing a strand of her hair from her graying face. "What's your name?"

Barely blinking, her pale eyes darted to me. "Carly," she said, choking around her words.

"Just hold my hand and I'll help you cross," I said softly, forcing myself to meet her gaze so that someone would witness her ending as they had her beginning.

She smiled slowly, and I saw that in life she had been pretty. When she'd believed. When she'd had hope.

"The light?" Her eyes widened, glittering green for a brief moment in their otherwise colorless depths at the prospect of going somewhere beautiful after this life had been so cold.

I nodded, although I didn't really know where she would go. I was only in training, but I hoped it was someplace good, where her tormented soul could rest.

She had small, feminine hands, I thought, as she laced her slippery fingers around my longer warm ones. She didn't last long, her pulse giving one last flutter before sputtering out.

The room was suffused with the silence left behind in the absence of such a simple thing. The thundering lack of a person's heartbeat had never seemed quite so loud. As life departed Carly's mortal coil, her soul lifted from the body, but unlike some souls I'd seen that were light and buoyant, at peace with the next step in their existence, hers was outlined in darkness, and it rippled, suspended in space like a special effect in a bad horror film. Her gaze turned from her body to me, sorrow coming to settle on the slope of her bowed shoulders and in the recesses of her eyes. Regret was a fickle creature. It always came too late.

"I hope you find what you wanted," I whispered to her soul, waiting to feel the energy that usually infused my body during a crossover. As she blinked out, all air was ripped from my lungs and I was left clutching the bedpost for purchase, grappling for oxygen and drowning on the echo of Carly's anguish. The room spun around me, and my rasping heaves hurt my chest as I struggled to survive the sharp, bitter sting of loss that clung to the drapes and walls and assaulted my nose with its acrid scent.

I inhaled deep breaths when air returned, staring at the pool of red on the floor, thankful the bedspread had been black. She looked like a zombie, gray and without light, her once green eyes staring into a void that held nothing for her now. Without thinking about it, I reached forward and closed her lids with the lightest touch of my fingertips. The hands of Death.

"Blake," my mother warned again, a chastising edge to the velvety lilt of her voice. I turned to look at her and sighed, feeling the darkness in the girl's room overwhelm me, irritation surging inside me at my mother's emotionless manner.

"Don't you care?" I asked.

She stepped forward from the shadows, her shroud of black hair sweeping around the marble pallor of her face.

"Of course," she said. But I had a hard time believing her when her features remained composed in an expression of sculpted apathy. "But it is what it is, Blake."

"This was the worst."

"I've seen much worse," she said, her voice lacking the deep resonance of human compassion. It was flat, a monotone observer in a world colored by grief and heartbreak.

"Gee, thanks, way to make me feel better about this whole gig."

"That wasn't really my intent. This is who you are. You will have to deal with tragedies that far surpass this. Tragedies far more encompassing. This was one girl. Be grateful it wasn't thousands."

I could barely look at her, nauseated by the way she acted as if one girl hadn't been everything to someone. I opened my mouth to retort with something equally nasty, my body tensed to storm past her for the last time, but I was caught in mid-motion by a soft knock at the door.

My head swiveled.

"Carly?" A soft voice came from the other side, concern coating the lightness of her tone.

Oh god, I absolutely could not stick around to watch Carly's parents find their daughter dead from suicide on her comforter.

Turning quickly, I pulled a fleecy black blanket, folded so carefully before, up over the girl's chest, trying to make the scene look less gruesome before I headed to the window.

"I'm outta here," I told my mother. To her credit, she didn't try to stop me with more inane platitudes.

"You could just flicker out," she said dryly. The doorknob was turning, and I shook my head. I'd tried her way of traveling through realms to no avail. If I was going to make an exit, it was going to have to be the human way.

I hurled myself through the open window onto the tree outside without thought of my physical safety, only glancing back once to see that my mom had already disappeared.

Sliding down the tree, I hit the ground with a grunt, my sneaker-clad feet stinging from the impact. I didn't pause, pumping my legs to power myself down the sleeping streets as fast as I could to get as much distance as possible from the death scene. But I didn't run fast enough, because her mother's shrieks of agony followed me from two blocks away. *They don't ever think about who they leave behind.*

I blocked my ears and kept running, the late winter air biting at my cheeks with the hope of spring hanging heavy in the wind, even on such a desperate night.

When I got to my own house, I paused at the stoop, sucking in a few breaths and trying to make the images in my head go away. Smoothing back my long, dark hair, so like my mother's, I checked my hands for hints of blood. But just like any normalcy that had previously existed in my life, the blood I'd seen stain my fingers had vanished. Licking my lips, I put my key in the door and pushed it open, stepping into the foyer.

My dad looked up from the living room, where his nose was buried in a book. "Hey, B," he said, taking off his glasses and rubbing tired eyes. "What are you doing here? I thought you were staying at the dorm tonight." He arched his brows and glanced at the cable box clock that glowed a green 11:15 p.m.

"Yeah, I was going to, but Shelby wanted me to stop by her parents'—you know, it's weekly game night—so I figured that since I was so close, I'd just crash here tonight. I'd better get a little reading in though, so 'night, Dad."

He didn't stop me or question me, which I was thankful for. I bounded up the steps to my room. Movies always made it look so easy, but living a double life was going to be the death of me. Pun intended.

After closing my bedroom door behind me, I sat down on my bed, tossed off my shoes, and quickly headed for the bathroom to shower. My skin felt dirty with the cloak of death, and I wanted to wash it away. Even though I knew it was impossible.

I was struck by my reflection as I closed the door behind me and turned to the medicine cabinet. It was like looking at a younger version of my mother. Only my eyes were a pale crystal blue. Hers were black. I was thankful for the difference.

But what we had in common even more than looks was a legacy. A long one. You might have heard of her before; she's really quite famous, although most stories have gotten it wrong and made her out to be a dude. She goes by the name Grim, but her full name is Grim Reaper. Do you know what that makes my mother? Yep, that's right. She's Death.

So what does that make me? The Reaper's daughter.

PART I

CHAPTER ONE

Six Months Earlier

"THE SPECTERS ARE BLACK! The Specters are white! The Specters will haunt you and fight, fight, fight!"

My breath fogged in the air as I shouted the cheer, and my fingerless gloves muffled my claps in the early autumn afternoon. I marched and clapped my way into formation and prepped myself for the lift. I felt my base, Brandon, wrap his strong hands around my calves and ankles, and then the wind encompassed me, stinging my cheeks on my way up through the air. My feet instinctively planted onto his shoulders and my muscles worked to keep myself balanced. The adrenaline kicked in, giving me that rush, the one that made it seem as if my blood sparkled within me and my heart danced in symphony to the head thrashing of eighties hair bands. The only reason I was on the squad was to be a flyer. It was like I had a death wish, sailing through the air like that, propelling my body in a way most sane people wouldn't dare. Plus, I got to satisfy both my physical need to be hurled through space and my dad's need for me to do it in a structured environment while furthering my college career.

Just as I got my balance atop Brandon's shoulders, I noticed the crows. The cheer pounding out into the air caught in my throat and died on my lips. Those bloated black birds were littered all over the field like a bad omen—just sitting there, not doing anything but staring. Or maybe they were watching. I didn't know why I focused on the birds in that moment, but they had always creeped me out. Maybe because they tended to hang out in my backyard like they were waiting to pick someone off.

Turning my focus back to the stands, I flung my arms up in the air in time with the whoosh of the other girls' hands clapping together, feeling the beat of the cheer rhythm sound inside me once more. I wasn't looking at anything in particular; I was concentrating on balance. And that's when I saw him, my eyes sticking on him as if by gravitational force.

He had caramel brown skin and his silky black hair was pulled back into a ponytail. But it was his intense dark eyes that made me pause, because there was no way I could look away. He was sitting amidst the crowded stands, but he was the only person I saw. And I was pretty sure I was the only person he saw, because his gaze was locked on me from where he was leisurely sprawled on the bleachers. A secret whirled in the depths of his eyes, and even from my airborne, muscle-locked position across the field, I could see it. And it was a secret about me. How I knew, I wasn't sure, but that boy knew me. I was supposed to be jumping, flipping through the air into my base's arms, but I blinked instead, and with the connection disturbed, I felt my leg slip. I tried to recover, my arms wind-milling around me, the gasps of the audience sounding in my ears as a backdrop to my certain demise. Then there was just air around me, and the rushing of the world coming to take me back.

My eyes clenched shut, but arms swooped around me, partially cushioning my head and body from the hard ground. Despite the save, my foot slammed down, a searing pain ripped through my ankle, and I heard a sickening pop. The acidic swirl of bile hit my throat and filled my mouth as I attempted not to wretch, but I managed to swallow it back down, glancing up at Brandon and nodding a jerky thanks. I curled over my ankle, trying not to cry in front of the whole university. I didn't want to give anyone fodder for harassment, especially since Hailey, the team captain, deeply resented my presence on the team. I guess the fact that I was dating her ex-boyfriend didn't help. *Must. Not. Cry* ... I sucked in a deep breath and exhaled as the team crowded around me.

"Oh god, Blake, are you okay?"

I looked up to see my best friend Shelby's pale green eyes, outlined heavily with eyeliner, staring at me. Her Kool-Aid bright orange hair was tucked under a beret-style hat, and her pretty face scrunched in concern. I smiled wanly, realizing she must have hurtled down the stands the moment she'd seen me go down. Despite her natural athletic prowess, she'd refrained from joining any school sports. Her excuse had always been that she refused to play into the monarchy that was high school. But now we were in college, and she still wouldn't join in the school spirit, acerbic and defiant despite the change of scenery. Basically, she just liked being that cool, alternative chick. It was an image she pretended not to care about.

Sipping from the chilly, fresh air, I managed a nod. "But I think it might be broken or something." I heard how weak my voice sounded, and I cringed.

"Are you sure? It doesn't look that bad to me," Hailey's sugary sweet voice said from above me. I blinked, looking up at her, unsurprised that she would try to downplay my pain.

"Give her some room!" Coach Jill parted the cheerleaders with a stern look and a sharp tone, her petite frame belying the steel rod in her back. Her heart-shaped face and aquamarine eyes made their way to my level. "Blake, what do you feel?"

"Umm, it feels like pain," I managed to say.

Grinning as if I'd told a joke, she looked down at my ankle, which was already turning black and blue. "It looks like a sprain, Blake. Who can take you to the hospital?"

"I'll take her." Hailey's smile was even sweeter than her voice.

"Um, no, you won't." Shelby elbowed her ungracefully out of the way. "I've got it, Coach."

Coach Jill nodded, ignoring Hailey. Coach Jill was the other reason I had joined the team. She was laid back but tough, and she had begged me to join, having seen my acrobatic abilities and fearless nature when I'd competed as a cheerleader in high school. Looping one of my arms around her neck, she gestured for Shelby to get my other side. "Here, I'll help you get her to the car."

* * *

Later, when I was reclining on the couch at home with my dad, my mildly fractured ankle in a brace, I remembered the boy. He'd been good looking, definitely, but it wasn't his good looks that had made me fall like that. It was something in his eyes, no ... something I sensed. I had felt an instant kinship with him, like we were cut of the same cloth, similar souls.

I was trying to muddle through my thoughts when my dad entered the room carrying a glass of ginger ale and saltines.

"Here, B, I brought you the remedy for everything." He grinned and set the tray down on the coffee table in front of me.

"Dad, I'm not sick." But I smiled, eyeing the fizzy bubbling soda. My dad was totally a Mr. Mom, and I loved him for it, especially since I didn't remember my mother.

He wrinkled up his face in a grin and sat next to me on the couch, patting my good leg. "I know this sounds strange, but I hate that you're a cheerleader, seems too risky."

I laughed. "And to think, Dad, when I told you I was going to try out back in high school, you were so excited I was actually participating in an extracurricular activity."

"Well, it would have been fine if you hadn't insisted on being one of those fly girls."

"Flyer, Dad ..."

He chuckled and patted my arm. "Same thing." I shrugged and sipped my ginger ale through the straw my dad had so nicely included.

"I know you're probably upset you won't be 'flying' for the rest of the season, but I'm not," my dad said.

"Well, I guess I'll have to put my life at risk in some other way," I grinned, enjoying his worry ... My smile eased into a straight line as I realized I was making my father nervous on purpose and enjoying it. What was wrong with me today? I stuffed a saltine in my mouth anxiously at the thought.

Thankfully, he merely brushed off my response with a chuckle and a kiss to my forehead. "My daughter, the comedian."

I swallowed the salty cracker down and tilted my head at him. "You were laughing," I pointed out. My dad just rolled his eyes and headed toward the kitchen.

"I'm making dinner, lasagna?"

"Sounds good, I'm waiting for Geoff."

Geoff and I had gone to high school together, although he had been a year ahead of me and was now a sophomore at Spec U, while

I was a freshman. We'd always been friends, but last year something had changed, and when he'd asked me out, I'd surprised myself by saying yes. We'd been together ever since.

The doorbell rang, startling me from my thoughts.

"Dad?"

"Yeah, yeah," he said, heading toward the door and opening it.

"Hey, Geoff." My father grinned at my boyfriend as he swung the door open, jerking his head to where I lounged on the sofa with a saltine crammed in my mouth and crumbs littering my sweatshirt. "Lover girl awaits."

Thankfully, Geoff wasn't fazed by crazy dads, which was one of the things I loved about him. He strolled into the room with a rock band swagger, his dirty blond hair spiked out from his head. His tall broad frame wore jeans and a Nirvana T-shirt better than any real rock star I'd ever seen.

Instead of sweeping me with his typical nonchalant grin, deep lines gathered at the corners of his mouth, his normally sunny blue gaze storm-cast. "Are you okay, Blake?" he asked. He too was averse to my risky behaviors. While my friends wanted to party, I wanted speed and wind on my face. I wanted to dance with life and death and see who emerged the victor. Shelby called me an adrenaline junkie, and maybe I was. But every time I was tossed through the breezes, every time I flew down the side of a mountain on a snowboard, I felt as if I was searching for a piece of myself I had yet to find. I'm not saying I had to "find myself." But I wanted to know the secret that the boy in the stands was keeping. Because I was sure it was about me.

I shook my head and grinned at my hot boyfriend. "I'd be better if the warden in the kitchen would give me some stronger drugs. He keeps insisting all I need is Advil. I swear it's just evil," I said, shooing all of the Shelby-like thoughts of secrets and cosmic connections from my painkiller-fogged brain. Who was I kidding? That boy knew as many secrets as I did, which was none.

Throwing his head back, Geoff laughed. I loved when he did that. He was handsomest when he laughed. He just had one of those laughs that was contagious. I felt my cheeks heat as I stared at his mouth, barely able to stop myself from grabbing him and pressing my lips to his, which were smooth with the telltale signs of a recent

ChapStick application. The presence of my loud, clattering father in the next room was reason enough for restraint. But I could dare a kiss.

"Kiss me," I whispered. Despite what I'd told him, the drugs from the hospital still hadn't worn off and I was feeling a little loopy. My inhibitions didn't seem quite so present, and I had to keep myself from giggling at random thoughts that popped in my head.

He turned his head toward the kitchen and then looked down at me. I could only imagine how I looked—tufts of my usually straight black hair stuck out of my sloppy mess of a ponytail, and my pale skin was whiter than usual. But his lazy grin said he didn't mind at all that I looked like death, or that my father was only a few feet away, separated by a thin wall and an open doorway.

"How can I refuse?" he whispered back, his lips already closing in on mine. When he finally found my mouth, I relished the taste of him on my tongue, the spicy trace of clove cigarettes lingering on his breath and clothes. I relished all of him, and I was so lost in the moment, I heard myself cry out in protest when he broke the kiss.

"As much as I love making out with you, Blake, your dad is about to come in here and check on us any minute."

Sighing, I sat back, but I was still feeling the heat clinging to my cheeks when my dad sauntered in casually only moments later.

"You hungry, Geoff? I made lasagna, Blake's favorite."

He looked up from staring deeply into my eyes with his blue ones and grinned. "I could eat," he announced. It wasn't news to anyone that the 6'2", nineteen-year-old boy in the room was hungry.

Later, when my dad went to bed, Geoff and I cuddled in close on the couch to watch a movie. With my foot elevated on pillows on the coffee table, I laid my head on his chest, his warm arm automatically curling around me. After a long day, the comfort of his embrace made it seem as if my eyelids were weighted, and I found myself beginning to doze off. I'd fought the effects of the painkillers, but I was no match for them or the security and love I felt within Geoff's arms.

I was half asleep when the image of the boy from earlier that day drifted across my thoughts, and I remembered how he'd been staring at me right before I fell. I shivered again, feeling a deep sense of familiarity overwhelm me. Why had he been staring at me? I was certain I'd never seen him before, but I couldn't quite push down a nagging desire to see him again.

CHAPTER TWO

"COME ON!" SHELBY BEGGED, pulling her orange hair into a bun on top of her head and gesturing to the magic shop, which bore a sign touting guaranteed dragon's blood essential oil and all the herbs and incense anyone could want. I sighed. She was always so into the New Age crap.

One hand on her hip, she wore a cropped sweater and a flouncy skirt. Looking at me over the top of her aviators, she was catalog chic despite her sugar-coated dye job and the overly dramatic make-up. She was an old-school throwback, and she insisted on dyeing her hair with Kool-Aid packets, changing the color so often I rarely remembered that her true color was light blond.

"What?" I asked. "Are you going to join the ranks of so many hopeful, impressionable girls who've come before you and buy into this stuff? We're in college now, that's so passé," I laughed, knowing full well that she'd be horrified at the suggestion that she would ever do anything to be trendy except dress stylishly. She couldn't get enough clothes.

But she didn't take my bait and instead grabbed one of my crutches and tried moving it to the door, causing me to stumble forward in order to hang on to it.

"Come on, gimpy, being interested in the occult has nothing to do with being trendy. We're young and thus must indulge in our innate curiosity of all things related to nature, spirituality, life, and death," she said philosophically. "Besides, I'm taking a class right now about witchcraft. It's more history and symbolism and stuff, but there's a contemporary Wiccan section in this store, and I want to check out what they've got for the paper I'm writing," she added, batting her lashes over her glasses at me before sliding them back into place and revealing the light spattering of freckles on her tanned nose.

She was a sun-kissed girl all over, while I was forever ghostly pale with skin that was so blindingly fair that I never went anywhere without tons of sunscreen on. Even at the end of August, I was still as white as I would have been mid-winter, my dark black hair making the contrast all the more noticeable.

"Well, I suppose I can't argue with that logic," I relented and allowed her to grab my backpack as I hobbled after her into the shop. The moment we entered, my senses were assaulted by the smoky musk drifting up in a thin plume from a burning stick of incense.

"Blessed be," a woman said from behind the desk. I had been expecting someone hippy-ish, but the woman had short, spiked black hair, piercings all the way up her ears, and tattoo sleeves on both forearms. She looked more like a punk motorcycle mama than a New-Ager. She held a cigarette and blew out a waft of smoke, tapping the ashes into an ashtray with her pointer finger and smiling warmly. I pegged her to be in her mid-forties and noticed a coffee cup nearby stained with red lipstick.

"Hi," Shelby said brightly, her heavily shadowed green eyes darting to the jewelry on display. I could see she was already eyeing a large pair of thickly engraved silver hoops, each with a circlet attached bearing a dangling black stone.

"Hi," I nodded, turning to a shelf with crystal balls and dream diaries, feigning interest.

"You girls looking for anything specific? Any spells I can help you with?" I could tell she was used to humoring girls our age.

I laughed and shook my head. "No thanks, my friend just wanted to come take a look." I looked up and smiled politely.

The woman smiled and stamped out her cigarette. "Well, I'm Rae. If you girls need anything just holler." She smiled at me again, looking into my eyes. "You know, you have startlingly blue eyes. They're very eerie," she said. Unsure how to take her matter-of-fact comment, I nodded.

"Thanks ..."

She must have sensed the question in my voice because she laughed, a deep throaty sound. "They're beautiful, hon. Almost otherworldly, which is cool in my book."

I nodded and suddenly decided I liked this motorcycle mama witch. "Thanks," I said again, more sincerely this time. I'd often been told that my blue eyes were one of my best features, but I'd also been told they were creepy.

"Lemme know if you need anything, I'll be right back." Rae rose from her chair behind the counter, her skinny, tattooed, wifebeater-and-leather-pants-clad form disappearing behind a curtain.

I watched her go and then sauntered over to take a look at the jewelry, examining a large turquoise pendant that caught my eye.

Shelby, who had quietly been perusing the merchandise, looked at me sharply with a glint in her eyes. "She does palm readings," she said quickly, a gushy ring bringing her voice to a high pitch as she gestured to a sign nearby.

Arching my brow at her, an ability I had perfected from long hours practicing in front of a mirror, I shook my head. "What?"

"Palm readings. It could be fun!"

"I don't know … It's usually expensive and really a bunch of crap."

"Oh, come on, I'll pay for you—it can be your birthday present!"

"I don't want to be told I'm going to meet a tall, dark, handsome stranger for my birthday when I've already got my tall and rock-star-hot boyfriend," I argued. "Why don't you get it done; I'll watch."

"Because it's not as much fun if you don't do it too," she whined, clasping her hands together under her chin and pulling out the dramatics. "Also, maybe she'll tell you something about Geoff, like whether he's your true love!"

I sighed, more at myself than her, so easily tempted by thoughts of Geoff and the tiny little voice inside of me asking if perhaps there wasn't something to cosmic connections and palm reading. The boy from the bleachers popped in my mind for a split second, but I shook the thought away.

"Well, let's make sure it's not like fifty bucks first," I partially assented and was rewarded with Shelby's killer smile. Her father was an orthodontist and she had the whitest, straightest teeth of anyone I knew. She'd had braces for like six years and unlike any other friend I'd had, she strictly wore her retainer every night. For such a wannabe rebel, I always found it funny she was so conscientious about her oral hygiene.

Rae had come back into the room and overheard us. She smiled kind of strangely and glanced at the two of us, her gaze lingering on me. "You two girls interested in readings?

"Well, how much is it?" I asked.

"Hmm, well, I thought I heard your friend say your birthday was coming up?"

I shrugged. "Well, in like a week."

"Doesn't matter, I'll do you for free, it'll be my pleasure."

"Really? What about me?" Shelby asked quickly, shooting me a grin.

"I'll throw you in for half price at fifteen bucks."

"Cool." Shelby winked at me as if to say *look at our good fortune*, but I wasn't convinced. Rae had been staring me down pretty hardcore and seemed to have a creepy interest in me. I didn't think I was just imagining it either. There was something off here.

We followed her through the hanging sparkly curtain into the low-lit back room. The flickering glow of candles cast shadows on the walls, and a table sat covered by a blanket with pictures of moons and stars embroidered into it.

"Sit, stand—do whatever suits you girls," she said in her rough, scratchy smoker's voice, flicking a tatted arm. We both decided to sit, not knowing what to expect.

She followed suit, but sat opposite us and pulled out a drawstring velvet bag, which she opened to reveal an array of crystals. "For good energy," she explained.

"Who's first?" Shelby asked, her anticipation palpable in the candle-scented room.

Rae spread her faded red-lipped mouth into a smile and nodded at her. "You."

Shelby grinned, took in a deep breath, and struck a melodramatic air. "Tell me my future."

I snickered, which bought me a glare from Shelby before she once again got on with her dramatics by adopting a pained look.

"Give me your palm, girl." Shelby handed it over almost reluctantly, although I could easily read the eager glow in her peridot eyes. "Hmmm." Rae traced lines with her index finger, as if exploring a determined route on a map.

Glancing up at Shelby, she started to speak. "Your life line indicates you've had a pretty easy ride up until now." Rae wasn't buying herself any favors with Shelby, who frowned, as she liked to pretend she was persecuted based on her decision to be an individual. I held back my laugh.

"Unfortunately, you're in for stormy weather," Rae continued, following the sudden zigzag of the top main line of her palm. "But I do foresee adventure, some love and ..."

"What?" Shelby asked breathlessly.

"Well, I see death."

"Like I'm going to die soon? When?"

"No, not death for you, but just ... death. You and death will have a close encounter, I believe."

Shelby turned a panic-stricken face to me, and I grabbed her hand to reassure her, feeling annoyance bubbling up inside of me at Rae, our would-be fortuneteller.

"Okay, I think you've freaked out my friend enough for one day, why don't you move on to me," I said, feeling protective of my BFF, who was way too impressionable when it came to spiritual mumbo-jumbo.

Rae lifted her heavily lined eyes to me and nodded. "Yeah, you're quite the intrigue. I think you have an interesting future ahead of you."

Rolling my eyes and rethinking my earlier feelings of warmth toward the woman, I held out my left hand, already thinking about what Shelby and I would do for lunch.

She took my hand almost a bit too eagerly, turning her gaze to my palm, a psychic hungry for futures. Minutes stretched on while she held my hand and looked at it, searching for unseen answers.

"So what's the deal?" I finally asked after shooting Shelby a look. But she was still so caught up in her own fortune, she barely paid me any attention.

Rae didn't say anything at first, but then she slowly lifted her dark eyes to mine. "Your lifeline is long, very long," she said in a precise way, choosing her words carefully. "I know this sounds like some cheesy line from a movie," she added briefly, looking up at me in all seriousness, "but life is going to change, and you too will experience death, although in a different way than your friend. It looks like you will be visited by death and ..." She paused and finally said, "I don't understand. It's like your fate and death's fate are intertwined."

There was a full pause where I looked at her incredulously. "Really, whatever happened to tall, dark, and handsome?"

She smirked, not realizing I was trying to be sarcastic. Or else she was just ignoring my tone. "Oh, you have one of those in there as well, it just seemed to take a back page to meeting death."

"Meeting death?" I laughed. "Okay, well thanks for the fortune, hopefully neither one of us is going to drop dead for a few minutes or encounter a brush with death. I think we'll be going," I said as politely as I could muster, given that Shelby was obviously freaking out even more now that death had been mentioned in both our fortunes.

Rae nodded and looked at me casually. "Blake, if you ever need someone to talk to, I have an open ear."

I frowned, not remembering when she could have possibly heard my name, but I figured Shelby must have said it at one point, and these psychic types were good at picking up on small cues.

"I appreciate the offer," I nodded, trying to keep the snark from my tone. Grabbing Shelby's hand, I threw three crumpled fives onto the table and I pulled her out the door before the weird witch lady could feed us any more of her garbage.

"Shelb, what do you want to grab for lunch?" I felt my stomach rumble and turned to her, but she was shaking her head.

"Food? How could you eat at a time like this? We're best friends and she said we're both going to meet death."

"No, she actually said you would experience death while I would meet it."

"Right, and if you read between the lines, Blake, that means I'm going to almost die and you're just going to full-out bite it."

"Don't buy into it, Shelb, she's obviously got a lot of time on her hands between motorcycle mama meet-ups and dive bar socials. We're not going to die."

"Well, I'm not, but apparently you are," she continued stubbornly, although I could tell she was really worried.

We were nearing my favorite pizza place. The slices were like three in one and it was the closest thing to thin crust New York-style pizza you could get. And I was really wishing Shelby would just drop the whole subject.

"Okay, name one thing that woman said besides making stuff up that wasn't something she couldn't have read off of us—our jewelry, our conversations. For all we know, when she left the room she was listening to us to try to learn more about us so she could swindle us. And near death—come on, I'm on crutches."

Shelby stopped walking, dragging the corners of her sweater around herself and shivering, even though it was an unseasonably warm seventy-degree day. Her intense gaze found mine and locked on. "Well, when you were first talking to her did you tell her your name?"

"No, she just offered to help us find stuff and told me my eyes were strange."

Shelby smiled somewhat sadly. "Well, I never said your name the entire time we were there."

"Are you sure?"

Grabbing my hand she looked at me hard. "Yes. So how did she know what your name was?"

"You know what, I did tell her, stupid me," I said, hitting my palm against my forehead in a gesture of mock stupidity.

Shelby smiled, gazing at me with loving green eyes that were filled with worry. "Sure?"

"Totally." I nodded. Reassured, Shelby shrugged and moved on. "Well, that makes me feel better, I was really creeped out when she said it."

Laughing, I felt a rock in my throat and tried to push it down. "Nah, I totally told her after she introduced herself."

The pizza shop's sign dangled in front of us, and Shelby gestured to it with a still semi-shaking hand. "Shall we?"

"Sure," I nodded. But I knew I wouldn't be eating any pizza. A sickness was rising in my stomach and I knew it wouldn't be going way soon. As we entered, even the yeasty aroma of rising bread and greasy cheese couldn't take away the turn of my stomach. How the hell had she known my name?

CHAPTER THREE

A WEEK LATER, I was still thinking about what the woman from the magic store had said. I crammed my Psych 101 textbook into my backpack, zipping it up and turning to head out early from where I'd been studying in a school lounge. I had an appointment with my doctor to check my ankle. I slid the backpack over my shoulders and adjusted it on my back before grabbing my crutches.

"Happy birthday!" Geoff was standing in front of me, his come-hither grin banishing my dark thoughts as he thrust a bouquet of bright orange and red Gerber daisies at me.

I took them as he leaned in and brushed his lips against mine, sending a flare of desire through me. I nearly gasped when he lingered for a moment before drawing away and fixing me with his droopy gaze. "I thought I'd give you a lift to the hospital, so I called your dad and told him not to worry."

I lifted the flowers to my nose and inhaled deeply. They were my favorite.

"Best birthday present ever. Stolen flowers and a hospital escort in the Red Baron," I said, grabbing his hand between mine and smiling teasingly at him.

His bright red Chevy truck had seen its day. It sported a bed made of wooden planks painted red to match the truck that we likened to Snoopy's doghouse. Geoff had opted to live at home rather than dish out the money to stay on campus, and he didn't get along with his father all that well. Luckily, his father traveled a lot on business. But when he was home and they had fights, Geoff often slept in the truck, weather permitting. He used to call it the doghouse, but I liked the Red Baron better and we'd called it that since.

Geoff blushed at the word *stolen*; I knew he'd probably picked them from his mother's immaculate gardens. "Your mother will have your head," I warned.

He shrugged his lanky frame and brushed back a strand of my hair, pushing it behind my ear and cradling my face with his hands. He donned a rock-star sneer, but his eyes were gentle when he spoke. "Well worth the risk," he whispered, before kissing me again. Yep, best birthday ever.

*   *   *

It was nearly twenty minutes into our wait in the waiting room of the Orthopedics unit that I decided I couldn't hold it in any longer and notified Geoff, who was lazily flipping through a *Rolling Stone*, that I had to go to the bathroom. He offered to go with me, but I shook my head and with the help of my crutches, got to my feet easily enough.

I hobbled through the waiting room and down a hallway, having seen a bathroom that way earlier. It was several minutes and an entirely different wing of the hospital later that I realized I wasn't going the right way. But I continued because I figured I had to find a bathroom somewhere.

I finally found one, but by that point I didn't even know what unit I was in. I made my way into the handicapped stall, the only one big enough to deal with me and my clunky crutches. I managed to get toilet paper on the seat without falling in and took care of business.

I examined myself in the mirror as I was washing my hands, frowning at the left leg of my old skinny jeans, which I'd had to slit up the side in order to fit over the brace. It was my birthday, after all, and I had wanted to look good. The hot weather had finally broke and dipped down into the forties over the last day or so, so I'd donned a light, loose-fitting blue sweater that hung off one shoulder and highlighted my eyes. I'd decided to wear makeup that day, and I was leaning into the mirror to check my eyeliner, not quite as thick as Shelby's, when I gasped. Out of the corner of my eye, I caught a face in the mirror.

I shrieked, straightening up and catching the golden brown eyes of the boy from the bleachers, but when I snapped around to look behind me he wasn't there. I wasted five minutes tromping up and down the bathroom aisle and kicking open each door with the butt of a crutch, certain I'd find him crouching in one like a stalker. I only stopped shouting at him to come out from wherever he was hiding when a nurse walked in and looked at me strangely. I saw her do a cursory look at my wrist, so I fled before she could get me committed to the psych ward, flashing her the sanest smile I could manage.

Back in the hallway, I leaned into the crutches and figured I should head back quickly so I didn't miss my appointment. I was only partially down the hall when I realized where I was: the ER. A nurse came flying around the corner, followed by a stretcher pushed by a team of medical professionals.

I couldn't move as they rolled past me, my eyes on the elderly woman whose face looked like it had been hit by shards of broken glass. I knew she was dead—if not in that moment, she would be in the next.

As the group with the gurney started to round the corner and I turned to gimp my way back to the right wing, I saw the old woman sit up. I shrieked and pointed before I could stop myself, my heart jumping in my chest, but no one was paying attention to me in all the commotion. I lowered my arm and bit my lip. What was happening?

The elderly woman stretched and bent her body around Gumby-style, a smile stretching her liver-spot speckled lips as she stood on her tiptoes and did an arabesque. I frowned. Huh?

I glanced at her and then looked back at the gurney that was being swiftly wheeled away. She was still on it, a lifeless shell. Then I looked back again to where I'd last seen her, and she was twirling gracefully all over the hallway.

The old woman, who was looking increasingly younger, glanced over at me and met my eyes. For a beat I couldn't look away, too drawn into the insanity of the moment. My gaze was pulled away for a brief moment by a black shadow that seemed to have slipped behind the figure of the dancing dead woman. I blinked and it was gone, but the woman continued her twirls. Was I actually seeing a ghost?

"She's a soul, soon to be lost," a husky male voice whispered from behind me.

Hobbling around to face the voice as quickly as I could, I stepped back a few paces, my heart pumping in my chest as I took in the boy who'd been in the bleachers and in the mirror. This time he was standing right in front of me, staring deeply into my eyes with his own soulful golden brown ones.

"Who are you?" I panted, the rest of my normal calm leaving me at his sudden reappearance. His full lips curved up into a smirk that made me want to deck him.

"We need to talk, Blake," he said.

I almost wobbled off my crutches, feeling vindication settle in as I realized he really *was* some skeezy little stalker. Although he was hot ... Who was I kidding? I was almost flattered he wanted to stalk me. No, I wasn't! I chastised myself, hearing Shelby's voice in my head telling me I had just set back women's lib a century.

"Are you following me? How do you know my name?" I accused, narrowing my eyes at him and shifting my weight fully to one side in case I had to lift one of my crutches to meet his face.

He grinned again. It was like he couldn't stop smiling, and I felt like screaming because of it. "That woman you just saw, she's a lost soul. I know she looks free, dancing around like the ballerina she was when she was young. But that will change. Over time, these things get ugly. Souls shouldn't stay on earth, they need to pass on. That's why I'm here."

I gaped at him. Who was this guy and why was he talking crazy? That's when I remembered where I was. I was at the hospital, duh. He was probably some guy who'd escaped from the psych ward. *That doesn't explain how he was at your cheer meet*, interrupted my quiet voice of reason. But I ignored it. This was a disturbed individual.

"Uh, sir. Do you need a nurse? I can find one and have her take you back to your room," I said and tried smiling compassionately, wondering if I was missing my appointment. Maybe they hadn't even come to get me yet. I mean, seriously, I'd waited like an hour to see the doctor here last time.

The golden-brown-eyed boy laughed, holding up his bare wrists with an amused grin. "I'm not a patient, Blake."

I shook my head and wobbled on my crutches. He reached out a strong hand and stabilized me, his eyes meeting mine in a way that made my heart flutter in rebellion against my good reason.

"I'm sorry, I just don't know who you are. Have we met before? Why would you need to talk to me? And what are you talking about?" I finally blurted out, sick of the strangeness of the situation and wishing Geoff was by my side instead of in the waiting room, likely wondering where I was.

I looked past the boy and watched the old woman, who was now young, continue to arabesque down the hall until she passed through a wall and disappeared. I shook my head, not believing what I'd seen. Ghosts? Lost souls? Whatever. I'd probably taken a few too many painkillers that morning and was seeing things, including this boy.

Focusing my gaze on him once more, I arched a brow, which by now I was getting really good at, and frowned sternly. "Go away, you're just a delusion."

He laughed, chuckling in a way that made me grit my teeth in annoyance.

"I'm not a delusion, you crazy girl. Try to explain seeing me in the bleachers the other day at your school."

"Ha! So you admit you're a stalker," I said, glancing around furtively to see if any doctor or nurses were nearby in the event that he was trying to make me his next basement love muffin. Shelby had apprised me of many real-life horror stories. I wasn't going to be one of them.

He laughed again and I hated him for it, conjuring up images of Geoff to ward off the way this guy's voice made my nerves fray.

Suddenly, his amusement vanished and he looked straight in my eyes, drawing closer so that he was merely inches away, and his breath, smelling all the world like chocolate, beat against my senses. "I need you to meet me later. We need to talk."

I laughed, feeling happy I could return the condescending gesture. "Why would I meet up with a crazy guy who is stalking me? Like that's a smart thing to do," I said.

"Because your mother is looking for you and if you want to ever meet her, you're going to have to do what I say," he said, his tone dropping.

At the mention of my mother, my comebacks faltered and I couldn't do anything but stare. "My mother is dead," I finally said, my words falling like stones.

"Your mother has never been dead," he said, stepping back and finally giving me the breathing room I needed. "She's been watching you, waiting for you. And now she needs your help."

Hope flickered in my chest for a mere moment, butterfly wings beating against a fading sun. My dad was perfect. He was a better mother than some mothers, and he was certainly an awesome father. But still, what kid who was missing a parent didn't want to know them, see them, feel their embrace? I don't think my dad could have done a better job trying to be both parents, but I didn't look like him. There were no pictures of my mother anywhere in the house. I'd looked for them for years, asked him for one. But he'd always just said she had avoided cameras.

My dad liked to stay safe at home behind a book. The most dangerous thing he did during a typical week was play basketball with his friends. He was a worrier, a gentle soul—an amazing cook. I wasn't. I was sharp, and I liked danger. Cliff diving seemed like a fun afternoon adventure, and I couldn't cook a noodle, let alone a soufflé. Hell, even my chocolate chip cookies came out bad. But spicy foods, high speeds, and shark-infested waters made me happy. So there was a part of me that wanted to believe my stalker—that wanted my mother to be alive so I could finally meet the other person who had created me and see if my looks and my need for thrills came from her. But I couldn't. It was all too strange.

Tossing my hair, which didn't work so well since it was in a ponytail, I glared at him. I was sure now that he was either sick or joking. Hobbling away from him, I shook my head.

"My mother died in a car accident when I was a baby. I don't know who you are, but just leave me alone," I said, staring him straight in the eyes so he knew I meant business.

Going to get an orthopedics check-up had never seemed so enticing. Not even giving him another glance, I crutched myself around him and started back down the hall I'd come from. But of course he had to call out after me.

"Blake, if you want to meet your mother, I'll be at Mount Clave Cemetery at nine."

I turned back to shoot him a disbelieving look. "You're sick," I spat and then turned on my crutches and thumped away from him. I didn't look back.

When I got back to the waiting room, I found that they hadn't even called my name yet and Geoff was flipping through a different issue of *Rolling Stone*. He barely glanced up when I returned. "You fall in?" he joked, cracking up.

I laughed along with him, but I didn't feel it. The echo of the guy's words stayed with me even when we left the hospital an hour later. I was free of my brace and crutches and was walking gingerly, but without pain.

"You wanna grab something to eat?" Geoff asked, catching my hand in his and bringing it to his mouth for a quick kiss.

I smiled at him, feeling my heart skip a familiar beat. But I shook my head. "Can you drop me at my dad's? I have to catch up on some studying, and I can't deal with the crazy partying at the dorms with the big game coming up. But I'll see you later for my birthday date," I said and gave him my most brilliant smile.

He nodded, as always just as lost under my spell as I was under his.

CHAPTER FOUR

I STARED at the search engine screen on my laptop and typed in "Grace Rayne." My mother's name. I knew it was ridiculous—my father wouldn't tell me my mother was dead unless she was. But still … a part of me wanted the strange boy's claim to be true so much. And it bothered me that my father had never shown me one picture of her. I mean, there had to be one somewhere. My parents weren't together very long before they conceived me. They were young, my father had said, and they'd fallen in love at "first sight," whatever that was supposed to mean. He'd told me about their whirlwind romance, but he hadn't really told me much about her, only to say once in a while that I reminded him of her. Mostly, he was pretty closed off about the topic of my mother, except to say that she'd been a wanderer before he'd met her, traveling the country and the world. But I did know her name.

As expected, her name yielded little in the way of search results, bringing up some teenage girl's social media pages. I sighed, knowing that it had been a foolish attempt anyway. She'd had no family and had been an orphan, my father had explained when I was old enough to ask about grandparents. "We know more about freaking Jesus," I muttered, startling when I heard my dad's soft knock.

"Hey, B, happy birthday," he said, popping his head in and smiling, the corners of his eyes wrinkling beneath his glasses.

"Hey, Dad," I said, closing my laptop as quickly as possible without looking suspicious.

He brushed back his floppy, sandy hair and walked into the room bearing a small ice cream cake on a plate, an "18" candle burning a trail of black smoke through my room.

I grinned. He knew I was going out with Geoff in a little bit, but he couldn't stop himself from making sure I got my birthday cake every year. "Thank god you didn't actually put eighteen candles on the cake, I don't know if my lungs could withstand it," I laughed.

My dad chuckled and put the cake on my desk in front of me, singing a quick rendition of the Happy Birthday song. "Make a wish," he said, as he had every year since I could remember.

I paused and thought about it, and then I knew the right wish to make and blew, extinguishing the flame.

"What'd you wish for?" he asked me, sinking down on the end of my bed.

He said this same thing to me, as well, every year. I shook my head. "If I tell you, it won't come true." I humored him with a dry smile and a roll of my eyes, letting him know that I was much too old for this game.

He just laughed in response, his blue-green eyes sparkling. He knew I loved it.

"So what are you and Geoff up to tonight?" he asked, handing me two plastic bowls so that I could dish ice cream cake into them.

I licked my fingers before I slid the knife through the melting chocolate and vanilla cake and carved out another piece for my dad. I handed him his bowl, dipped my spoon into mine and savored the cool, silky ice cream on my tongue before answering.

I shrugged, licking my arm where chocolate had somehow magically appeared. "Not sure, he said it's a surprise," I grinned. "But Shelby is supposed to meet up with us early for a bit." I was looking forward to the night—it felt like it was going to be memorable. The ballet-dancing apparition of the old woman clouded my vision for a moment, only to be taken over by the strange boy with the golden brown eyes again. I shook my head and pushed all thoughts from my head other than those of hanging out with my best friend and best boy.

"Well, that boy better not think he's taking you parking," he said sternly, looking at me over his glasses.

"What is this, the fifties?" I laughed and stood up, having devoured my cake in a matter of minutes. He was only joking; he loved Geoff. The two hung out sometimes when I wasn't around and watched golf together, a sport I truly didn't get. Although I did suspect my father was getting concerned that Geoff and I might be taking our relationship to the next level. And he wasn't far off. We'd talked about it a few times, and I knew I wanted my first time to be with Geoff. We'd been dating for a year, but we'd been friends for a lot longer, and he was one of the best guys I knew. I was in college, I loved him, and now I was eighteen. It felt like it was right.

But as much as my dad fulfilled my parental needs, I really didn't want to talk about all that with him, so I hopped to my feet and held up sticky fingers. "I should probably shower. Geoff texted me a little while ago and said he'd be here in an hour."

My dad gathered my bowl and the melting cake and leaned in to kiss my forehead. "I can't believe you're only two years away from being twenty. It makes my poor old heart hurt," he said as he walked to my door, balancing the dishes.

"Yeah ..." I said, my voice trailing off. Eighteen and I didn't know anything about my mom. Surely he would tell me a little more about her now. I couldn't help it. Ever since Mr. Criminally Insane—as I'd decided to call him in my head—had said she was alive, I couldn't get rid of the nagging feeling that there was truth to what he was saying. No matter how crazy it seemed.

"Dad," I swallowed, trying to find the right words that wouldn't upset him. "I know that you said you don't have any pictures of my mother, but ... I guess I just feel like it would be cool to have something of hers—did she leave anything behind? I mean she must have had something." I fixed him in a stare, feeling a dark boldness creep up that made me want to keep him in place until he gave me something to hold on to.

He looked at me strangely and nodded slowly. "It's funny you asked that, because your mother did have something that she wanted to give you on your eighteenth birthday. Your question just jogged the memory. If you wait a minute, I'll take this stuff downstairs and go get it. I put it in the safe after she died," he said and paused, suddenly averting his eyes. "I'll be right back." He glanced at me once more as if checking me for strange behavior and then disappeared from my room.

I looked around my room, my heart racing. *She left something for me!* For the first time it seemed I was going to be given proof that my mother had existed.

A few moments later, he returned carrying a small envelope. He handed it to me and then sat down next to me on my bed to watch me open it.

I looked down at the plain, white envelope and swallowed, wishing my throat wasn't so dry and my mouth so sticky with leftover traces of ice cream sugar. I gingerly slid my finger under the flap and began to open it. I tried not to breathe too loudly, but I was nervous, wondering what this woman who had birthed me had left behind and bequeathed to me, her only daughter.

Slipping my fingers inside the envelope, I pulled out a pendant attached to a short chain and dangled it between my fingers, staring at it with parted lips and widened eyes. Placing the necklace in the palm of my hand, I leaned my head forward to study it, taking in the detail of the charm that bore the shape of an owl in flight. It bore no resemblance to the trendy owl paraphernalia I'd seen in stores and around girls' necks. No, this had been hewn from wood and was more finely crafted than anything I'd seen before. The eyes were two turquoise beads and the wood was stained in a rainbow of colors. It was roughly as big as my thumb and came to rest in the middle of my chest when my dad put it around my neck for me.

"Do you like it?" he asked quietly, his voice tight with worry.

I nodded, feeling a quiet reverence fall over me. My mother ... She was really with me now.

"Gracie always wore that necklace. She called it the harbinger, but I thought that seemed morbid so I renamed him Sam. She liked that," my father said, a soft smile on his face and a distant look in his eyes. I knew he was remembering, and I wished in that moment I could jump inside his head and see it too.

"Did she say where she got it?" I asked, encouraging him as lightly as I could when he didn't go on.

Shaking his head, he seemed to snap from his reverie and met my gaze with his blue-green eyes. "You know, I don't remember specifically, but I feel that maybe she said something about it being carved by a Native American man. There should be a note in that envelope too."

My head snapped up to look at him, and then I dug my fingers around the inside of the envelope until my fingers snagged a small, rectangular piece of paper. I was practically panting in my excitement to see what my mother had written to me, almost as if she was reaching from the grave to talk to me. I uncurled the stiff piece of paper and stared at the looping and curling script, uncomprehending until I saw that she wrote her "B" exactly like I did, with the bottom bubble line extending out and looping down. I was nearly halted by the tears that threatened to spill at this peek into my history, into my own blood.

Finally, after I had stared at the "B" for longer than was sane, I took in the words:

Dearest Blake,

Let the harbinger lead you above the darkness.

Love,

Mom

It was short and it was sweet, and I'd take it. I'd take anything I could get. Eighteen years old and I'd found a piece of my mother within myself. Finally, I folded the square back up and looked at my dad. "Thanks, I think this is one of the best birthdays I've ever had already."

He looked at me sadly, opening his mouth several times to speak, but instead shook his head and squeezed my shoulder. "I'm glad you liked it, kiddo. I've also got a little something for you," he said and handed me several pieces of paper. I looked down and grinned—they were vouchers for whitewater rafting lessons.

I laughed and threw my arms around him, happy to feel the warm embrace of my father. He was forever trying to keep me from doing one dangerous activity by paying for me to do another dangerous activity that he found safer. I'd been talking about skydiving lately, and this was his way of throwing me off track. But I loved it.

"Now it really is the best birthday. Angry rapids here I come!" I laughed, and he shook his head chastisingly.

"Now no more talk of skydiving for at least a year," he ordered.

"Yeah, yeah, this wasn't a birthday present, it was a bribe," I teased.

He stood from my bed and winked. "You know me too well. Now go get ready, I've got to run out to the store. Casey is coming over tonight and I haven't even gotten the movie."

I shooed him out and closed the door behind him, happy he'd found a girlfriend in the last year. It had been good for him and focused his never-ending parade of worry off of me. I marched to my full-length mirror and leaned forward, admiring the way the owl looked against my chest, resting against the pale blue of the sweater.

I touched it and smiled softly, watching the smile reach my sparkling pale blue eyes. Tonight was going to be fun.

I turned to my closet and examined my wardrobe. I wrinkled my nose at the pickings, wishing I could raid Shelby's robust closet. All it usually took was for me to try on a few outfits from my own closet and her disdain would get the better of her, and before I knew it she'd be bustling me off to her house. Her mother was as fashion obsessed as she was and so the two of them were forever shopping and bringing home the latest styles.

I decided to dress nice for once, instead of the usual jeans and sweater getup. I eyed a red wrap dress that had three-quarter length sleeves, a V-neckline, and a skirt I knew was far above sea level. My dad would have a fit. I'd bought it on a whim when out with Shelby, and she'd convinced me it would look striking against my pale skin and black hair, but I'd never worn it. Never dared to put it on. I hummed and tilted my head, pondering the dress. I could have worn it in school, away from parental eyes, but I'd left it here on purpose, honestly thinking I'd never find use for it. I smiled to myself and hurried to the shower so I could get ready. Tonight was the perfect night.

CHAPTER FIVE

LATER, when the red dress rippled over my body like soft silk and my dark hair rippled in ringlets past my shoulders, I grinned at my reflection. Shelby had been right. All I needed was deep, red lipstick to finalize the fiery effect. But I knew it would be over the top, and besides, Geoff hated lipstick. So instead I fastened a pair of silver hoops in my ears and slid my feet into a black pair of heels—my only pair. I knew I'd be cursing myself later that night, but I couldn't very well wear my sneakers with the dress. I eyed my ballet flats in deep thought. I could probably get away with wearing them, given that I had long legs and really didn't need the heels. I shifted from foot to foot, debating, but after only two minutes of being in the heels I realized I couldn't deal. Plus, it probably wasn't good for my ankle to be walking in heels so soon. Flipping them off my feet, I slid my toes into the black, pointed-toe flats and smiled in comfort.

Turning to the mirror, I made sure I didn't look ridiculous and was still happy with the effect, even if I looked a tad less daring. Halfway through my perusal of myself, I realized I was planning to seduce my boyfriend. It hadn't been a conscious thought, but in that moment, when the smile slipped unbidden to my pale, pink lips, I realized it had been my plan all along. I loved him. I wanted to be with him. I was eighteen. No more waiting.

While I was usually honest with my dad, talking to him about my love life was another matter. And I guess that's where a mom would have been nice. Because Mr. Mom as he might be, he was still a dude.

I sighed and touched the owl, which was framed by the red neckline of the dress. Glancing at the time, I saw that it was only a few minutes before six. Geoff would be at the house any minute. Casting one last cursory glance at myself, I grabbed a long black cardigan and my cell phone, and then headed down the stairs to watch for the Red Baron.

I liked to pretend I was so cool that I didn't wait by the window watching for the telltale sign of the broken headlight and the red wooden truck bed pulling in, but I couldn't. Obviously, because that's just what I did—what I did every time I knew he was coming to get me. Anxiety made my stomach do flips, and I thought out a plan to get Shelby out of the picture so Geoff and I could be alone before it got too late. She'd understand but would probably be totally freaked out that I was planning to lose my virginity tonight. But she'd known it was coming eventually, and we'd talked about it before. She'd promised to get my roommate out of my dorm room if needed when the moment was right.

I glanced at my phone to see if I'd missed any texts. It was 6:10 p.m. Geoff was often late, but I had been hoping that because it was my birthday he'd actually show up on time. Sighing, impatience rising in my chest, I headed to the kitchen for a glass of water, trying to fill the rumbling of my stomach. "Hurry up, Geoff," I said under my breath. I felt beautiful and sensual and I was in a hurry for him to see me.

I walked back out into the family room a few moments later and glanced out the window again, fully expecting to see him pulling in the driveway. But it was empty, the sky growing dimmer by the minute although it was still relatively light out. Sighing, I dropped down into a chair and scrolled through my social media postings on my phone, barely glancing at the updates, just trying to pass the time until my night could start. I'd just clicked my phone off when I heard it—the sound of an owl screeching through the house so loudly I turned my head expecting to see one perched on the fireplace mantel, staring at me.

I got up to look around, but my phone started vibrating in my hand at that moment. It was Shelby. I swiped the screen to answer the call and put the phone to my ear. "What's up, please tell me you've got some ridiculous scheme planned and that's why Geoff is so freaking late."

"Blake," she said through a sob. I could hear loud noises in the background. It took me a moment but as I focused on them, I could tell it was the whir of sirens ... which only grew louder as I realized they were coming from somewhere outside my house and down the road.

"Shelby! What's going on?" I demanded, my skin prickling and crawling as I heard someone scream from a distance. "Are you okay?"

"Blake," she said again, her voice strangled with pain. "Blake, it's Geoff," she breathed as if she couldn't or wouldn't go on. But then she did. "There was an accident."

I felt my stomach drop, and bile threatened to rise up in the back of my throat. "Shelby, is he okay?" I demanded again, but I was already out the door and running down the street toward the roar of sirens in the distance.

As I ran, I irrationally thanked my blessings that I'd worn the damned flats. But I wouldn't have felt the pain, and I didn't have to go far. I only had to run around the corner, and the scene was laid out before me, a horror story for my birthday.

I found Shelby still blubbering into the phone, a conversation I was no longer a part of. I realized I had no idea where my phone was, nor did I care.

I grabbed the phone from her hands when I reached her and shook her until she focused, her orange hair in disarray and her pale peridot eyes ringed by mascara. "Shelby, what's going on?" I asked, beginning to feel like maybe she was overreacting, like maybe I was. It was a hope. I was obviously in denial, because I could hear and see the emergency vehicles and crew running around.

Her eyes looked wild, looking at me without seeing me, but then I saw comprehension return and her face crumbled. "He ... He was taking too long, so I-I started walking toward your house. Then I-I heard the crash and-and ... Oh, Blake ... Look," she said, unable to go on, her lips trembling and her face streaming tears.

I choked back a response and really focused on the scene. Immediately, red dominated my vision. It was at a corner, one that was rife with accidents because of a stoplight that often took way too long to change. People blew through the red light all the time, this being a pretty small town. Of course they usually looked both ways before going through it. Geoff was almost a perfect boyfriend, but he had one fault: he was impatient. I'd seen him on more than one occasion barely glance at what was coming, assume no one was approaching, and go through the light. I'd yelled at him for it plenty of times myself, pointing out that he was going to get us both killed.

But I'd been wrong. It was just him.

Shelby tried to grab my hand when she saw the realization hit, but I shook her off, barely able to zero in on the wreckage. A black SUV probably bearing the right of way had smashed into another vehicle, the bright Red Baron, which was crumpled up from being hit on the driver's side. I could barely focus my eyes, but I had to find him.

"Where is he?" I mumbled, lurching toward the wreckage and snapping my head to the side to look at the ambulance. "Geoff!" I screamed, noting there wasn't anyone inside the decimated truck.

Snoopy's doghouse, our private joke together, destroyed. I could hear the shrill piercing arch of my voice, the hopelessness that already knew. And then I saw him. He was standing a short distance from the destruction, near the line of trees, looking fine. Well, fine in the sense that no bodily harm seemed to have come to him. His bright eyes found mine and a relieved smile curved his lips, as if I were his savior.

I reached out to him, a sigh of relief getting stuck in my throat. But I knew something wasn't right, because when I looked to the right, a crew of EMTs were crowded around a man on a stretcher. I could see his head through their arms, the shock of sandy hair and the familiar curve of his bumpy nose.

I glanced from the lifeless form of what looked to be Geoff, to the figure standing there apparently unharmed. I looked back and forth, and then I heard them call it. His death. I shook my head, not understanding, and barely realized where I was heading until I was standing next to the emergency personnel who were lifting the stretcher into the ambulance, wearing sadly drawn expressions. The body was mangled; the left side of his face was unrecognizable and covered in glass while his neck twisted sharply to the side. He'd been dead on impact, I knew then and there. And there was no doubt in my mind that it was Geoff.

Clasping my shaking hands, I tried to clench the tidal wave of grief that threatened to empty the contents of my stomach. And I would have let it all go if it wasn't for the Geoff that was still living and walking toward me, doubt and confusion on his face.

The image of the old woman at the hospital twirling down the hall crossed my mind. I headed toward Geoff and then he was in front of me. Was he a lost soul too? The image of the golden-brown-eyed boy came back to me. I couldn't stop trembling, and I wondered where Shelby was and if she could see him too.

"Blake," Geoff whispered, reaching out and touching my hand. My eyes widened, amazed that he could still make contact. I looked up from our hands and met his gaze, wishing we could always stay like this—just him and me.

"Geoff," I managed to say without completely falling apart. "You didn't stop and look both ways, did you?" I sobbed, failing to bite it back this time.

He seemed to realize that all wasn't right in the world, because his eyes filled with tears and he shook his head. "I should have listened to you, I just wanted to see you ..." He trailed off, stepping forward to embrace me.

But I couldn't. Not in that moment. I pulled back, halting him, and stared into his pale face. "You're dead, Geoff." The words, when they left my lips, were cloying and hard to extract from my tongue.

He started to shake his head but stopped, incomprehension choking his ragged voice. "Dead?"

I nodded, my own throat feeling swollen and bruised from the grief cutting through me and trying to make its exit, but I sucked it down, trembling to keep it contained.

"Blake," he breathed, glancing down at his hands as if they could give him answers, as if they could explain how he'd ended up without a body, without a life. His eyes were red and bright with pain, and his face crumpled. "H—how am I here ... How are you seeing me?"

I shook my head mutely, knowing if I attempted to speak I'd start crying and possibly never stop.

"I mean, I saw my body. But I just can't believe ... I'm gone, you know? And yet, I'm here," he said, meeting my gaze, his expression so deeply furrowed that new lines creased his face with sorrow. Confusion and his grief clouded his usually clear blue gaze. Something seemed to break within him as his shock began to settle into mourning, and he must have seen the ruin of my face, reflecting the breaking of my heart. "Oh Blake," he breathed, reaching up a large, rough musician's hand and caressing my cheek. I didn't pull away this time, but instead leaned into his hand, into his touch. "It's your birthday, and I ..." He stopped and shook his head. "You look so beautiful. I mean, that dress."

He leaned down and pressed his lips to mine, and everything I'd been hoping for that night shattered around me. He pulled back and met my gaze, his own seeming to have grown old in only a few minutes of despair.

"I'm so sorry. I should have been more careful," he said, his voice thick with agony.

I bit my lip, but I couldn't contain it any longer and the sobs came crashing out. He grabbed me and pulled me to him, holding me fiercely in his strong, lanky embrace. I sank into him, wishing I could hold on forever.

We stayed there for a long time, long after the sirens had whirred away and all that was left was the wreckage and us. I wondered what had happened to Shelby, but I couldn't be too concerned about her when I was holding my dead boyfriend and beginning to wonder why he was still here. Not that I wanted him to go, but where was the white light, the big show?

We finally separated, and I looked up at him and heaved a shaky breath. Tears still fell from my eyes, but I let them stream, unable to stop them and no longer caring if they flowed until I died myself, or dried up altogether.

"Do you feel like you need to go somewhere, like a higher force is calling you?" I asked softly.

He frowned for a moment before shaking his shaggy head. "I just feel like I need to be with you."

I nodded, glancing around and seeing that traffic had opened up again. "Do you want to come home with me, then?" I didn't know what else to do, and I didn't really want him to go into any white lights. As long as his ghost—or whatever he was—was hanging out with me, I could pretend the night hadn't happened, that I hadn't seen his body disappear in an ambulance headed to the morgue.

I shivered. The night had grown darker, although total darkness hadn't fallen quite yet, and I'd forgotten my sweater. He wrapped his arm around me and nodded. "Take me home with you, Blake. We'll figure it out."

I nodded, hoping that figuring it out included how I could get him to stay with me. I didn't care if he was a ghost. For some reason I could touch him and kiss him and I was okay with that. As long as he was here and not gone forever.

We started to turn, and I truly believed that whatever cosmic forces existed were going to let me get away with keeping my boyfriend. But then of course I should have been expecting the golden-brown-eyed boy to show up.

One moment he wasn't there and the next he was striding up to us in snake-skinned, steel-toed cowboy boots, faded jeans, and a Star Wars T-shirt with a ribbed, long-sleeved shirt underneath. His piercing eyes found mine, heavy with secrets and compassion he had no business putting on me.

"What are you doing here?" I asked roughly, my hand clasped in Geoff's. It had started to sprinkle, and I could feel the first few drops splatter on my face and hands. Good. Maybe it would wash the horror away, I thought, glancing back at the road that was red with paint and blood. People in cars zoomed by, going about their Friday nights as if someone hadn't died, as if the intersection hadn't been a war zone only an hour before.

Snake Boots tilted his head, his shiny black hair pulled back in that ponytail. "Blake, you really need to come with me. Now. Especially if you want your boyfriend here to have a happy ending."

"Go with you where?" I asked, averting my eyes from his steady stare and imagining me and Geoff cozied up in my room, away from the terrors that lit the late September night.

"To see your mother, Blake," the boy said, the faint lilt of an accent coloring his words with a richness that was too thick for my mood.

I shook my head. The mother stuff again.

"Blake?" Geoff turned to me, his brows rising to his hairline. "Your mother?"

"She's dead, Geoff," I reassured him. "This guy is just crazy."

Geoff stared at me, but he didn't seem convinced, eyeing the guy as if something about him smelled familiar.

"What?" I asked Geoff impatiently, wishing the stranger was far away so I could wrap my head around tonight and my arms around Geoff.

"It's just ... Well, he can see me, Blake. No one else could until you got here. And this guy can too."

I frowned, disliking the logic that was coming from his mouth. I turned to the boy with the golden brown eyes and gazed at him for a long moment, noticing a plea that hid in the stillness of his breath. "Why can we both see him? And what's your name anyway?"

He inclined his head and spoke. "Rishi," he said, his face a stoic mask. I had thought him annoying at the hospital, but now I saw kindness crease the corners of his eyes. "And to answer your other question, I have to bring you with me. Your mother can give you the answers you seek." Although I sensed he was empathetic to our current plight, his voice was tight with urgency and his fingers flexed into fists at his sides, possibly holding himself back from dragging me with him rather than waiting until I acquiesced to his outlandish claims.

"Why should I listen to you?" I asked a bit more petulantly than I meant to, but he was asking a lot of me on a night my boyfriend had died and stuck around as a ghost.

His deep gaze met mine and he inclined his head, speaking as softly as he had before, but with no less impact than if he'd shouted. "Because your other option is to stick around here, take your dead boyfriend home, and watch him slowly deteriorate. And that will happen, Blake. He's a lost soul now."

I shook my head, ready to argue once again, but Geoff squeezed my hand that was still clasped in his own. "Blake, I think we should listen to him. I'm dead, I'm not seeing any light, or whatever is supposed to happen when you die, and the only thing I feel is that I'm supposed to be with you. But if I'm not supposed to be here, I think we should figure this out."

I turned to him, ignoring Rishi's quiet presence and looking up into Geoff's eyes. "I don't want to lose you," I whispered.

He cocked a half smile, the one I'd always loved, and leaned down to kiss my forehead. "What if your mom's alive? We should go, Blake. I'm convinced that there's something to this dude's claims."

I cast one last searching glance up into my dead boyfriend's eyes and turned to Rishi, narrowing my ice blue gaze and crossing my arms. "Fine, take me to her. But this better not be some sort of sick joke or even weirder, some strange trap, stalker boy. I want to see for myself this woman you claim is my mother. And I want answers. This is the second dead person I've seen walking around today."

Rishi smiled mildly and nodded, although the smile didn't touch his eyes. "Follow me," he said and took off at an amble across the park toward the line of trees.

I glanced up at Geoff. He smiled reassuringly and took my hand again, and together we set off after Rishi. I was still holding my boyfriend's hand despite his lack of heartbeat, and I was possibly going to meet a woman I thought had been dead my entire life. It all made me sick with fear. It gnawed at my empty stomach and caused my heart to skip along at a frantic pace, leaving behind a heartbeat here and there. Everything was about to change. No, everything already had changed, and the darkening night fell down on us like a shroud of doom. I knew without a doubt that after tonight, nothing was ever going to be the same.

We followed in silence for a time, going deeper into the trees until I remembered how he'd told me to meet him at the cemetery.

"Oh, you've got to be kidding me," I muttered. "He's actually taking us to the cemetery, where my 'mother' will probably be a gravestone."

But Geoff didn't chime in with a laugh, and when I glanced up at him I could see that he'd known all along where Rishi was taking us. He had secrets in his eyes, and I suddenly was hit with the thought that he knew more about the situation we were in than he was letting on.

"What do you know?" I hissed up at him, but he merely gazed down at me with a lost look in his eyes and shook his head.

Right about then, we stopped short behind Rishi, who had paused at the entrance to the cemetery and was looking back at us. He put a finger to his lips to hush us, and then he beckoned us in, moving through the grass and around the gravestones with a singular grace.

Finally, he brought us to a large crypt, the stone archways intricately carved with the face of the crying Virgin Mary. I stopped and shook my head. "Seriously, serial killer. You want us to go into a dark crypt with you? We'd have to be insane."

He merely paused and met my gaze, his golden brown hues steady and deep as usual, but also demanding and challenging. It was that glint of a challenge that slayed me, and he must have known it. I had never been able to back down from a dare.

Meeting his gaze full on with my own eerie blue eyes, I tried to get him to falter beneath my stare, but he didn't waver. It was only when Geoff started to rock from foot to foot that I sighed.

"Fine, lead the way. But I've got pepper spray if you try anything," I muttered halfheartedly. I had a slinky red dress and no purse; I'm sure no one was afraid of me.

The crypt door gave a loud groan as he pulled it open easily. He beckoned us to go inside first, but I stood my ground with a shake of my head, every bad horror movie I'd ever seen flickering through my imagination.

He shrugged his shoulders and went ahead. Gripping Geoff's hand tightly, I followed. But I made sure the door remained cracked. I was not going to get locked in one of these things, and definitely not with a stalker.

When we were standing fully inside the crypt, the dark was almost pervasive except for a slit of moonlight coming in through the door I'd left cracked open. I looked around until my eyes adjusted and found Rishi.

"So, what's next?"

As if an answer to my question, I heard the striking of a match, and then I could see Rishi standing beside me with a lantern in his hand. He turned and set it on a ledge and leaned against the wall.

"She'll be here any minute."

I shivered. It was dank and cold in the dampness of the crypt. I idly wondered if Shelby was okay and frowned to myself because she wouldn't know that Geoff was alive. Well ... a ghost, or spirit, or whatever. I hugged my arms around myself and smiled gratefully at Geoff when he wrapped me in a hug. But he didn't warm me up, and that's when I realized he was frigid, devoid of warmth.

I shivered again, stepped away from him, and sighed. "You're cold," I said softly, daring a look at Rishi who was staring at us with his unblinking gaze.

Geoff looked at me sadly and sighed as well.

"You were warm before," I said, remembering when I'd hugged him immediately after encountering his spirit self.

"That's because his condition is worsening," a new voice cut through the dimness of the space, throaty and without humor.

"His condition?" I asked. I spun around to take a look at the newcomer, my heart quickening. Was this my would-be mother? She was in the shadows, so I couldn't see her face, but I could see a cloak draped around her head like a shroud.

When she stepped forward a moment after speaking, I could see she hadn't been wearing a hood at all, just her long, curling black hair that was so dark it became a part of the shadows. The flickering light caught her face, and for a moment it looked almost skeletal, making me back up a quick step.

But when the light caught her face again, it was that of a beautiful woman. She had elegant features, high-boned cheeks, plush pink lips, and a narrow chin. Her nose tapered to a soft point, and her eyes were large and fringed by a coating of thick black lashes. I gasped, hardly able to breath through the revelation. Although her eyes were pitiless, black, and deep, and mine were a striking blue, as clear and pale as the sky, we were almost identical.

I struggled to wrap my head around it, thoughts darting in and out of my mind before I could grasp on to any one of them. Was it possible? Was this really my mother? I felt Geoff's icy hand squeeze mine and I was happy for it despite the chill it gave me.

"Who are you?" I asked softly with a tremor in my voice, afraid to say it too loud.

"I think you know, Blake," she said, her features emotionless. But I saw the spark of warmth light up her deep gaze, and a small, almost hesitant nod.

"How is this possible? I thought you were dead. My father told me you were dead. Where have you been all this time?" The questions rushed out all at once, and my eyes narrowed as I thought of all the nights I'd wished for my mother. I hadn't really believed it before when Rishi had said my mother was alive. I'd hoped, but I hadn't really believed. But looking at her, my world altered and shifted. When it stopped again, everything I had thought to be true had changed. Everything real was now a lie.

The woman, my mother, stepped further into the glow of the light, and I could see she wore jeans, black boots up to her calves, and a black, long-sleeved V-neck. She looked like a chic mom, but there was something I couldn't quite put my finger on. There was a darkness that surrounded her. The shadows never truly lifted from her silhouette. She smelled like flowers, but which kind I couldn't decide.

"Blake ... I couldn't come until now, until today, your eighteenth birthday," she said, confusing me more.

"Couldn't come?" I heard the pain of abandonment and disbelief edge my voice, my confusion making me feel a thousand different emotions and nothing at the same time. I didn't even know what I was feeling in that moment. My mother was alive. And yet, something bigger was happening. Geoff and the woman at the hospital, they were somehow connected with my mother's return. "And why are we in a cemetery? My world is already colored by death," I said desperately, my gaze jumping between this woman who claimed to be my mother and Rishi and finally, resting back on Geoff.

"Grim, maybe you should explain it to her," Rishi spoke up from the corner, his soft tone failing to mask the terseness laced in his voice. "It's going to be a shock no matter how you say it."

My mother looked at him and seemed to entertain his suggestion, a look passing between the two of them that I couldn't explain. Wait, Grim?

"My mother's name is Gracie, why did he just call you Grim?" I asked. I knew where the signs pointed—all I had to do was look into her face—but I just couldn't yet accept that my mother was standing before me. Even though I felt my inner being long for her, she wasn't what I had imagined. She seemed sharp and unforgiving. The mystery hanging over our encounter made me uneasy—that, and the fact that I'd recently seen my boyfriend's body being wheeled away on a gurney.

Grim broke the look and glanced back to me, meeting my eyes with her own. "I made up a name when I was with your father. Grim is my real name. I always liked Gracie though, it sounded so ... normal," she said, a faint smile etching her lips for the first time. "And I chose the cemetery because the lost often come here, and seeing is believing."

"I don't understand any of this. Why did you leave me? Where have you been?" I said, still clutching Geoff's freezing hand and worrying about this "condition" Rishi and Grim had mentioned. "I want to know what's going on now." A sharp edge rang in my voice as I met Rishi's steady gaze with my own and felt my pale blue eyes go stony. He finally looked down, and satisfied, I turned my stare on my mother. But she didn't look away. A glimmer flickered in her eyes, possibly something akin to amusement, and she nodded.

"After all, that's why we're here, isn't it? So I can claim you as my daughter and you can find out the truth. But first, you should know what's going to happen to your young man if you allow him to continue here. The condition I was speaking of only a few moments ago is death, and it is destroying him."

"How?" I asked, glancing at Geoff and meeting his grave gaze with my own.

"When souls aren't passed over to the underworld, they begin to decline, lose their humanity, and become what we call lost souls," my mother said. "The longer they stay on Earth, the worse they become, until who they were gets so lost it's hard to retrieve."

"So, he's turning into a ghost?" I asked, my confusion, disbelief, and sense of loss growing deeper with every revelation. And yet I couldn't refute that I was literally seeing spirits.

"He's not a ghost," Rishi corrected me.

I glanced at him with a small shake of my head. "You corrected me before, telling me souls aren't ghosts. What's the difference?"

But it wasn't Rishi who responded. "When you call him a ghost, you suggest he has a purpose here," my mother said, lifting a hand and gesturing to him as she spoke. "Ghosts by nature are souls who evaded crossing over because of unfinished business, whether it is to relay a message to a loved one, exact revenge, or due to ties so great they are simply unable to leave behind the life they once lived unless they're forced to or their feelings somehow are resolved. They are profoundly tied to this world by a strong bond."

"Okay ... and lost souls aren't?" I didn't like the sound of what she was saying. Geoff loved me, why wouldn't he want to stay with me?

"No. They're people who died and should move on, people who are willing and wanting to go on to the next life but are prevented from doing so. Look at Geoff. He's certainly sad to have died. He loves you, and he doesn't want to leave you. But that essential bond a ghost needs to stay here is missing. It's the bond that keeps ghosts from being driven mad by the pull between the physical world and the next life, because they have no desire to go anywhere. For a soul like Geoff, however, languishing here on this realm serves no purpose. He should be crossed over. But he hasn't been. He's lost."

"I'm his purpose," I said, my voice coming out more impassioned than I meant.

Her gaze flickered over me with only slight interest before she went on without ever acknowledging that I'd spoken. "Lost souls' sadness at being left in a world they can no longer be a part of creates a tide of emotion, so that if more than one of them congregate around the living, their emotions begin to affect the general atmosphere, poisoning those that still have life. Geoff being here only adds to that sickness."

I shook my head, glancing at Geoff. It sounded like an awful existence, but my boyfriend could never be poison.

"But then how do they pass through to wherever it is they're supposed to go?" I asked, locked within her unfathomable gaze.

"That is where the truth comes in, daughter. Let me explain before you run out of here cursing my name for the rest of your life. You need to know about me and why I left you. You see, I'm much older than I look. You asked me why I wanted to meet you at a cemetery, and it is because the call of the souls is so great, I often cannot withstand their need. And yet I can no longer help them."

"What are you saying?" I asked, feeling a pit yawn open within my stomach. Because I'd seen the skeletal shadows flash fleetingly across her face for a moment and dismissed them. Because I'd been plagued by death twice that day and claimed by a mother I'd always thought deceased. It just wasn't possible ...

"I am older than the first archetype of Death," my mother went on, deaf to my inner turmoil. "I reap souls. I am leader to the death deities ..." She started to go on, but I let out a laugh so loud it rang from the stone.

"What are you talking about? Are you trying to tell me you're Death? Like, as in *the* Death?" I laughed so hard I had to catch my breath, but my laughter was laced with hysteria and my breaths were gulps as I clung to life. Was I going insane? Even Geoff was staring at my mother with a certain amount of horror written on his features and glittering in his eyes.

I straightened up, taking one last heaving breath and squeezed Geoff's hand before slipping mine out of his. My fingers were going seriously numb. I wiggled my fingers for a moment in distraction before finally meeting my mother's haunting gaze once more. "That's just crazy," I finally whispered.

"She's not just Death," Rishi said, and I glanced over at him, dread making my chest clench. "She's the Grim Reaper," he added, pride coating his tone. He glanced at my mother, and I saw the adoring look that flashed through his eyes. She was obviously his hero.

"And what are you? The Grim Reaper's groupie?" I spit out, my voice acerbic and steady despite the anxiety attack sweeping through my body. I was unable to get a hold on the mixture of contradicting emotions threatening to overwhelm me.

He didn't bite, merely curving his full lips in a grin. "I am like you, a hybrid: part human, part death deity."

I gaped and swallowed the "ewww" that wanted to escape because I'd thought he was cute. "You're like my brother?" I asked, horrified.

He laughed, shaking his head so that his shiny ponytail flashed in the light. "No, my father is Yama, Hindu death god. My mother is dead. Your mother found me in an orphanage and took me with her when I was very small, sensing what I was. She showed me the way of the death deity."

I stared at him, finding no words. I did believe them. My physical and emotional reactions were proof enough of that. How else could I explain Geoff's soul standing next to me while his body lay in a morgue?

"Um, okay." I tried to sound sarcastic, grasping on to what sanity I could, but I was losing the battle. I turned to Geoff. "Do you believe any of this?" I avoided looking at the woman calling herself my mother. If I chose to accept her story, I didn't know if I would cry from happiness or sorrow. All I knew was I was exhausted.

He turned toward me, his eyes having grown so light they were almost as pale as mine, and sighed. It was like the sound of someone's last breath leaving their body, as if he had no more in him. When he met my eyes, he looked heartbreakingly sad and nodded. "I don't just believe it, I know it's true, Blake. I'm drawn to your mother as much as I am to you right now. I know without a doubt only you two can set me free."

I turned to my mother, wanting her and not wanting her to do it all at the same time. "Are you going to send him away?" I whispered.

She shook her head, and for the first time, I saw sadness wash over her sculpted features. "I cannot, unfortunately. But you can."

"Me?" I asked, glancing quickly between the two self-proclaimed death deities.

"You're my daughter," Grim said slowly. "That means you have the powers to cross souls over. You're a death deity as much as Rishi is."

"You're more," he said to me intensely. "Because you're the original," he added to Grim, who smiled faintly.

I shook my head, blocking out the mumbo jumbo and zeroing back in on the part where I was supposedly a death deity. "So what are you telling me?" I asked, still confused by just about everything going on around me.

Geoff took the moment to intercede, taking my hand within his icy grip. "They're telling you that you have the power to cross me over to the next life."

"He is right," my mother said in her velvety, lush voice. "But there is so much more to this. You see, on your eighteenth birthday—today—you came into your reaping abilities. I've seen it happen before with other deities' children, like Rishi here, and it is always on their eighteenth birthday. It is your duty to reap souls and help them pass on to the next life."

A deep sadness crashed over me along with a riptide of anger. Reap souls? "I don't want to do that," I said softly, barely able to believe that this was my life.

"You have to," Rishi said, stepping forward. A bright fervor lit up his eyes and he pinned me with his intense gaze. "It's your birthright," he added.

I shook my head at him and looked at him with disgust. "You're sick. It's my birthright to watch people die? No, thanks," I said, barely able to keep the tremor from my voice.

I tried ineffectively to temper myself with a deep breath, but I didn't really want to. I was overwhelmed by the entire night: realizing Geoff was dead, encountering his soul, and meeting a woman I thought had been dead my entire life. I felt numb, angry, as lost as they claimed Geoff would eventually be. And even though there was a light inside of me that had unfurled with happiness the moment I'd seen my mother standing there with her face so like my own, the entire thesis of the night was finally revealed, and I found myself unable to cope with the emotions roiling through me. So I chose to go on the defensive. The one thing I had was Geoff, and I wasn't giving him up. Not tonight.

Rishi's eyes widened in shock, but when he tried to speak I cut him off. "You both listen to me," I said, my voice taking on strength. "I don't know what this is about, but I am not Death. I am a college girl who wants to go home and cuddle with her boyfriend."

"Who happens to be dead," my mother interjected with a sardonic arch of a dark brow.

I glared at her, almost having forgotten that fact, almost able to pretend I was talking to two clinically insane people.

"Fine. Even if what you say is true, I want no part of this. I'm not going to watch people die over and over again. I don't want to be a part of the darkness," I hissed, feeling the night already invading my life.

"It doesn't have to be dark, it can be beautiful," Rishi said softly, but his words fell on deaf ears, because I wasn't having it.

"Listen, both of you." I turned to Grim. "If you're really my mother, I'm glad you're alive, but I don't want this in my life and I've been fine without you up until now, so I think I'll stay that way." I looked at Rishi. "And you, I'm glad you've kept my mother company, but I'm leaving. With my boyfriend. Now. Please don't find me again."

I locked eyes with both of them, and they did nothing to react at first. Turning, I whipped around and grabbed Geoff's hand, which felt even icier than before, if that was possible. "Come on, we're going home," I said and started to drag him after me.

But he didn't follow right away. "But Blake, I don't want to turn into anything that's not me. I don't want to hurt people."

"Don't listen to them," I insisted. "I won't let anything happen to you. Trust me." He stared deeply into my eyes and must have seen the fear I felt at losing him, because he finally assented with a quick nod of his head.

We started up the stairs out of the crypt, but my mother made me pause with her words. "When he starts to go bad, Blake, come find me." As if he was milk that would go sour, I thought bitterly.

I didn't even bother to respond but hurried up the steps with Geoff in tow, feeling the purity of the cool night hit me like a refreshing shower after being bathed in darkness. The soft light of the full moon had never seemed so welcoming. I glanced at Geoff, and the crushing weight that held my chest in a vise didn't ease with the decision to leave my mother and Rishi behind.

Echoing from within the crypt and following us into night air, I heard Rishi ask my mother, "Why did you let her go? You know what's going to happen to him. It will only hurt her more."

"If she's anything like me, she'll learn quick enough what needs to be done. She'll be back, it's in her blood. The Reaper's song will have her."

Geoff held my gaze for a moment, obviously having heard them as well.

"Do you want to go back? She looks just like you, Blake."

I shook my head hard and fast. "The Reaper's song? You think I should go back to a woman who claims to be Death and believes the 'Reaper's song'"—I held up two fingers from each hand and put air quotes around the words I'd heard my mother say—"is going to 'have' me? I mean what does that even mean? No, I just want to go home."

I grabbed his hand, leading him away from the crypt and away from the people telling me I had to say a final good-bye to my boyfriend. I wasn't going to let that happen, and so denial became my new best friend. A voice inside of me whispered that I was being selfish, that I should consider Geoff in all of this, but I couldn't seem to let him go. I was determined to be his purpose, his bond to this world.

Finally, when we were nearing my house, Geoff spoke. "Where will I go?" he asked.

"With me, of course. My dad won't even see you, remember?"

He grinned the way he always used to, slowly and crookedly confident like a rock star. "Like in your bedroom?"

I laughed and stopped to face him, sliding my hands up around his neck and pressing my lips and body to his, wishing I could blister him with my heat. When we pulled apart, I tried to ignore the trembling that touched every fiber of my being. I was so cold. Not wanting him to see, I smiled back. "Yes, in my bedroom."

* * *

When we got to my house, I was relieved to see my dad wasn't home. He'd probably gone to Casey's for a sleepover. Sure enough, when I glanced at the kitchen table, I saw a note. He had a thing about letting her sleep at the house. Not that I wanted to think about my father hooking up with his girlfriend, but I really just wanted him to be happy.

I went to the fridge and grabbed a bottle of water while Geoff glanced around the house aimlessly. I felt like my lips had been scorched by the cold, and I was freezing from the inside out. All I wanted was a hot shower to chase away the chill. The thought of cuddling with

Geoff up in my bed, which had seemed like a hot idea a moment before, now conjured images of hypothermia.

I turned to Geoff and held out my hand to him, and he took it. I tried not to shiver—I didn't want to make him feel bad. As we passed through the family room on the way to the stairs, I noticed my phone. I grabbed it off the end table and saw that I had fifteen missed calls. All from Shelby.

I glanced up at Geoff with a frown.

"What is it?" he asked, his face looking paler than I'd ever seen it.

"Shelby called."

"You should call her back, she's probably a mess and worried about you," he told me.

I knew that what he said was true, but what was I going to say to her? I shook my head. "I can't, you're not dead to me. I'm talking to you right now."

He reached out and touched his frigid hand against my cheek, knowing how it was affecting me. "But I am dead, Blake. And Shelby doesn't know what you know."

I went to tap her name on the screen, but instead I shook my head and shut the phone off, avoiding his disappointed gaze. "Come on," I said, and without waiting for him, I marched up the stairs.

I closed the door behind Geoff as he followed me into my bedroom, turning to him and wishing I could jump into his arms. "I'm going to take a shower," I said softly.

He nodded, avoiding my gaze. "I'll be right here," he finally said with the ghost of a smile. His sandy hair was shaggy and tangled, and the circles under his once warm, cerulean eyes made him look ill.

I tried to smile back, but this moment when I finally had him in my room was nothing like I'd imagined it. Longing emanated from him, but it wasn't from a desire to make out with me. My hand trembled against an urge to take his, to set him free … Shaking my head violently against my own thoughts, I turned to the laundry basket of clean clothes in my room.

Grabbing a pair of sweats and a long-sleeved cotton shirt, I hurried out the door into the hallway, careful to close my bedroom door behind me en route to the bathroom, as if my dad might come home and see a boy in my room. But no one could see him. No one but me. I blocked the mental images of Grim and Rishi and stripped off my clothes.

When I was done showering, I took my time blow-drying my long, black hair, basking beneath the heat of the dryer. I sighed, wishing for nothing more than to crawl into Geoff's arms, to hold my boyfriend, even if he wasn't really there. But I knew I couldn't.

I finally made my way back to the room and crept in. Geoff looked up and smiled at me crookedly with a dimple in his pale cheek. He was stretched out on the bed. "I have an idea," he said softy, light coming to his eyes for a moment once more as if life had never left him. "Go get the electric blanket downstairs. I would have, but I can't seem to hold anything except you."

"For what?" I asked.

"Just go get it," he insisted. I shrugged my shoulders and flew down the stairs, grabbing the fleecy blanket off the couch and unplugging the cord from the wall. I carried it back upstairs and stepped into my room, shutting the door behind me.

"Plug it in and put it on the bed, so we can cuddle," he said gently.

Tears sprung to my eyes. It was the kind of thing he always considered. The kind of thing that had made me want to date him in the first place. I smiled tremulously and crawled into bed next to him, wrapping myself in the blanket, which quickly began buzzing with heat. He lifted his arm and curled it over me along with the rest of his body, the blanket protecting me from his chill, making me feel snug and secure in the arms of my boyfriend.

"That's funny," I said, noticing his hand resting on the blanket. "You seem to be able to touch it now."

From behind me he grunted his agreement. "I think it's because it's touching you. You seem to have almost like a force field around you and everything within that field is attainable to me. Are you warm?"

I smiled to myself, nodding my head and then speaking. "I love you, Geoff," I whispered. I'd never quite said it before, although he had plenty of times. I wanted him to know, right then and there, that I'd always loved him.

He pulled me in closer and for a moment I smelled the familiar hint of Geoff: vinyl and the faint whiff of cologne.

"I love you, Blake," he murmured, his lips momentarily against my hair like an ice cube on my scalp. But I was so warm and content everywhere else, nothing mattered. I drifted off to sleep, almost able to forget the earlier events of the evening.

CHAPTER SIX

I WOKE UP with a start. The room was a dim gray and frost left my mouth when I yawned. I shivered in the gloom, the electric blanket tossed to the side. *Geoff!* I sat up and gasped in relief. But when the figure sitting on the edge of the bed turned to me, I realized it was my dad, his crinkly blue eyes sagged with grief, and when he met my gaze, I saw his own sadness weighed him down as much as his hurt for me.

"I heard about Geoff. How are you doing, B?"

I almost ignored him, peering in the shadows for Geoff. Where did he go? It must have been early morning, and when I looked at the clock, I saw the glowing green numbers click to six o'clock.

Turning back to my dad, I nodded. I cleared my throat before I could find my voice and looked away. "I'm having a hard time feeling anything right now," I finally said. And it was true. I didn't know what to feel. My boyfriend was dead, even if his soul lived on to hang out with me and cuddle in bed with me. Even in my delusion and denial I realized we couldn't go back after what had happened. I just wasn't ready to face what was to come, either.

And for some reason, that's when it hit me. The psychic. She'd said I was going to meet death. But it hadn't been my death, it had been my mother: Death. I had to go see Rae, see if she knew how to help Geoff. Maybe she knew some sort of spell. I looked frantically around and that's when I saw him leaning in the corner, waiting for my dad to leave before coming to sit back down on the bed with me. Probably out of respect.

"That's normal, sweetie," my dad said.

I looked up at him. "Huh?"

He peered at me as the room lightened, and he reached out to put his hand against my clammy forehead. "Are you feeling okay?"

I shook him off and looked away again, calculating in my head how I could get out of the house without rousing suspicion. Then I remembered how early it was and figured I'd have to wait a few hours before the store opened. But I couldn't stay here, not with my father breathing down my neck and watching me with his worried eyes.

"Dad, do you mind if I go to Shelby's? I feel like I really need to be around her right now. She saw it happen, and I haven't really talked to her yet."

My father arched his brows, the auburn slashes reaching up and wrinkling his brow. "Right now?" he asked, glancing at the time.

I nodded. "I won't be able to get back to sleep, and I was so upset last night I didn't return any of her calls."

The wrinkles in his face increased, and he nodded understandingly. "Of course, Blake. I'm going to call Geoff's parents later and see if they need anything. Do you think you'll go see them as well?"

I frowned, biting my lip and inwardly sighing. With all that had happened, I hadn't even thought of them. I still had Geoff, and they didn't. I really should go see them, but not until I saw the woman from the shop.

I nodded. "Yeah, I'll stop by later ... I just, I need to see Shelb."

"Okay, honey. Call me if you need anything."

"Can I take the ca—" I didn't finish my sentence because Geoff was in the corner shaking his head, and I instantly understood that he had no desire to get in a car again, dead or not. "Never mind, I want to walk."

"You sure? It's cold out this morning."

"No, I'm good. I'll dress warm."

He nodded, and standing, leaned down and kissed my forehead, brushing my hair tenderly away from my face. "I'm so sorry that this happened, honey. Geoff was ... Well, he was an amazing guy. I'm here if you want to talk about it."

"Thanks, Dad," I said, forcing a wavering smile.

When he had finally shut the door, I rifled around my room for a sweatshirt. Finding a gray, zip-up hoodie, I pulled it on over my shirt and glanced at Geoff. "Close your eyes," I whispered, grabbing a pair of jeans off the floor.

He had come to sit back down on the bed and he chuckled. His chalky face and newly gaunt features were ghoulish even without his laugh. "Oh, come on, throw the dead guy a bone," he grinned.

I shook my head and glared at him. Finally, he shut his eyes, but I suddenly didn't trust him, so I went to the bathroom anyway and slipped my pajama bottoms off and the jeans on. I glanced at myself in the mirror and saw that I looked almost as bad as Geoff, and I wasn't even dead. "No, I'm only Death," I whispered to my reflection, taking in the dark hollows under my eyes, the shadows against the white planes of my face, and the dark shroud of my tousled, raven's wing hair. My mouth was pinched, but what struck me the most was the grief that glittered like ice in the pale, ghostly depths of my blue eyes. It was a grief I didn't feel, and yet it was there, almost as if innately I knew it was to come. I very nearly hissed at myself for what it showed me.

When I walked back into my room, I grabbed a hairband and twisted my hair into a puffy bun on the top of my head. I looked to Geoff, who was shimmering and glinting in and out, and the creepy effect reminded me of a bad reel of film. He looked over at me and grinned disturbingly widely before rushing at me like a whoosh of wind. I bit back a scream and backed into the wall, shutting my eyes and biting my lower lip so hard I tasted blood.

After a few moments, I slowly opened my eyes and saw Geoff sitting on my bed normally, watching me curiously. "Why are you huddled over there like that?" he asked, confusion clouding his usually cheery expression.

"You, why did you do that?" I gasped, spreading my arms out in a gesture of question.

"Do what, Blake?" He frowned, tapping his fingers against his leg as he often did when sitting idle, listening to a beat in his head.

I smiled at the motion. It was so him, so like he'd been when he was alive. A sandy shock of his shaggy hair fell into his eyes. I shook my head, rubbing my temples for a moment, trying to massage away the pounding that lanced through my skull. "Nothing, nothing. I think I must be seeing things. Come on, let's go to Shelby's."

"How come? Last night you couldn't be bothered with talking to her."

"I just didn't know what to do. But I have an idea, and she can help."

He looked at me doubtfully, but he dutifully stood up to follow me. It was really all he could do at this point. For a moment I paused, hearing my mother's and Rishi's warnings add their cacophony to the banging in my head, but I quickly pushed them out. I loved Geoff, and I had to believe he was better with me than in some other realm.

We stepped out into the early morning, and I was gratified to see the night had lightened to day, chasing the nightmares and shadows away. Ribbons of light cast their glow across the horizon and warmed my soul, even if the air was crisp with the chill of fall. Around us the houses were mostly still silent. The neighborhood had been built up in the 1970s; the houses were a bit worn, and the trees thickened the suburban landscape with life and a wholesomeness that made the world a bit brighter.

We walked mostly in silence to Shelby's, which was several streets removed from my own house. I assumed that given the tragedy that had befallen our town just the night before, she'd be staying with her parents. When we got there I clicked on my phone and, ignoring the ten voicemails I had, texted her to come open the door. I didn't want to wake her parents, who liked to sleep in on the weekends. She didn't respond, but only moments later the door swung open and she rushed out into the morning and flew into my arms, her orange hair catching the sun and glittering with a fiery glow.

"Blake, oh my god, it's so horrible! Are you okay?" Shelby asked, her voice a sob. I breathed in her essence and at once felt comforted by her open-minded presence. If anyone would believe me, I knew it would be her.

She pulled back and met my gaze. Her pale green eyes were puffy and swollen and dull, and her face was devoid of the heavy makeup she usually wore. Her hair was a tangled mess, and she was wearing a stained T-shirt with an unzipped hoodie and sagging sweats. She looked worse than I did, but of course I had spent the night curled in my love's arms. Even if he was a sub-zero temperature.

Shelby stared at me for half a beat and, cocking her head, the tears stopping for a moment, she sighed. "You look sad," she whispered. "But something is up, why aren't you the mess I am?"

Despite everything that had happened, it almost seemed magical to me how perceptive my best friend was. I'd always taken it for granted before, but she really was *seeing* when she looked at the world.

I glanced over at Geoff, who stood quietly behind me, the faint signs of grief etching his own face. I'd never thought about what it would do to him to see me mourn him, especially when it was so raw and fresh.

Shelby followed my glance, but seeing nothing, looked back at me with her light brows arched in question.

"I have to talk to you," I said softly.

"Sure, sorry. Come inside," Shelby said, shaking her head and gesturing for me to follow her into her house, a tissue clutched in her fist. I closed the door only after I made sure Geoff had followed me in, and then we headed through the hall and into the kitchen, where a door led to the basement. Shelby had taken up residence there about a year ago when her parents had made a whoopsie and popped out their fourth child. Shelby's older brother was away at college, but she still had a fourteen-year-old brother and now a toddler for a sister. She'd gone crazy from the baby crying and had complained that her grades were suffering because of it since she'd had to share a room with her. Her parents, generally being laid back and reveling in the new baby, had relocated Shelby to the basement. It's usually where she could be found when she wasn't at school in her dorm.

We clattered down the stairs and passed through the beads she had hanging from the doorway that lent additional privacy to her space. I plopped down on her futon couch and Geoff sat next to me. Shelby came over to sit next to me as well, and panicking, I shrieked, "Don't sit!"

Jumping back, startled, she gave me a funny look, her brows arched again. "Is there a problem?" she asked, walking to her bureau and picking up a package of makeup remover wipes. Pulling one out, she put it to her face and rubbed away some of the smudges on her cheeks. I was worried she was going to come back and sit on Geoff, but instead she ambled shakily to her bed and sat with her legs tucked under her, staring at me with her pale green eyes.

"What's going on, Blake?" she asked softly.

I glanced at Geoff again, and she followed my gaze once more.

"What do you keep looking at?" she asked.

I cleared my throat and looked down, trying to work out in my head the best way to tell her that he was still here. We sat in silence for a while before Shelby broke it.

"Blake?" she asked. "Just spit it out. You know you can tell me anything. You've got to be going through hell right now, although you just look anxious at the moment."

Taking a deep breath I darted another glance toward my boyfriend. Geoff, who'd been staring off into space, looked back at me and smiled wanly. His lips had grown so pale they were almost white. I had to get to that store. He nodded at me, and I inhaled deeply again. If I was going to do it, I might as well just come out with it.

"Okay," I said, flashing Geoff a brief smile before turning back to Shelby, who was watching me as if I was the old homeless man down at the bus station who was always talking to himself.

"So, I know you think Geoff is dead, but ... Well, he's still here."

Instead of telling me I was crazy right from the get-go, she just mutely stared at me. Which meant she thought I was certifiable.

So I went on, ignoring the silence. "Like, he's sitting right beside me. Wave, Geoff," I laughed a little hysterically. "Oh right, I forgot you can't see him. So anyway, I saw his body, just like you did, you know. But when I looked again, I also saw Geoff alive."

"Like a ghost?" Shelby finally said, incredulous.

"Well, no, it's his soul, at least that's what Rishi said."

"Who?"

"He works with my mom," I said, realizing that I was sounding so insane I didn't even believe myself.

"Your mom?" Shelby's eyes widened, her gaze darting to the door so quickly I almost didn't see it. She thought I'd gone off the wall.

I glanced at Geoff for support and frowned when I saw he was laughing at me. "Seriously, Blake. You sound like you're on drugs," he cackled.

I laughed in response and shook my head. "I know, it's just hard to put into words," I told him, the ludicrousness of my night making me laugh even harder.

"Just go slow, tell her everything. Even about your mom."

"You think I should?"

"You have to, Blake. She's the only person who might believe you." I nodded, and he smiled so sweetly back at me, I almost cried. God, I loved him.

I turned back to Shelby, who was gaping at me. "So was that a little convo between the two of you that I just witnessed?" she asked, disbelief weighing her tone even as she waggled her pointer finger between me and the space beside me on the couch.

"Okay, I know this all sounds crazy, so I'm going to start again. But Shelb, the only reason I came to you is because you're the one who has always said anything is possible. You believe in psychics and all that crap, and so now I need you to believe me. Because I can't do this alone, I need you," I finished in a whisper, struggling against tears that had been strangling me since I'd seen Geoff's body. Even so, one single tear escaped and traveled down my cheek. "I swear I'm not crazy," I pleaded.

Shelby stared at me with her green eyes, looking slightly less puffy but dull with exhaustion, and she analyzed me. I could almost feel her brain working, trying to figure out if I'd gone off the deep end or if I was, in fact, getting up close and personal with the paranormal.

Finally after a few moments her eyes cleared, and I could see the decision physically make its way across her pretty features as she nodded. "Okay, Blake. You've always been the sanest person I know, and the most rational, so if you say this is for real then I believe you. I'm here for you."

I smiled gratefully, and gulping down a huge breath, I began the story with seeing Rishi at the game the week before and then at the hospital. And finally, I told her about my mother.

"So you're telling me, your mother is Death? Like Death, living, breathing, and walking?" Shelby exhaled the words, rocking back on the bed from where she'd sat leaned forward for the last ten minutes as I'd relayed my story.

"Not just Death, she's the Grim Reaper."

"Did she, like, have a scythe?" Shelby asked.

"Well, no, not that I saw. But then again, I wasn't really in the mood to talk. She and Rishi kept telling me I had to lead Geoff over to the other side because apparently, and this is the clincher, I'm Death too."

"What!" Shelby shrieked, and then covered her mouth with her hand. The last thing we needed was her parents down here.

"I don't know why she didn't do it herself. She told me she couldn't. But she wanted me to lead Geoff over. They both did. They said that the longer souls stay here, they change, and then they become lost souls."

"And that's when you ran away, right?"

I nodded. "I can't lose him," I said with a shake of my head.

"Have you asked Geoff what he wants?" Shelby asked, arching her brows.

I glanced over at Geoff, who was staring off into space with a blank look on his face, the usual life of his expression faded, his weary features grown ancient overnight.

Frowning, I turned back to Shelby. "He said he doesn't want to become a lost soul," I said softly, avoiding eye contact.

"Then, Blake, why is he still here?"

Finally I looked at her, and I could feel the intensity of my expression bore into her. "I think the palm reader might be able to help."

"The palm reader? How?"

"Remember our fortunes. She told you that you'd have a close encounter with death and I'd meet death. Think about it, your encounter was Geoff and mine was my mother," I said hurriedly, before she could poke the inevitable holes in my argument.

"Yeah, she nailed it, I won't argue there. But how is she supposed to help us?"

"Maybe she knows a spell, a charm, or some ancient voodoo ritual—anything that will help Geoff. I mean it's worth a try, right?"

Shelby nodded slowly, and I could tell she was unconvinced. "Ask Geoff what he wants," she insisted.

"Fine," I said, turning to my dazed boyfriend. "Geoff, what do you want to do?"

Geoff turned, blinking, and life once again flooded his face. He studied my expression and finally smiled softly, compassion lighting the dimming glory of his once blue-green eyes. He reached over and touched my hand, making me shudder from the cold of his skin. But I didn't pull away; I continued to lie to myself that there was a way I would be able to stop something that was already done.

"I want what you want," Geoff finally said, squeezing my fingers with his own.

I turned back to Shelby. "He said let's do it."

Shelby turned a pretty frown, but she nodded. "Okay, but promise me, Blake, if this turns out to be a dead end, I think you're going to have to do what your mother told you to do."

I avoided looking at her as I rose to my feet and turned toward the door, itching to get to the New Age store and see the witchy palm reader. "I won't have to," I insisted, my faith in a woman I didn't even know as implausible to me as it probably was to Shelby. But I continued to lie to myself and let hope bloom in my chest as the three of us headed out. It was the only way I could go on.

CHAPTER SEVEN

IT TOOK SOME COAXING, but I was finally able to get Geoff into Shelby's car with the promise that she'd drive extra carefully. She drove like a grandma anyway, so I knew we had little to worry about. Geoff seemed content, but his form faded in and out the entire ride to the store. One moment he'd be there, and the next he'd be a faint outline. I sat in the back with him, and the car ride was a silent one.

As soon as Shelby parked in front of a meter, I jumped out of the car, panic flooding my chest with each ticking moment, and speed-walked along the sidewalk to the door. Turning, I jumped from one foot to the other as Shelby and Geoff hurried after me, only Shelby's breath coming out in pluming puffs in the chill of the morning. My boyfriend's lack of breath reminded me once more that he was no longer of the living. But the sun was shining, lending a hopefulness to the crisp, clean air as it took hold for the season, and I pushed the dark thoughts away.

When they reached me, I wasted no time and tried pulling on the door. Letting out a frustrated grunt, I pulled out my cell phone and glanced at the time. 10:55 a.m. We had five minutes before the store officially opened. I glanced at the hours on the door just to make sure Sunday hours were the same.

"Okay, we have to wait a few minutes," I muttered and turned away, scuffing my Adidas sneakers against the loose stone on the ground, my hands crammed into the pockets of my hoodie.

Shelby leaned against the side of the building and reached into her purse, pulling out a stick of gum that she delicately unwrapped and shoved into her mouth. She held out the package to me, but I barely glanced at her with a quick shake of my head. Geoff looked at the gum longingly when Shelby held out a stick in midair in his general direction. Shrugging, she slipped the pack back into her purse, a wallet-sized bag that was made out of a vibrant green threading and had a long strap she draped across her body, shoulder to hip. Her orange hair was pulled into a messy bun atop her head and gleamed almost as brightly as the sun, and her eyes were hooded by sunglasses.

She snapped her gum and I shot her a withering look. I was in no mood—I needed silence and the quiet thrum of traffic as I waited. When the door suddenly opened, I whirled around. But standing in front of me was a completely different woman. This one looked more like your stereotypical seventies flower child castoff. Her long, light brown hair swept down over her shoulders, and she wore a loose, flowing skirt, a peasant top that went out of style before I was born, and a large, crystal-adorned ring on each finger. Her eyes were kind when she met mine, and I felt all my anxiety flow away.

"Hi," I said. "Is Rae around?"

The woman smiled apologetically. "I'm sorry ladies, she's not in, can I ..." Her voice broke off and her gaze stopped exactly where Geoff was standing. I glanced back at him and then at the woman again, and she was definitely staring at my boyfriend. But how was that possible? Was she a death deity? She just didn't have that quality my mother and Rishi had. That detachment. Although my mother certainly more so than Rishi.

The woman, whose eyes were soft brown, turned back to me. Her expression grew serious as she studied my face. "Why don't you come in," she offered and stepped back while the three of us filed into the store. Only when Geoff had stepped through did she lock the door and turn over the sign on it to indicate the store was closed.

Shelby was watching the woman strangely, her eyes widening. "You can see him, can't you?"

The woman smiled gently and nodded, turning her focus back to me.

"I guess you aren't crazy, Blake," Shelby offered generously, the surprise evident in the way she now darted her eyes around as if Geoff was going to jump out at her and yell "boo!"

I shot her a dark look. Unbelievable. She'd been humoring me all this time. "It's nice to know my best friend has such faith in me," I snapped, before turning to the woman.

Once again, the shop smelled like incense and I could see the steadily burning stream of smoke coming from a stick held between the ceramic paws of a dragon.

"I'm Wendy," the woman said softly, her plump cheeks rosy without any makeup. She looked to be in her fifties, and where I'd been suspicious around Rae, I felt comforted by this woman's round, motherly presence. "Why don't you children come in the back room with me and we can have a chat. I can see you have troubling issues you need to deal with."

She gestured for us to follow her, and single file, we all headed toward the room where Shelby and I had been serenaded with our readings only a week prior.

When we got to the room, Shelby, who kept glancing over her shoulder, hissed, "Where is he?"

I chuckled, finding her anxiousness amusing, especially after she'd doubted me. "You're stepping on him," I whispered with a snicker.

Gasping she pulled up short. "Sorry!" she said.

Wendy glanced over at her from the seat she'd taken at the familiar table and furrowed her brow. "My dear, he operates on a different plane than you do now, so you can occupy the same space and it won't hurt either one of you."

"Oh," Shelby said and glanced at me with a scowl. "You're messing with me," she complained.

"Yeah, that's for only pretending to believe me," I bit back.

Shelby and I both took seats, but Geoff started to float around the room, whispering in and out of visibility, his sandy hair suddenly sporting frosted tips. Occasionally he would laugh, unsettling me beyond explanation. I couldn't keep my eyes off his eerie presence and the strange way he was acting.

I turned worried eyes back to Wendy, who was watching me with sadness lurking in her eyes and compassion softening her already sagging features.

"Blake, is it?" she asked me softly.

I nodded, trying to shake off the sympathy that was radiating from her.

"I know what you are."

"What?" I widened my eyes, startled. "How?"

"I am what you would call a medium. I speak with the dead who haven't yet moved on. They whisper to me, the lost souls who walk this earth, unable to pass beyond this plane of existence onto the next. Many of these spirits are drawn to you. Have you experienced this yet?"

Not knowing what to say, I just mutely shook my head. I seriously did not want a bunch of dead people following me around. I was trying to avoid this little birthright that had so inopportunely been thrust on me.

"No one has come for them, and I do not know why. But I have noticed their numbers growing, and the existential planes are becoming overwhelmed with the noise of them. The other day they got quiet, though, and then like an explosion there were whispers of you. They need you to cross them over, there's so many of them," she said, her voice threaded with sadness. "That's why you're here, isn't it? You want to pass your young man over? Already I can see the lostness taking over, he's not acting right."

Just as she said it, an overwhelming tide of misery washed over me with such force that I felt the pits of despair welling up around me, my chest heaving with emptiness, and then it was gone. I glanced at Geoff, who disappeared for a moment and came back laughing.

Horrified, I watched him and then glanced at Shelby, whose eyes were wide, the whites overwhelming the pretty pale green of her irises.

"What was that?" she whispered.

"Did you feel it too?" I asked.

She nodded quickly in response.

"It's the sickness," I whispered.

Wendy met my gaze and nodded. "He's feeding off nearby lost souls, and their misery is being projected on us. He's doing it on purpose because he's losing himself," she said firmly.

I looked at her and shook my head. "I don't want to cross him over, I want to save him. There has to be some way I can bring him back, make him whole. Or at least stop him from changing," I said, hearing the desperation thick in my voice.

"The only way to save him is to pass him over," she said softly, reaching out and putting her hand over mine.

I jerked my hand back. I refused to be comforted. There had to be a way. "What about Rae, maybe she knows a way. She's the one who said we were going to meet Death," I countered.

But Wendy was shaking her head, and I could feel the concerned stare coming from Shelby. I was off my rocker and they all knew it. The lone rational voice in my head knew it too. But I still couldn't accept it.

Finally, Wendy was unwilling to deal with my denial gently anymore, and I was startled by the sound of her fist coming down on the table.

"Now you listen to me. There is no bringing him back, he is gone. And you'd best deal with this sooner rather than later because your refusal to help him or accept who you are is only hurting him more," she said, her gaze now forceful as she pinned me to my chair with just her look. Her face softened after a moment. "I know it hurts, but you have to move on. Everyone has to move on. And then you can get to the grieving part."

I nodded. Her words made sense as I stared up at Geoff's maniacal laughing. But then he stopped, and he floated back down to my side and gave me his familiar crookedly confident smile. My chest tightened around my inner pulsing pain, and I shook my head.

"No. No." I stood up. "I refuse to believe that. There has to be something that can be done, someone who can help him. Come on, guys, let's go," I said, refusing to meet any of their eyes and face their worry and pity.

"Blake," Shelby tried to argue with me, but I cut her off with a look. She must have read the desperation in my eyes because she closed her mouth and nodded.

"Okay," she whispered.

As we headed out, Wendy spoke one last time. "Blake, when you allow yourself to see the truth, I believe all you'll have to do is take his hand and let him go," she said.

But I blocked her out, I blocked the world out, and the only thought that echoed in my head was to save Geoff.

Back outside the shop, I charged off toward the car, ignoring Shelby's calls for me to slow down. When I got there it was locked, so I waited impatiently for Geoff and Shelby. "Come on, hurry," I said.

Shelby stopped and stared at me. "Hurry where, Blake? Where are we going?" I could hear her patience with me wearing thin, but there was nothing to be done about it.

"I don't know, but we have to figure something out because I'm losing him," I said, glancing at my former boyfriend who, when he wasn't floating and laughing, looked like a sleepwalker.

"No kidding. I pretty much had that figured out back at the shop, when I momentarily thought downing liquid detergent would be a good way to escape the sudden, inexplicable depression I sank into for a few seconds. 'The sickness,' as you and Wendy both called it, was pretty brutal."

"Listen, if you don't want to help me, I get it. But standing here arguing with you is only wasting my time," I said and glanced over at Geoff. "Come on, Geoff." He didn't register my command, only floated my way, no longer walking like a living human person. "I'll just walk," I yelled and marched off. My throat was so dry and my eyes felt parched, but I knew there was a deep well of tears just waiting to pour forth. I refused them access to the air.

"Blake!" Shelby shouted after me, but I ignored her. I heard her pounding the pavement behind me until she grabbed by my shoulder and spun me around.

"Listen to me, you insufferable hardhead. I'll help you, okay? Just promise me that you're really thinking about this. Because the longer he's around—as you've been told twice now by authorities on this subject—the more likely it is you're going to lose the boy you once knew."

Shelby had removed her sunglasses so that they perched on top of her head, and I looked into her bloodshot eyes and nodded. "I know, and if we can't find a solution soon, then I'll do it," I said, masking the truth—that I couldn't let him go.

She searched my face, but my lies must have been believable because she nodded.

"Where do you want to go? I'll drive."

"Let's go back to my house for now. I want to hit the Web and do some research. I don't think driving aimlessly around is going to accomplish anything."

Relief spread across Shelby's face and she nodded with a small smile. "Now that seems like a rational next step. Let's go."

*   *   *

I was thankful my dad seemed to have stepped out when we got to my house. I honestly didn't think I could deal with more sympathetic stares and worried glances. Shelby and I headed up the stairs to my room and Geoff floated up after us.

The changes he was going through were really starting to scare me. He was acting insane at times, and other times he seemed barely present. The boy I'd once known was going farther and farther away from me, and I felt the urgency to do something building up inside me. I hated the nagging feeling that my mother had been right. He was deteriorating.

Once we were in my room, I locked the door and headed to my desk where my laptop sat. "Shelb, why don't you use my tablet and you can help with the research."

She nodded and flopped on my bed, sliding back up against the headboard and positioning a few pillows behind her. "What do you want me to look for specifically?"

I wiggled my mouse to get my screen to light up. "Maybe lost souls, reanimation, stuff like that. I'm going to search for local witches," I said.

She glanced over at me. "Witches?"

"Yeah, maybe the local Wiccans know something, right?"

"Wow, you sure have come a long way since last week, when palm readers were 'mumbo jumbo,'" she said, using air quotes.

"Yeah, well, I've since been informed that my mother is the Grim Reaper and my boyfriend is floating around my room right now, so I had to adjust my previous beliefs," I said dryly, turning toward the screen and typing "witch covens, Specter, New York."

I was scanning my findings when I felt an anger so fierce it set my teeth grating against each other, and I felt my fingers hook into tight claws as my skin crawled with loathing. As it had last time at the shop, the feeling faded but the aftereffects left me with a sour taste coating my mouth. I turned around slowly in my chair to see that Geoff was floating eerily close to me, and his once beautiful blue eyes so filled with life were almost white, the color had leached out of them. He was no longer solid, but partially transparent, and he had the most horrible grin on his face.

"Blake," he sneered. "Worst girlfriend ever. A good girlfriend would have saved me. Instead, my body is rotting … or should I say, getting embalmed. My insides filling with chemicals, replacing my blood, my organs," he cackled.

I lifted trembling hands to my mouth, barely able to hold back the plea for forgiveness that wanted to tumble out of my mouth.

"Blake," Shelby shook me. "What's he doing?"

I shook my head. "He's, he's, he's saying such horrible things," I said in a wavering voice as he circled above us. I could feel his rage, and an energy seemed to surround him in his fit, a force that affected the space immediately around him. He was drawing energy from me. I shuddered, gasping for air but finding it hard to suck any into my lungs. I saw all color drain from Shelby's face and I shook my head, finally heaving in a breath.

"No," I shrieked to Geoff. "I'm sorry! I should have saved you." I knocked into the desk with my knee as I struggled to my feet, sending an old picture of Geoff and me at a high school game crashing to the floor.

I crouched down to pick up the ruined frame and pulled the picture out, staring down at it. Geoff was giving me a sloppy kiss on my cheek and I was smiling into the camera, the happiest girl in the world, my vivid blue eyes sparking with the joy of having the love of such a cool guy. I'd totally failed him. The tears I'd been keeping in check started to bubble up, wrenching out of me.

I felt the push of his twisted anger once more. I sucked in my breath and Shelby lurched to my side, clutching me against her and petting my hair.

"Stop it, Geoff!" she shouted to the room. "Cut this out right now."

The room went silent, and I looked up for any sign of my lost soul boyfriend, turning my head fast as the shadowy edge of something wavered out of my perception before I could truly see it. I frowned, wondering what it was, but I was distracted by Shelby speaking.

"Hey, he listened. Maybe I'm a ghost whisperer," Shelby quipped.

I couldn't help but give a tremulous laugh. I glanced at her and nodded, showing her I had it back under control, and I looked around the room. While only moments before the room had been unimaginably loud with the force of Geoff's twisted emotions and his wrathful voice, now it was utterly still.

Getting to my feet, I set the picture I'd been clutching back down on my desk and tried to stop the trembling of my hands. Shelby was on guard, swiveling her head around quickly, trying to ward off the attack of an entity she couldn't see.

When he did come back, it was with a mournful wail. He appeared before me on his knees, his face in his hands, sobbing. My heart broke for the millionth time in the last twenty-four hours as I watched him cry.

I sank to the ground and put my arms around him, happy that even as he grew more intangible that I could still touch him. I ignored the cold and kissed the side of his face, caressing his hair. Finally, he lifted his head and stared at me, his eyes carrying the last hint of cerulean blue.

"What's happening to me, Blake?" he whispered. "I didn't mean those things I said. I don't know why I said them."

"Shh, I know," I said soothingly, brushing my fingers through his hair.

"Blake," Shelby whispered from behind me. "Is everything okay?"

I nodded. "He's himself right now, he's Geoff."

Geoff glanced at Shelby and then to me. "Blake, I know you love me, and I love you. I never felt for a girl the way I do for you," he said with a wobbly smile. "And I'm pissed as hell that I died, that I didn't get to kiss you more, to get to third base, go all the way." He cocked his smile and waggled his eyebrows lecherously, and I laughed despite the pain swelling within me. I knew what was coming. "But seriously, I'm pissed that I didn't get to love you longer on this Earth and see you graduate and stare into your beautiful blue eyes longer."

Tears streamed down my face unchecked as he lifted his fingers to stroke my cheek, and leaning forwards, pressed his lips to mine. And maybe I imagined it, but they were moist, and soft and warm, just for that instant.

"I love you too, so much. I want to do all those things with you too," I said.

He smiled, and the sadness that etched his smile carried up into his face until every crinkle and wrinkle and smooth plane of his face was heavy with the hopelessness of our predicament.

"Blake, I wish we could. I wish I could be here to help you, because what you are, who your mother is—I think it's going to be a hard road. And I wish I could be there for you to lean on," he said, reaching up his hand and wiping tears from my face. It did no good, because more came after.

I sniffled and wiped my eyes, my fingertips coming away laden with salt and sadness. "What are you saying?" I asked, but I already knew. I just needed him to say it, to tell me it's what he wanted.

"You need to cross me over, Blake. I can't—I can't become this thing."

"But maybe I can find a way to stop this from happening," I insisted again, but he was already shaking his head.

"I died, Blake. There's no coming back from that. I need for you to let me go," he said gently.

"I don't know if I can," I whispered.

Taking my hand in his, he met my gaze and held on to it, the need in his eyes so great I knew that he was right. "Please," he said softly.

After a few moments, I nodded. "One last kiss?" I asked.

His lips curved in his signature smile and he bent down, covering my mouth with his own and clutching me to his cold body as if he'd never let go. Finally after a few blistering moments amidst his frigid temps, he released me. And now it was my turn to release him.

Heaving a shaky breath, I wiped my tears from my face and struggled to regain control of myself. I glanced at Shelby, who'd quietly been watching my exchange with Geoff, although of course she'd only seen me.

"I'm going to cross him over, or I'm going to try," I told her.

She nodded and smiled faintly. "Yeah, I'd gathered that. Do you know how?"

I shook my head with a humorless laugh and glanced at Geoff who nodded supportively. "I don't know anything, really. But Wendy mentioned that all I needed to do was take his hand and let go, and there's a feeling I've been having, an urge, and I think it might be related to this. So I'm going to try."

I held out my hand toward Geoff, and he slipped his large, callused one into my own. I started to close my eyes, but he stopped me.

"Hey, Blake," he said. "Thank you for loving me."

I nodded. "Thank you for loving me back," I whispered with a soft sob.

Then, I closed my eyes once more and focused on Geoff's hand. The room fell away and I envisioned letting him go, allowing him the peace he'd wanted from the very beginning. The peace I hadn't allowed him because of my selfish need for him.

At first, I didn't feel anything happening, and I cringed with the thought of having to go see my mother and show her she'd been right.

But it was then that I realized I was still holding on to him and standing in place, when I needed to lead him. My mind altered and shifted, and when I opened my eyes I saw the different planes of existence shimmer before me. I lifted a finger and pointed where a shivering rift in the two planes had opened, surrounding me, encompassing me. I was the rift. I was the gateway.

I kept my fingers around his as he stepped toward me, the mixture of his emotions rushing through me. He met my gaze, lifting his fingers to his lips and releasing the symbolic kiss in a wave, and then he walked into my arms, into me, and I felt his joy at the union pound through me. "Good-bye," I gasped, and he blinked out of existence. The planes and the doorway within me collapsed so that when I refocused, all I saw was Shelby sitting on my bed, watching me curiously.

I was silent, the high I'd gotten from Geoff's crossover running through me like an addicting adrenaline. It was the most amazing feeling—the intermingling of our souls and his feeling of release powered through me and gave me a rush like nothing I'd ever experienced. I'd like to say it lasted, but it came crashing in on me and I slumped to the floor. I still felt the joy he'd felt, and it was a deep comfort. But the rush disappeared and I was left with my grief.

Shelby dropped to the floor and gathered me into her arms while I sobbed. My tears strangled me and wrenched my body as I cried and cried.

There was a knock on my door and then my dad was standing in the doorway, the grief still fresh in his eyes. "Blake, oh, sweetie," he whispered and hurried in. I turned toward him and fell into his embrace, into the soothing sounds of my father's voice and his strong, comforting arms. "He's gone, Daddy," I whispered. "He's gone."

CHAPTER EIGHT

WHILE I'D BEEN trying to keep Geoff on this plane, his parents had been planning his funeral. When the grief wasn't wracking my body with the force of my sobs, the guilt weighed heavily that I hadn't yet visited them. But the day after I sent Geoff through into the underworld, I was getting dressed for his funeral.

I donned a long-sleeved black wrap dress, black stockings, and the black pair of heels I never wore. Shelby met me at the house. She'd dyed her hair black for the occasion, the only time since our freshman year of high school that I'd seen her with hair that hadn't been colored by packets of powdered juice.

My own black hair was natural and curled around my shoulders in thick, heavy waves.

"You ready?" she asked with a raspy voice, which she cleared of the tears I knew she'd already been crying.

I shook my head. "No," I said and grabbed a long, gray sweater from a hook by the door. "Dad? You coming?"

My father appeared in the kitchen doorway wearing a dark gray suit, and he'd actually given his floppy blond hair some order. His pale blue eyes so like my own watched me with concern from behind his glasses.

"You ready?" he asked us both, echoing Shelby's question from only moments before.

We both shook our heads. I'd never be ready for Geoff to be gone.

We all turned to the door, but I stopped and grabbed a piece of paper off the table that we always put the mail on in the hallway. The day before, mere hours after I'd sent Geoff's soul off into another plane of existence, his uncle had called and asked if I'd give a eulogy for Geoff. But I'd declined. I knew I wouldn't be able to keep it together long enough to even get a sentence out, let alone pay him the dues that were called for. Instead, my dad had offered.

"Hey, Dad, don't forget your speech." He smiled at me in thanks, taking the paper from my outstretched hand, folding it, and placing it in his suit pocket.

I sighed. I'd already said good-bye. I really didn't know if I had it in me to do it again. But I slipped my arms into my sweater and pulled it tightly around me as my dad opened the door and Shelby followed him out. I glanced around the foyer of my house as if I might catch a glimpse of Geoff floating maniacally through a wall. And as much as even lost soul Geoff would have been a welcome sight, I knew he was better off where he was, a Geoff that was unfettered by the trappings of this cold, bleak world.

I followed them out the door and shivered. The sky was overcast and the chill of the fall wind had taken a turn for the colder. Leaves on the trees danced and dangled, brilliantly enflamed with the bright hues of the season. It was the only color in the dull grayness of the world.

"Come on, Blake," my dad called, already sitting in the driver's seat. "I don't want to be late."

I almost laughed in despair. Late for what? It was already too late.

* * *

It was only as I was standing at Geoff's gravesite after the memorial service that I remembered the joy I'd felt crossing him over, the peace he'd felt that he was moving on. It took some of the ache away, and I knew that even though I wished he could have stayed here with me, I'd done the right thing.

The pastor was saying a last few words and then it was time to toss our flowers into the grave. When it was my turn I looked down at the box his body was in and let the snow white rose fall gently into the grave. *Good-bye.*

Turning, I fell into his mother's arms and she gripped me to her petite, bony frame in a surprisingly firm embrace. "Blake," she whispered, choking through my name.

I hugged her back, feeling the tears I'd hoped to keep down strangling me as well. "I'm so sorry I haven't been over to see you," I said, feeling color brighten my cheeks with my shame.

She pushed me back so she could look at me and shook her head firmly, her wavy, shoulder-length, silvery blond hair bouncing with the movement. "Don't be silly, Blake," she hissed. "I know you loved my boy and must have been going through hell. Just make sure you come and visit me soon," she sniffled and dabbed at her eyes. She'd always been a tough lady, rough around the edges, but sharp and insightful and kind.

I nodded, sniffling as well. "I promise," I whispered and hugged her again.

She patted my cheek with a firm hand and gave me a wavering smile. "He loved you a lot, Blake girl," she said and then turned to someone else.

I spoke with a few more people and gave my condolences to Geoff's father, who I hadn't really gotten to know since he was away on business a lot. And then everyone was heading to their cars, the sharp nip of the day driving them to the warmth of Geoff's parents' home, where everyone was gathering after the service.

I turned to find my dad and Shelby, and instead I took a quick step back when I saw a gathering of roughly ten people staring at me a short distance away. At first, I thought they were mourners at another funeral ceremony, but then I noticed that a few of them shimmered in and out of focus at times. Souls. Lost ones, I gathered.

I turned to go, shuddering as my flesh crawled with the intensity of their stares, but I didn't make it too far. I shouldn't have been surprised. Only a few feet away from the host of souls was Rishi. His dark, demanding gaze met mine with an intensity I couldn't look away from. I started toward him, resigned to this meeting. I should have been angry he'd seek me out minutes after my boyfriend's burial, but it was the nature of everything that now consumed me. Death.

"Blake." I turned, and Shelby was walking over, her face smeared with black from her tears mingling with her makeup. "Are you coming?" she asked softly. "Your dad is waiting in the car."

I glanced back at Rishi, who was still waiting for me, and nodded before turning back to look at her. "Yeah, I'll be there in a minute. There's someone I have to talk to," I said, looking back at Rishi.

She followed my gaze and her eyed widened. "Is that ...?"

I nodded, cutting her off. "It's him. And there's about twenty lost souls watching me right now over by that cluster of trees, so I feel like I should at least talk to him really quick."

I noticed the number of souls had grown in the last few moments, and I could feel their need, their desire. Not yet fully lost, they had moments of awareness, and they wanted out of this realm and into the next. Their longing beat against me in waves. I felt like the lone standstill in a pit of moshing teens. It was a feeling I didn't relish. Agitated, I ran my fingers through my hair, ripping at it slightly.

"I'll be right back," I said shortly, and without waiting for an answer, headed toward Rishi.

When I got to him he smiled sadly at me, lifting his arms to hug me and then dropping them, obviously thinking better of it. We weren't friends.

"Why are you here and why are those souls stalking me?" I demanded, hugging my sweater around my body against the sharp chill, even though after days of embracing a frigidly cold Geoff, I'd practically grown immune.

"I came to pay my condolences ... and I wanted you to know, letting him go was the right thing to do," he said softly.

I didn't meet his warm, penetrating gaze and instead looked off to the souls haunting my boyfriend's funeral. I gave a short jerk of my head to acknowledge his words.

"Thanks. Is that it?" I asked, breath coming out in bursts of white as I finally met his stare.

"No ..." He seemed at a loss, but he finally spoke after a few moments. "I was hoping you'd come hear Grim out. She's your mother, no matter how angry you are at her."

"I'm not angry, I'm ... disturbed, horrified, and a whole dictionary of feelings I don't have time to say right now. And I'm sad. Now tell me why they're here," I said again, unwilling to soften any more, unwilling to bend, not on this day of all days.

He sighed, making me look at him curiously. Geoff had often heaved great sighs when he'd been frustrated with me. Was Rishi finally getting annoyed with me? The thought almost made me smile. If I could have made my mouth work that way.

"They're here because of you, Blake. They felt you pass Geoff over and now they know that it's possible for them. There's a lot like them, souls stuck on this plane who have lost themselves completely to the soul fade."

I shook my head. "But why don't you or my mother just help them over?" It didn't make any sense.

Rishi looked off at the souls and I could see pain flicker in his eyes. Their pain was his. "I would if I could, but it doesn't work that way. Your cultures and beliefs dictate which death deity you get. I am a Hindu death deity. And Grim, well she just cannot. That is why you need to come tonight and hear her story. You'll understand it all then," he said, his gaze once again beaming against my own.

I realized for the first time that he was gripping my arm, as if he wished he could drag me along with him. His other hand slid down and grabbed my hand, slipping a cold metal key between my fingers. I glanced down at it. "What is this?"

"It's a key to the B&B where we're staying."

I tugged my arm away from him and stepped back. "Listen, I have to go, my dad is waiting for me." I turned to walk away, a cold and comforting numbness settling around my shoulders like a shroud.

"Will you come?" he asked.

I turned back to him, ready to tell him no, but I saw something akin to fear flicker in his eyes. Was he afraid of me saying no? I couldn't worry about him, I thought, especially with so many stages of grief left to go. But then the overwhelming longing of the souls hit me again. Hard. And I gasped, barely able to suck in a breath. Finally, after a moment I gulped in the air and turned to him, nodding. "I'll come," I relented, and I walked away before he could say anything else, slipping the key into my sweater pocket.

In that moment I knew with frightening clarity, I knew against my will: I wasn't going to be able to fight this. My life was coming for me—or more accurately, Death was coming for me.

CHAPTER NINE

IT WAS EARLY EVENING by the time we got home from Geoff's parents' house, and I felt numb. Every part of my body ached from exhaustion. I hadn't had a bite to eat. A sick feeling in my gut had kept me from taking any nourishment all day, aside from a few sips of water.

My dad closed the door behind us and sighed, releasing some of the tension of the day. His shoulders sagged as much as his face with the weariness of the grief that was wearing us both down.

I turned to him and glanced at his disheveled hair and the creases at the corner of his eyes that seemed to have folded down only in a matter of hours. "I think I'm going to go crash for a while," I said, my heart twisting for a moment as I contemplated a life without Geoff.

He studied my face in his quiet way before he finally nodded. "Okay, honey," he said. "Do you need anything? A hug? Ice cream? Dishes to break?" he attempted to joke.

I smiled half-heartedly, appreciating the humor on this, the blackest of days. "Thanks, Dad, but I think I just need to sleep and not think."

He nodded understandingly and pulled me into his embrace before I could bound away, forcing the comfort of his arms around me and nearly breaking the dam I'd created against my tears. "Sleep well, hon. Call me if you need anything," he said, pulling back and giving me the best smile he could manage before turning toward his study.

I also turned and slowly ascended the stairs, thinking about sleep, a dreamless and peaceful sleep. Because in only a few hours, I'd be creeping out into the street and into the dark I'd already spent way too much time in. I'd be seeing my mother, once again.

* * *

I woke to a dark room, the light of the moon vacant from the corner of my window. I sleepily wondered if it was a new moon. Shelby loved to go on and on about the phases of the moon and how it impacted her mood. She was just so into that stuff. Except now I was starting to think it wasn't so much crap or so much "New Age."

I glanced at my alarm clock, and the glowing green numbers told me it was eleven-thirty. I kept an alarm clock because I hated fumbling for my phone in the middle of the night to see what time it was. Shelby always scoffed at my old-fashioned sensibilities. But it served me well now, telling me it was a good thing I'd woken up. I was supposed to meet Shelby in ten minutes outside in my yard. I couldn't help the smile that curved my lips when I thought about how annoyed Rishi and my mother would most likely be when Shelby tagged along. But I didn't care. It was my last rebellion before joining what I knew was probably my destiny or fate or some BS like that. I just wanted to piss off my mom, even though I barely knew her. Maybe it was because she was telling me I had to be something I didn't want to be. We already had the makings of a typical mother-daughter relationship.

It's not like I had to crawl out of my window or anything, I wasn't as dramatic as that. Since I didn't technically live with my dad anymore, I pretty much did as I wanted. He was also one of the deepest sleepers ever. It was amazing the man woke up so early every morning, but at 6 a.m. sharp he would be in the kitchen trying to get something wholesome into me.

Instead, I slid out of bed, put on a black hoodie over my light, long-sleeved T-shirt, and pulled on a pair of black leggings. I fumbled in the dark for a pair of soft, woolen gray boots that I pulled up to my knees, and I quietly slipped out my bedroom door.

I stepped as lightly as I could down each step until I was at the bottom of the stairs, which met the foyer and the front door. I grabbed my keys off the mail table and curled my hand around the doorknob, turning it with ease until I was able to squeeze out into the brisk night.

I glanced around into the dark, and the chill in the air invigorated my soul, so much that I felt the color rush to my cheeks at once and my eyes widen to awareness. I could see Shelby's shadow in my driveway, and I hopped down the stoop to meet her.

She looked up from beneath her own hood, although she had a fleece jacket on as well as gloves. "That's all you're wearing?" she asked, peering at my thin sweatshirt and bare hands.

"It's not that cold," I shrugged.

"Yes it is," she insisted, her breath turning into white fog in the night.

I shook my head and jerked my head toward the road. "Ready?"

Her thickly black-outlined eyes met mine seriously. "Are you sure this is a good idea, Blake?" she asked. "I mean, your mother is like the Grim Reaper; that's really creepy. What if she decided to off me? They probably have like a death code or something about not telling mortals who they are."

Although I thought she was probably right, I shook my head condescendingly and laughed. "You watch too much TV," I said.

"I don't watch TV, I read books," she muttered, following me as I started to walk, my fists jammed into my hoodie pockets and my thoughts on what was to come. How could my life change any more?

As we walked in a contemplative silence, the earth-smoked scent of an early fall campfire made me nostalgic for simpler times. Like last week. I sighed and glanced over at my best friend, whose head bent down as she walked.

"You think it'd be okay if I just turned around and went home, forgot about all of this and tried to move on?" I asked, picturing my warm bed and a life where death wasn't hovering around my consciousness.

Shelby glanced at me, pausing at the crosswalk and looking both ways before walking across the silent intersection that led past the field I'd first seen Geoff's soul in only days before.

"Is that what you want to do?" she asked softly, neither one of us stopping to examine the telltale signs of the crash.

"With all my heart," I said. I actually was contemplating it when a flicker caught my eye. It was a person, but I knew it was a dead person, standing on the edge of the field staring at me, pleading at me with his dead eyes. He was turning. I could already see the signs. It didn't make me warm and fuzzy that I had already acclimated to being part Death, or whatever it was that I was supposed to be.

"You see a soul, don't you?" she said, her pale green gaze keen on me, her scary powers of observation, as always, just a little too right on for my comfort.

I nodded and ducked my head so as not to have to look at the ghoul's pained eyes anymore. "Let's just go," I said as we passed the field and crossed an intersection, taking the sidewalk right into town toward Lake House Bed & Breakfast. Apparently, Mother liked to stay in style. I had been worried for a while there that she had actually been sleeping in that crypt. It really would have been so cliché.

Shelby didn't say anything, but I could feel the weight of her eyes. I knew she didn't judge me, but I could almost feel the question. Why hadn't I helped cross him over? She understood, I knew she did. But I guess the problem was that I didn't understand why I hadn't. He'd probably still be there when I came back through, I told myself. But something like guilt hugged my soul, and I knew that this gig was going to wear on me in ways I couldn't even begin to understand.

As we approached the B&B, Shelby stopped and gaped at me, her eyebrows arched in disbelief. "She's staying here?" she asked.

I gave a short laugh. "What were you expecting, a cemetery?"

"Um, yeah," she said.

"Come on," I hissed, noting the spark of fear that had taken hold in Shelby's eyes. We stepped into the house and I sighed inwardly. Maybe I shouldn't have brought her. Reading the look on my face, she jerked her head in a quick shake, her hood sliding halfway down as her midnight hair caught the last bit of moonlight that crept in through the open door.

"I'm fine, Blake," she said, and I saw resolution and stubbornness come to roost in the lines of her face and the set of her eyes.

"You sure? Because I understand, Shelb. This is some crazy stuff."

She shook her head again. "Seriously, I'm fine. You're my best friend and I want to be here for you. Even if that means meeting Death," she grinned.

I laughed softly and nodded. "Okay, well prepare to enter the *Twilight Zone*," I whispered.

I shut the door behind us and glanced around the foyer. It was dated, and it reminded me of an old person's house. The walls were covered in a faded, flowery patterned wallpaper. I turned to the stairs, which were on the left. I didn't stand around too long because I wasn't sure if the owner was wandering the halls and I just wanted to get to my mother's room.

We mounted the stairs and drifted down the hallway until I found room number five. I lifted my hand to knock, but the door swung open ominously before I could do so. Rishi peered out and glanced from me to Shelby, his dark brows shooting up in question.

"Seriously?" he said.

I flashed a grin. "Seriously."

I pushed past him, towing Shelby by her arm, and walked into the old-fashioned room with its canopy bed and hard, high-backed chairs and couch, also upholstered in a floral print.

My mother glanced up from her seat in one of the uncomfortable-looking chairs arranged around an old, circular wooden table. She seemed so normal sitting there with one leg draped over the other and her head bowed over a book, but the ordinary stopped when I met her gaze. Her hair once again seemed like a shroud around her ivory complexion. Her black eyes were deep and startlingly dark and seemed to penetrate beyond emotional barriers.

Without so much as a hello, her gaze rested on Shelby. "You brought a friend?" The inflection of her voice remained the same, and only the arch of a dark brow showed any expression at all on her stonily molded face. *My mother is cold*, I thought with an inward shiver.

I lifted my chin defiantly, trying to hide the smile that wanted to curve my lips in rebellion. I knew it was silly, but I didn't care.

"My best friend," I said, finally letting the smile show on my face.

My mother laughed and glanced at Rishi, who shot me a wink. Frowning, I turned to Shelby, whose eyes had slightly widened at the sight of my mother's mirth.

Annoyance bubbled up inside of me at the shared secrets between my mother and Rishi. *She's my mother, why is she so buddy-buddy with him? And for that matter, she's lacking in serious people skills. Why does he think she's so great? It's like he's a little teacher's pet.*

"I think it's nice you have a friend who you're willing to share this with, Blake. But was tonight really the best night?" Disappointment flickered in the recesses of her dark eyes and I couldn't help but feel that I'd let her down.

Rishi pinned me with his overwhelmingly intense gaze and nodded, reaffirming my mother's words. "These are the secrets of the death deities, Blake. How could you tell someone about this? There's rules, you know?"

I glanced over at Shelby, who mouthed, "I told you."

Turning back to my mother and her sidekick, I shrugged my shoulders once again. "She's my best friend and she's here to stay. I need someone in my corner. I'll join your little death deities club, but she's coming with me. Got it?"

I paused, glancing between my mother and Rishi, surprised when neither one of them argued with me. *Hmm, well, that was easily won.* Feeling a bit more confident, I leveled my gaze at my mother. "So now I want to know—why? Why do you need me? I know this little meeting isn't because you're concerned for my welfare," I said evenly, narrowing my eyes at both of them. But inwardly I was surprised at my own words. I hadn't even realized what had been bothering me about this whole thing until now. Yeah, sure, being Death really wasn't cool. But I was more upset that my mother had only deigned to show up when I could do something she couldn't. Pass souls over. She'd mentioned it before, and now I wanted to hear why, and what she specifically wanted from me. She didn't care, that's what hurt. This was pure business.

"You have no idea how Grim feels," Rishi started hotly, once again coming to my mother's defense. I glared at him, not even caring what he had to say, nor that it was the most fired up I'd seen him since I'd met him.

"Rishi," my mother said coolly, "that's enough. Blake wants answers and that's why she's here, for answers." Turning to me, she nodded. "I came because you turned eighteen and that is when I knew you would come into your death deity calling. Would you rather I had pulled you into this life as a child? I knew your father would create a nice life for you." She inclined her head in my direction, the darkness of her eyes less chilling for the moment.

I refused to respond, the truth of her words compelling if useless. She still wanted something from me.

"Please, take a seat." She lifted her arm, gesturing to two chairs at the table. I glanced at Shelby, who nodded, and the two of us sat down.

My mother reclined back, recrossing her black-legging-clad legs. I watched her drum her fingers on the cover of the book, showing more humanity in this mannerism than I'd ever seen cross her face. But it could have also been the environment. I mean, crypt versus hotel room. She was less scary, and maybe that's why she'd had me come here this time. To make it all seem less grim.

Rishi's long, lean form continued to lounge against the wall, looking bored. God, what was with that guy? I felt my teeth begin to grind.

"Would you like a drink?" my mother asked, suddenly putting on the guise of hostess.

Shelby opened her mouth to answer, but I cut her off. "I want the story," I said, meeting her dark gaze with my own blue one.

Grim opened her mouth to say something, but obviously thought better of it before finally nodding. "First, Rishi, please get Blake's friend here some water, my daughter is being a bit rude."

I tried to glare at her, but I knew she was right. I glanced at Shelby apologetically, but she'd grown bright red.

"Um, thank you," she said nervously, shooting me a look with wide eyes.

Rishi returned with three glasses of water, holding my gaze for a moment longer than necessary. "Thank you," I said with forced politeness, taking the glass from his hand and glancing back at my mother with a shake of my head.

I found her smiling at me, a secretive glow lighting in her eyes. I frowned at her and almost at once the composed mask of nothingness came back to her face. I arched my brows at her but she'd already begun.

"I have told you before that I cannot reap souls, have I not?"

"Rishi mentioned it," I said, shooting him a look out of the corner of my eye and seeing that he'd taken a seat on the couch, one leg kicked over his knee, his head bent over some car magazine. Apparently he'd heard this story before. Big surprise.

I turned my focus back to my mother and nodded. "But I don't know why?"

"I am not the only death deity, as we've mentioned before. Each culture or religion has unique beliefs, and people are ascribed a death deity based on their beliefs. The Mexican culture has Santa Sebastiana, better known as Santa Muerte—your aunt, by the way. Egyptians have Anubis, Osiris, or Nephthys; the Japanese, Izanami. I could go on, but you see where I'm going with this. I am favored by Westerners and many European cultures."

"But what if you don't believe in anything?" Shelby piped up. Surprised, I glanced at her and found she was already intrigued by the story and my mother. I sighed. I should have known she'd get into this.

My mother glanced at her, shrugging a slim shoulder. "It is not an exact science, but if you believe nothing, your death deity is usually designated by the region of the world you were born in, or the culture your ancestors came from. Like you, Shelby. You would be mine," my mother said with a slow smile curving her lips. Something ancient flickered in her eyes, making me shudder. I quickly glanced at Shelby, who was showing the whites of her eyes, all color having drained from her face.

Snapping my head back to my mother, I instinctively kicked her under the table. "Ow." She looked back at me sharply, all humor and taunt missing from her face. "Don't kick your mother," she said evenly, although her voice was low with warning.

"Don't scare my friend," I shot back.

Reason returned to her, her face cleared and became a cold mask once more, although I saw a flicker of unease in her black eyes. What was that all about?

I glanced back to Shelby, who seemed to have recovered, although she still darted a spooked look at me from the corner of her eyes.

"As I was saying," my mother continued, "each culture has its own death deity. And we can't take another's soul. They must be crossed over by their own."

"Okay, but that doesn't explain why you can't do it," I said.

"At one time, I ruled Abbadon, which is what the underworld is called. I was head of the council, one of the oldest deities, and the most powerful. Much of my power comes from the scythe. You see, the scythe has the power to kill other deities, cut a path through space and time, and most importantly, open the gateway between life and death. And there was one deity who always wanted the scythe. He coveted it. Hades."

"You're kidding me," I interrupted. "Like the Greek god?"

My mother's dark gaze held mine blankly for a moment and then turned to glance at Rishi, who had looked up from his magazine. "They teach Greek mythology in schools," he said by way of explanation.

Turning back to me, her face darkened with the most expression I'd seen so far. And it was wrathful. "He's no god," she seethed.

"Okay, okay," Shelby said, holding her hands up as if to ward off the coming dark.

Shaking her head, my mother collected herself again and smiled without any warmth. "Hades would not yield when I refused to give him the scythe. In his hands it would be a truly scary weapon. So he secretly began to procreate with mortal women. What he did was create an army of death deity hybrids, whom he retrieved eighteen years later and brought down into Abbadon, beginning a war against me and those loyal to me."

"And you couldn't stop him?" Shelby said, her gaze still intent on Grim.

"Hades's one flaw is he shares a vessel with Pluto, his Roman counterpart. Pluto was a loyal deity where Hades is vastly flawed," Grim said softly.

"Was?" I asked. My mother eyed me and nodded.

"Hades framed me for Pluto's murder. Killing another death deity is the first cardinal rule, never to be broken. Hades has always been the stronger one of the two, and he got so powerful that he could repress Pluto. None of us knew that, so when Hades and I quarreled one night and he attacked me, I used the scythe in self-defense. I injured him but I did not kill him. He showed the council his wound and told them that Pluto was dead within him. No one could dispute his claim, and no one, that I know of, has seen Pluto since. But I didn't kill Pluto, I am certain of that."

"But you couldn't prove it?" Shelby guessed, her chin in her hands, her gaze never wavering from my mother.

Grim nodded. "Precisely. The council ordered me to hand over the scythe, and when I refused, Hades declared a war on me. There were deities who stood by my side, like my sister Sebastiana, but Hades had an army of hybrids fighting beside him and in the end I was overcome, the scythe taken from me. Then Hades banned me from Abbadon by closing my soul gate."

"Soul gate?" I asked.

Grim nodded, elegant and poised despite the disturbing nature of her tale. "When you pass a soul over, you serve as an exit from this world to the next. But to enter the heart of Abbadon, each deity's soul must pass through a gate. That gate belongs specifically to that deity only. No other deity is meant to know where another's gate exists in the underworld. It is secret and sacred and Hades found mine, although I am not sure how."

"So Geoff was the first soul to ever cross my soul gate?" I asked.

Grim nodded again. "Yes, he was your first ...," she said, something akin to compassion flashing in her dark eyes for a mere moment before she went on. "Many death deities are against Hades's rule and my banishment but have no power to thwart the strength of his numbers. There is no council anymore, it's a mockery. Hades is a dictator and his children are his army. Meanwhile, the longer I remain unable to pass souls over, the more lost souls populate the earth, creating havoc and imbalance."

I let out a breath, overcome by the way my world had become so vast. Hades was real? He'd gotten my mom banned from the underworld—Abbadon? It was all so crazy I didn't even know where to begin. But she wasn't done.

Leaning forward in her chair, her knuckles turning whiter than they already were from clutching the armrests, my mother met my gaze. "I don't know what his endgame is, but one thing is sure—I need to get my power back. The souls can't continue to linger, stagnant and lost," she finished softly, a sadness shadowing the sharp planes of her face.

I turned toward Shelby, who was even paler than the last time I'd looked at her. Shooting my mother a nervous look, she turned her gaze to me, asking the inevitable question, "So what do you want from Blake?"

"Well, first, it would be great if she could start passing souls over, because they've been building up for fifty years and it's creating a lot of turmoil in the Earth," Rishi spoke up, his long, denim-clad legs kicked up on the coffee table in front of him and crossed at the ankle. His shiny black hair was pulled into a ponytail and he clasped his hands behind his head, looking relaxed despite the rigidity of his expression.

I'd been afraid that this was what they were going to ask me to do, but I couldn't deny the truth of what I'd felt. Of what had been building inside of me for days—the longing, the need, the eyes that watched me now wherever I went. Pleading. Always pleading. I'd watched Geoff's transformation from cool dude to scary, shimmery lost soul, and I knew how badly they wanted to be released. But I'd selfishly ignored them, ignored the fact that I could help them.

"So, since Blake is a death deity, does that mean she's, like, immortal?" Shelby piped up, interjecting herself as quickly as possible before we could move on to the next story time.

My head swiveled as I was taken away from my thoughts. Shelby's question had never even entered my mind before.

"She's a hybrid like Rishi, which means one parent is mortal and the other a death deity," my mother explained. "She will age very slowly now that she's come into her reaper abilities, so that to most it would seem she is immortal. The oldest hybrid I know of is approximately a century old, and he is still youthful. I'm sure others have slipped through the cracks. Hades can't have been the only deity having affairs with humans."

"But can she be hurt or killed?" Shelby asked, her gaze rapt on my mother.

"It's hard to kill any of us and we're much more durable than full humans," Rishi said, drawing our gazes to him for the moment. "We are not invincible, though we do have specific gifts that make it easier for us to avoid certain death. The scythe is the only way a full deity can be killed. But all deities can feel pain."

I was listening to the conversation with interest, amazed to find out I could potentially live for so long, when suddenly a thought slammed into my head, and I pinned my mother to her chair with my gaze.

"Did you only have me so you could find some way to stop Hades?" I asked, trying to speak evenly over the lump forming in my throat. My poor father, he'd always talked about her with such love.

"Yes and no," my mother said softly.

I had to give her credit, she wasn't lying to me. If anything, she was a little bit too truthful. Her eyes suddenly dropped from my face to my chest, and I glanced down, realizing she was staring at the owl necklace. I glanced back quickly and I saw her gaze had turned dispassionate once more, but for a moment I thought I'd seen longing.

"How so?" I croaked, succumbing to all the lonely feelings I'd felt as a child when I'd just wanted a mommy. Now here she was, and I would gladly take my dad's warm cuddles over her chilly demeanor.

"I loved your father very much," she began. Looking at her, I could hardly believe she knew what love was.

"But I only had watched him from afar until the idea came to me. Don't hate me, Blake," she said softly, and I was surprised to see true emotion on her face. Her lips parted slightly as if from want of me, and she stared longingly into my eyes. For a moment I could almost see a real mother in her shining face, but then she shut it down completely. Had it been a façade? Or a glimpse of something that was really there? She was so confusing and emotionally draining to be around.

"I first saw your father when your grandfather died. I couldn't pass souls over at that point, but his call was so strong. Around that time, I'd sometimes visit with souls when they died and explain to them what was happening and why I couldn't help them. I was hopeful then, hopeful that I'd soon be at full power, hopeful that Hades wouldn't truly let these souls suffer for whatever my transgressions, real or false, might have been. Your grandfather was an interesting man; he'd seen a lot in the short life humans live. He made me promise that I'd keep a watchful eye on your father."

My mother paused, shaking her head, a wistful glimmer lighting her eyes for a brief moment. "I guess I felt sorry for him, or nostalgic for simpler times, because I promised him I would before he started to go lost. I had little else I could do, so why not? Over time, your father's quirks, the way his glasses were always lopsided, the way his shoulders were strong even when he was sad, the way he laughed aloud when reading even in a room full of people, started to affect me. And I realized I didn't have to follow the rules anymore and that maybe I could have a real life. At least for a little while, until you turned eighteen. And then I thought you might be able to help, although I couldn't be sure."

"But then why did you leave? You could have had a life with us for that time," I said, feeling my heart wrench at the idea of having had a mother.

For a few split moments, she appeared as lost as I felt, but she pulled it back in, looking frostier than before. "I'm the Grim Reaper. I had to do something about the souls, I couldn't be a mother," she said matter-of-factly, destroying the hope in my heart that had always imagined a kind, nurturing mother with mirth glowing from her eyes.

I swallowed down the sadness I regretted allowing myself to ever feel, and I met her gaze. "So what's next?" I said more evenly than I thought was possible.

Something flickered in her eyes. Remorse? Respect? I couldn't tell, so I pushed it away, waiting for her answer.

"First, you begin to clean up the imbalance of souls," she said, looking over at Rishi. He stood and walked to the window, glancing out into the night before looking back at me with his deep brown gaze.

"Then we get the scythe," he said with a slow smile, and it was then that I saw it. How Rishi and I were alike. He was an adrenaline junkie too.

* * *

It was inching toward 3 a.m. when Shelby and I quietly walked the streets of Specter toward home. "Unbelievable," she'd said as we'd hit the sidewalk, but she hadn't elaborated and I hadn't asked. It had been the only words said since we'd left the B&B.

I paused at the field and glanced across it, noticing the man's soul from before. He stared at me and blinked in and out, and I could tell he had gone to that lost place, the place where they change and morph into something spooky and dark. I turned to look back at Shelby, who had stopped just behind me. I didn't need to say anything; she read me as she always had.

"Go reap him," she nodded. "I'll wait here." I knew she was probably clutching pepper spray in her pocket, so I ducked my head, jammed my fists into my hoodie pockets, and began my trek to the middle of the field where the man stood wavering.

When I was only a couple of feet away I stopped and stared at him. "Hi," I said, not really knowing what else to say.

He continued to shimmer like a reflection on water until I got annoyed. "Hey, stop it!" I yelled. I glanced back at Shelby, who lifted her arms in question. I shook my head in response and turned back to the guy, at once noticing that he'd stabilized and was staring at me with deep blue eyes and light, tousled brown hair. And I recognized him—the deep set of his eyes and the wide jut of his jaw only just hardening as he matured into a man, losing the boyishness of high school youth. He'd been a freshman at Specter U on the basketball team, one of their star players, I remembered. His picture had stared out of the newspaper at me for weeks as the police had investigated his death. He'd died of alcohol poisoning, apparently related to a fraternity hazing ritual.

He stared back at me now, waiting for me to help him. I could sense it. Seeing the reason that existed within his eyes and the solidity of his form, I wondered just how long souls lived between states before they went fully lost. This guy obviously hadn't gone fully to the dark side yet, but I could tell it was coming soon. Desperation emanated off him, causing me to wrinkle my nose with distaste. It was musky and sour at the same time, and it clung to the breeze like bad whiskey and cheap cologne. But I managed to swallow my nausea back down long enough to focus.

"Can you help me or what?" he asked, his voice weighted by the dragging nature of futility but edged with hope.

"I think so," I said, watching his expressionless, hooded eyes widen a bit.

"What do I have to do?" he asked, suspicion still present in the set of his furrowed brow and the stiff tilt of his head.

"Hey, lighten up," I said, annoyed that he seemed to have so little faith in me. "I may be new at this but I *have* done it before."

"Right, right. To your boyfriend?"

"How do you know that?" I asked, surprised.

The guy shrugged his T-shirt-clad shoulders. It had been the end of summer when he died, so that must have been the outfit he passed in, I thought.

"Word travels," he said cryptically.

"What? Through the lost soul social media channels?" I asked.

A smile finally cracked his stoic expression. "Something like that, although I didn't hear that the Grim Reaper's daughter was such a comedian," he dimpled, casting me a wink.

I ignored his sudden cuteness. "And I didn't know lost souls were such pains in the butt. So color us both surprised," I retorted with my own smile.

We stopped, the air between us thinning as we locked eyes and our smiles faded, his first and mine an echo. Finally, he nodded his head as if my wisecracking had convinced him of my capabilities. *Hey, maybe I should rethink my future as a death deity hybrid and look into doing stand-up.*

"Do you want me to help you?" I finally interrupted the silence. The whiskey-cologne smell had faded, replaced by the faint scent of wet earth that reminded me of spring and rebirth. Hope.

He nodded slowly, taking a step closer to me. "What should I do?" he asked, his voice lacking the trepidation that had threaded his tone only moments before.

"Just take my hand," I said, reaching my own out and hoping I could remember how I'd done it before. It had been different with Geoff—there had been so much emotion involved, my heartache and loss. I barely remembered it aside from how painful it felt to feel his fingers vanish from my own.

"Hey," he said before he touched me. "I'm sorry about your boyfriend. That's rough."

I nodded, seeing the compassion heavy in his gaze.

His fingers wrapped around mine and I closed my eyes, but I didn't have to do much. The very connection of our fingers triggered something, and I felt him begin to slip through from the world. Once again I was hit with feelings, his relief, his grief at leaving behind his world. He hadn't wanted to go, but he knew he couldn't stay. His resignation saddened my soul, as did his reluctance at leaving his girlfriend. Her image flashed through my mind and was gone.

When I opened my eyes, he had disappeared, and I was left with the rush of his exit infusing my blood with energy.

That's when they came. A swarm of flickering figures with fearful eyes and the desire to be free of the trappings of lostness. The air was so thick with the cologne and whiskey smell that I doubled over, dry heaving on my knees and hovering over the shadowy blades of grass that looked almost silver when caught by the moonlight.

"Blake?" Shelby had come to see if I was okay. She stood over me, blocking out the moon, her face cloaked from my view.

"I'm okay," I gasped, although I was pretty sure I wasn't. How could I possibly send them all over? But I knew I had to. They circled me, staring silently at me. Begging me to release them. They'd waited long enough, and now that they'd found a way out, they weren't going to let me be.

"I think I'm going to be here a while," I said, taking a deep breath and looking up at her. "They're everywhere. I need to help them."

"Is that wise, Blake? Shouldn't you have your mom or Rishi around to assist? I mean they've waited long enough, what's another day? God knows how many lost souls exist in this town alone, waiting to be sent over."

I shook my head. "I have to, Shelb. I can't take the burden of it." My stomach was churning, but I shakily got to my feet, ignoring the agony of the souls' need, which sent shooting streaks of pain through my head.

"I'll be fine," I croaked, although I was sure I was about to have an aneurysm.

"If you insist on being stubborn and doing this, I'm staying right here. I don't trust this. You look like you're about to pass out," she said, stepping back into the pale beam of the moonlight with her hands on her hips.

I massaged my temples. "You should be more concerned about the mass of souls standing all around you."

Despite the pain I was in, I almost laughed at the way her eyes widened and she furtively glanced around. I shook my head and waved her off, then I lurched toward a woman who looked to be in her fifties and whose gray hair hung in two braids down the sides of her face, reaching to her waist. I reached out and took her hand and felt the electrical jolt sail through me as she crossed. My emotions melded with hers in those seconds, bathing me in everything she felt at her crossover. And then I did it again with the next soul. And the next.

The last soul said good-bye to this world as a new day dawned, and I stretched, inhaling the crisp smell of the fall morning, thankful to be rid of the lost souls' desperation. I glanced around as light slowly spread across the field, illuminating the figure of Shelby, who had long since fallen asleep in the cold grass. She shivered in her sleep and I felt my chest clench. My best friend.

I walked over to her and knelt down, the chill in the air making my senses buzz. "Shelb," I said, shaking her. "Wake up."

Her cheeks looked chalky against the pitch of her dyed hair, and she shuddered from the cold as she cracked her eyes open and lifted her head. Painfully, she rose to a sitting position and wrapped her arms around herself, teeth clicking together.

"You done?" she asked, glancing around the park as if she'd be able to see for herself whether there were any souls hanging around.

I nodded. "You ready to head home?"

"Are you tired?" she asked, blinking sleep from her eyes and staring up at me with surprise.

I shook my head and jumped from one foot to the other. Not from the cold, but from the energy that thrummed through my body, infusing my being and sending a pulsating sensation to burst through my fingers and toes.

"Just the opposite," I said, grabbing her by the hand and dragging her to her feet. "It's like I had five pots of coffee, but without the certain heart attack. I feel more alive than I ever have before. I remember I felt energized after reaping Geoff, but this is crazy. I could seriously run like three marathons."

Narrowing her eyes in disgust, Shelby stomped her feet to stay warm and jerked her head to the road. "Seriously? You get no sleep and you're like Death on speed. Meanwhile, I sleep on the ground in the middle of the cold and get a crick in my neck for my troubles," she whined. "Let's go get some coffee. We've both got classes today and I have no idea how I'm going to make it through."

I started to follow her, shaking my shoulders and wanting to fling off some of the excess energy that was coursing through me.

"Isn't your dad going to be expecting you at home?" Shelby asked. "I mean, he's up at the crack of dawn every morning, and we just buried your boyfriend yesterday."

"What time is it?" I asked, fumbling for my phone even as I asked the question, beating back the pain from the raw wound that was Geoff.

"Twenty after six," she said before I could look.

"Super," I hissed. "I just don't want him to worry. I don't think I'm up for going to class today."

"Just tell him you needed to go for a walk and so you called me," she said.

"I always leave a note," I said as we walked toward home.

"Tell him you forgot," she said. "And text him now before he thinks you went to jump off a cliff."

I took out my phone and started to punch in my message, but before I could, my phone vibrated in my hands. Great.

Where are you???? The text read.

OMW. Coffee with Shelb. Forgot note. Sorry!!!

I glanced at Shelby, whose eyes drooped heavily, her makeup smeared beneath her eyes. "We'd better go get that coffee because while you're buzzing like an addict, I look like I slept in a field. Oh wait, I did," she said with a sideways glare.

I laughed. "I love you, Shelb. You're the best. Does that help?"

"It'll do for now, I suppose," she said, somewhat appeased. "Hey, don't you have your big Death Deity 101 course with Rishi tonight?" she asked as we approached the coffee shop, which thankfully wasn't in the throes of its morning rush yet.

I shrugged in response to her question. "Looks like I'll be getting an A since I did a little advanced reading," I grinned.

Before going into the coffee shop, Shelby turned to me with a smile. "Hey, looks like you're taking to being a death deity better than expected," she laughed.

I smiled, but I didn't respond as we stepped into the shop. Sending souls who wanted to go wasn't that hard. I hadn't watched them die. It was the ones who were still alive who didn't want to go that scared me.

PART II

CHAPTER TEN

Present Day

I HAD HEADED BACK to my dorm the day after my encounter with Carly, my first suicide. I knew it wouldn't be my last. The thought nearly crushed me. The vacant eyes of the girl from the night before haunted me, as did the sound of her mother's grief as I ran from the scene. *How do I get out of this job?* I sighed. Rishi kept telling me it was my legacy. I told him where to stick it. I smiled momentarily to myself, picturing the rise I could get out of him.

I glanced at the clock, weariness making me sick to my stomach and still, my eyes felt glued open. The images of Carly's pale face and lifeless eyes shoved their way into my thoughts again. I tried to push them away, but I couldn't. My eyes stung, but I refused to cry. The dorm room felt tiny, my roommate Lisa's light breathing the only sound in the otherwise silent night.

I choked on the contained air. I needed to breathe. I rose, pulling a long-sleeved shirt over my T-shirt and sliding my feet into a pair of slippers. I was wearing my comfiest pair of yoga pants and figured I'd be warm enough. The cold just didn't bother me much anymore.

I grabbed my key and crept out into the hallway, closing the door softly behind me. I padded down the stairs and through the common room, which was strangely quiet. But a lot of the students had gone home to prepare for the ruckus of the upcoming spring break. I had a class tomorrow—actually, today—so I'd stuck around. I stepped out onto the small wooden structure that passed for our building's patio. My breath fogged in the graying morning as I slipped onto one of the beaten-up, fraying lounge chairs and inhaled the morning frost. My lungs welcomed the icy chill as I surveyed the trees that lined the university property, their barren branches not yet illuminated by the slowly rising sun.

Leaning back, I drew my knees up to my chest and hugged my arms around my legs. Thinking of Carly again, I hoped she'd found a better place. I gazed up through the gloom and watched the dying twinkle of the night's stars. So far away. Just like my hope that I'd wake up and find out I wasn't a death deity or that my mother wasn't the Grim Reaper.

"It doesn't get easier," a voice cut into my thoughts, and I jerked my head back, hitting the metal edge of the chair and yelping, although probably not loud enough to alert any students who had stayed behind, I hoped.

"What the—" Rishi's shape emerged from the fading shadows of the courtyard, appearing out from behind a large bush. "What are you doing here?" I rubbed my head, staring at him as he walked over and uninvited, sat on the edge of another faded lounge chair, just barely touching my leg.

"Sorry," he said, catching my gaze with his dark one. But he didn't look sorry, his full lips pulling up in a faint smile and his stare almost overwhelming me with its unblinking intensity. "I only wanted to check on you after Grim told me about your latest reaping. I was going to wait until you woke up, but then I saw you come out here."

"So let me get this straight. You came to check in on me at like 6 a.m. to see if I wanted to talk?"

Still unblinking, he nodded, although I saw the glimmer of amusement in his warm brown gaze. "You got it."

"You have no shame," I muttered, thankful that I hadn't put on the stupid retainer the orthodontist still wanted me to wear at night. "Oh, and great job with the comfort. 'It doesn't get easier'?" I asked, shooting a look at him while trying to avoid the power of his stare.

He ignored my previous comment, his face growing serious as he nodded. "It doesn't, I'm sorry to say. But you get used to it. The trick is to embrace your empathy."

The yard was slowly growing lighter with each passing minute as the sun started to creep over the horizon. I could see his face grow stronger in the light, and I knew he was the type of person that probably did feel real empathy. But could I?

"What do you mean?" I said, picking at a splintered piece of wood on the edge of the arm rest so as to avoid having to look at him.

"It means you can help those you cross over by being more than a gateway into their afterlife. You can comfort them. I think that's what every good death deity should be doing—comforting those who they must lead from life into death. Don't you?"

I did agree with him. I'd felt the fear and sadness of those I'd crossed over and they needed more than a hand. They needed a hug. Which I'd actually done for a teenage girl who'd died of a congenital heart condition earlier this week. She'd been so sad, and I had been so sad with her that I'd automatically just embraced her, and she'd passed through me into the other realm.

But I scoffed. "You say that, but my mother is the coldest person I know. She's the Grim Reaper and she can't even crack a genuine smile that isn't taunting someone. She's the anti-empath, and aren't I supposed to follow her example?" I spread my hands, wanting to laugh at the ludicrousness of sitting in a place of academia and having a conversation with a Hindu deity of death about the art of passing a soul over. At least we were diverse.

Rishi sighed, finally looking away from me. His dark hair floated just at his shoulders, and his hard jaw tensed as he seemed to play with the words he wanted to say. Turning back to look at me, he trapped me with his stare once more.

"Haven't you noticed the rush you get when you pass over those who are happy to go? Or the overwhelming sadness you feel when someone doesn't?"

"Yes, of course," I said, wondering where he was going with his train of thought.

"Reaping is what keeps full death deities human, Blake. It's been five decades since Grim reaped a soul. She's losing touch with her humanity. The passing over process infuses death deities with human emotion. It wouldn't be the same for you or me, because we're part human and we have the capacity for deep compassion. But the true deities, well, they were born from who knows where, but one thing is for sure. They aren't mortal. They're something else entirely."

I shook my head, tugging at my lip with my index finger and thumb. When I looked up, I noticed he was watching the gesture intently. He flicked his eyes to my own, but he didn't look away when I frowned. He winked. I was ready to tell him to get lost, but what he'd said about my mother had me intrigued.

"So are you telling me she used to be different?" Maybe my dad's memories weren't completely skewed after all.

He nodded. "She's always been composed, but when I was a little boy she was warm … loving. It had already started by then, the degradation of her humanity, but I witnessed plenty of instances of her kindness. It's been getting worse lately as she hits the fifty-year mark. She's losing her sense of empathy, or sympathy for that matter. Her ability to love. You may not realize this, Blake. But she's desperate to regain it, desperate to regain her sense of compassion. The darkness of her comments is out of character."

I barely listened to the last part of what he said. My desire for a mother who could laugh at a joke with me and even love me was so great that I felt it press in on me like a deluge. Was it possible that I could really have a mother like that? A mother who could laugh and smile without darkness permeating every gesture and lilting tone? Regaining the scythe had never seemed so important.

I looked up from my own thoughts and finally smiled at him. "You actually managed to be helpful," I said, unable to keep the sarcasm from my voice even though I didn't really mean it. It just came out around him. *Oh, who am I kidding? It comes out around everyone.*

But he took it well, grinning at me and grabbing my hand in his large one. With a gentle squeeze, he rose. "I should go. I'll see you tonight; we have souls meeting us in the cemetery to be crossed over. One specifically is about to turn full lost soon and hopefully he'll show tomorrow, or else we'll have to hunt him down," he said, his expression and tone serious once again.

The heart-to-heart was over, back to business. I sighed, but I met his gaze before he could flicker out of my view. "Thanks," I said softly.

He tilted his head, his eyes warming at the comment but the faint smile I saw that played on his lips was quizzical. "For what?"

"For being a stalker weirdo," I retorted and was rewarded with a mild crease of his brow. "For telling me about my mother. For caring enough to check on me," I said more seriously, annoyed that I actually had to be nice to him because he'd been nice to me.

He rewarded me with a curve of his lips. "Of course I care, we're going to be working closely together, I need to make sure you're emotionally ready to take on the challenge," he said.

Of course. "Well, then. If you've made sure I'm suitably stable, I'd like to try and get maybe an hour of sleep. You can see your way gone," I said, rising and heading to the sliding glass door.

I could feel his confused eyes on me, and then I felt his absence. Peeking back to where he'd been, I saw he had flickered out. I didn't envy the ability, no matter how convenient it might have been. Rishi had described it as accessing a plane of reality that existed solely for the purposes of traveling through realms. There was no light, no sound, no feeling. I'd tried flickering on several occasions, but I'd had no luck. Maybe it was because I had no desire to be thrust into a void.

Rishi had explained the rules to me so many times I'd lost count, but I did remember from his lessons that it was against the rules of the Council of Death Deities to flicker in view of living, healthy humans. Although, with practice, hybrids could elevate on a different frequency so as to stay invisible to the living just like full deities. It apparently drained hybrids a lot more to do it that way, though. I knew that until I could flicker I couldn't truly do my mother's work, but for all my daring jaunts, this was one I could do without.

As I closed my eyes back in my bed, I couldn't for the life of me understand why I was so annoyed. But it was Rishi. He generally irked me no matter what he did.

* * *

My bag felt heavier than usual as I shoved a book in and snapped it closed. Or maybe I was just exhausted from reaping souls all night and then having my early morning talk with Rishi. I slipped the bag over my shoulder as I headed toward the classroom door. I sighed as my cheer team's captain, Hailey, caught up to me just before I could claim my freedom by losing myself in the roving crowd of college students. She'd been nice enough lately, unusual for her, but then again she'd liked Geoff. He'd dated her at one time. Everyone had liked Geoff, and even she wasn't evil enough to get on my case following his death. But it had been almost six months, and apparently the giving-sympathy-to-the-dead-guy's-girlfriend period was over.

"Blake," she said, sidling up to me with a snide tilt of her mouth. "You've missed practice every day this week."

I turned to her, slinging my bag over my shoulder. "What of it?" I really didn't care. The only reason I'd joined was to satisfy my hunger for adrenaline kicks, and that was being fully satiated since learning I had the power to pass souls over into another realm—and that I'd soon have to venture into that realm and sneak past hundreds of scary death deities to steal back my mother's scythe. Yeah, flying through the air during a cheerleading routine was passé as far as I was concerned.

"Well, you're most likely going to be kicked off the team."

Rolling my eyes, I sighed, seeing Shelby approach. "Listen, I don't really care. I've got other things going on in my life," I said.

"You'll care when you lose your scholarship," she said.

In the mess that my life had become, I'd totally forgotten what was paying for me to go to school here. I glanced at her once more. "It's fine, I talked to Coach Jill," I said, hoping she wouldn't call me out on the lie. Now I really had to go and talk to her and plead my case. "I'll be back after the break," I added and turned to meet Shelby halfway down the hall, not giving Hailey another chance to speak.

A couple of girls walked by and started to whisper as they crept past me. I knew they didn't mean anything by it, but my god, I wasn't a fragile doll. I wasn't going to break if I heard Geoff's name. And yet, my heart still nearly shattered every time I thought about him.

But it wasn't Geoff they were talking about. "Did you hear about Carly Swanson?" one of them asked me, a sophomore Asian girl whose name was Mira, I remembered.

I gagged on my response, my throat feeling like grains of sand grinding against one another. I started to nod, but Shelby grabbed my arm and steered me away from the girls, throwing them a dark look over her shoulder. She had long since colored her hair from mourning black to watermelon red. It was about as red as you could get with the sticky Kool-Aid dye she used. It was amazing the sugar didn't seep into the pores of her skin. But then again, she did have a lot of energy, so maybe it did.

"Hey," I said, "ready to go?"

She nodded, her features set solemnly as we turned to exit the school together. The sky was already turning a dull gray, but we had a couple of hours yet until sundown. Not that I could only cross souls over in the dark—that would have been a little too cliché for my liking—but it seemed to be the time they were most abundant.

Since that night with Shelby out in the field, I'd barely caught a break. I was MVP of the lost souls, of the dead. Fifty years was a long time without a reaper. The lost souls had built up, and the ones left with any moments of coherency were tracking me down, one by one, in small groups, and by the dozen, when they had those cognitive illuminations. Although I supposed they weren't really cognitive, since the souls didn't have brains anymore. *Hmmm.*

I threw my bag into Shelby's VW. The Bug had seen its day, but she'd bought the thing for a few hundred bucks and then her parents had put in a good thousand to get it on the road. So much for independence. But she liked to tell everyone she paid for it herself.

I sat back and stared out the window, wondering what that night was going to be like. Would the soul Rishi had been talking about show up? Until then, Shelby was taking me to the cemetery a bit early so I could get a jumpstart on the soul passing. I couldn't take the stares anymore, and I wanted to clean out the town so I could have some semblance of peace. Not to mention that I was now feeling the buzz of people dying. That's the best way I could describe it, like a buzzing or tingling that reverberated through my body, pulling me toward the dying.

I thought about the night before and my conversation with Rishi. What he'd said had shed some light on my mother and had given me hope and motivation to get the scythe back. I couldn't help but want to know the woman who'd birthed me, and what she might be like with her humanity back in place. I had no delusions. I knew I wouldn't be walking home to Shelby's mom, who made dinner every night and tucked the little one in. But having a more fulfilling relationship with the woman would be nice. Even if it meant I had to embrace my role as a death deity.

Shelby made a quick stop at a local drive-thru and we filled up on the necessities—a cheeseburger, milkshake, and fries for me—and then stopped at the local grocery store so Shelby could get her sprouts and non-GMO snacks for the car. I was used to it.

The sky was still gloomy, but we had a few hours of daylight for me to pass some souls over before their numbers became overwhelming. I wondered if there was a way to do more than one at a time, but I figured that would be a question for Rishi. I suspected there had to be, though, because how else could Grim have been in a million places in one moment?

I'd told Shelby she didn't have to hang out with me day after day as I passed them over, but she'd insisted. She said it was interesting to her, and it also eased her mind to make sure that a crazy lost soul didn't hurt me. Although tonight she had to leave eventually and go home to study for an exam the next day.

We sauntered into the cemetery, the only one around, and headed toward the back. It might have been cliché, but souls did hang out around where they were last memorialized—it was their link to the living. Before we were halfway across the cemetery, they started to drift toward us, their pale eyes focused on me, hungry to be free of their earthbound status. Shelby didn't so much as nod as she trudged toward a grassy spot under a tree, plugged her earphones into her phone, took out some books from her book bag, and flipped them open. That's how commonplace it had become for her to see me standing in the middle of a graveyard passing over souls unseen to her eye.

I turned to those who gathered and heaved a weary sigh. I knew they'd fill me with the energy I needed, but for the moment, all I felt was tired.

"Who's first?" I said.

*　*　*

I trudged back to the car with Shelby in tow and took a long sip from the soda that was by then watered down with melted ice. The gray day had slowly faded to a more gently lit night, although the chill had unfurled in full force. Not that it was a problem for me.

"You going to be okay?" Shelby asked as she slipped on a long, black trench coat over her gray sweater and tied the belt tightly at the waist.

I nodded. "Yeah, go. Rishi will be here any moment now and I'm honestly not afraid of anything after the few weeks I've had."

"Yeah, but it's getting dark," she argued, surreptitiously glancing around, her eyes darting from a headstone to the pathway. I could tell she was anxious to hit the books. I was probably going to fail my classes, given my obsession with sending these souls over. They were so distracting, it was either study and not get anything done because I could feel their need pressing against me, or it was not study and do something productive for future studying opportunities by sending the souls on their way.

"Go, Shelby. The dark doesn't scare me. I'm Death, remember?"

She stopped, looking around for Rishi, and met my gaze, an ironic smile tilting up one side of her full, berry-colored lips. "Yeah, you've got a point," she laughed. Spreading her hair band with her fingers, she twisted her hair up into a knot. "Okay ... but call me if you need me. I feel like the worst friend in the world leaving you in an empty graveyard. I mean, listen to how that sounds. But I've seriously got to meet up with Cassie for that tutoring session, or else I'll never pass the exam."

"Go," I said emphatically, waving her on with one hand while I placed my cup on the cement-slab ledge of a bench. "I'm seriously fine."

"I'll meet you back at your mom's room later?"

I nodded. "Yes, I'll see you later. In one piece, I promise."

Giving one last glance around, she relented against her better judgment. I laughed with a roll of my eyes and shooed her on again. But in truth, I was thankful for the friend that she was, and I felt comforted by her concern. I watched her peacock-blue car disappear out the gates, and I turned in the darkening twilight to take a breather. Where was Rishi? I glanced at the clock on my phone reading 4:35 p.m. He was usually on the dot.

I sat down on a bench, trying to ignore several souls that had begun to drift my way, when I started to feel that itch on my spine—the one you feel when you're being watched. I tried to push it away with a roll of my shoulders, but that only served to make it worse. I shivered, but it wasn't from the cold.

Finally, giving into my impulses, I dared a look behind me, seeing nothing but the swarm of souls coming my way. I sighed and took another sip of my watery cola. I still burned with the energy of the passings I'd done earlier, and these souls were always happy to move on, but it was a never-ending task. They just kept coming. I shuddered to think of how my mother's lockout from Abbadon had affected the rest of the world.

I turned back around and glanced at my phone, wondering again where Rishi was. It was growing darker and even though the souls did little to bother me except stalk me annoyingly, I felt the presence of something else in the dark. Eyes that weren't quite so lost were watching me. I snapped my gaze to the side and that's when I saw the shadow approaching.

"Rishi?" I asked, thinking I was probably freaking out for no reason.

But when the shadow got close enough and the light from the rising moon illuminated his features, I saw that it wasn't Rishi.

I suddenly wished very hard that I hadn't told Shelby to go, or at the very least that I was as savvy as she was and carried pepper spray.

"Hold it right there, buddy," I said through my increasingly rapid breath, rising from the bench and trying to skirt around it without looking too obvious.

From what I could tell in the low light, he was big. He laughed and spread his arms to the side in a gesture of appeasement.

"Hey, little deer. I was just passing through town and I saw the souls here," he said, peering through the darkness and revealing a hard, wide jaw and dark, almond-shaped eyes. He had full lips that were curved around a thick set of teeth, and his chuckle was deep, hearty, and dark. "I can't do anything about them, of course—they're the Reaper's and we both know she was neutered," he said with the grin never leaving his face, his dark eyes holding mine uncomfortably. He was intense in a different way than Rishi. A bad way.

I felt like wiping his smile away. I really wouldn't be a good candidate for keeping the scythe, because I'd probably start injuring other death deities if they were all as bad as this guy. Little deer? What, did he think he had me in his headlights? He hadn't even said much, and I instinctively didn't like him. I also innately knew that he could not know who I was.

"But why are *you* here?" he asked, the curiosity obvious in his focused gaze.

I shrugged casually. Hopefully not too casually. "Same. I was wandering around and felt them. But whatever, can't do much," I said, trying to play if off that I didn't care.

He narrowed his eyes, scanning the dark, taking in the souls that hovered. I wanted to scream at them to go away. I thought it in my head. No, I shrieked it. And then they did, and I felt the trembling of my fingers stop as they departed. Had they heard me?

Despite the disturbing lupine curve of his grin, I held his gaze. "They need to go home. They search for the Reaper," I said, not knowing why I was engaging the guy. But I had a feeling he was one of Hades's boys.

If I thought I'd see guilt or compassion rise up in the narrowed tilt of his eyes, I was wrong. His big, white teeth shone at me beneath the moon as he shrugged. "Grim has to pay for what she did to my uncle, and for almost killing my father. Her suffering must be exacted across the souls so that she feels the wrath of all the deities for her trespasses against their codes." He spoke fervently, and I couldn't help but compare his zealot behavior to what I'd learned about Nazis in high school. The irrational hatred for a people that had done nothing wrong. In this case it was the souls that were innocent bystanders in a war that had nothing to do with them.

My hands, which I'd shoved into my pockets to keep from trembling, now clenched into fists. I jerkily pulled one out and swiped it against my thick, black hair that I'd attempted to pull back but that had fallen from its sloppy twist into a waterfall of wild waves that swept my shoulders. I looked just like my mother. If he'd seen her before, he could easily put the puzzle together. But in that moment I didn't care.

"So how long does it last? How long do these poor souls have to stay lost? How long does any person who was connected with my … with Grim have to suffer? It's wrong, can't you see that? Can't you feel the imbalance rocking the Earth?" My voice came out impassioned, a fiery thread riding through it like I'd heard in the speeches from members of the student government when they believed so strongly in an issue they couldn't understand why someone else didn't. I heard that same plaintive note mixed with the disbelief of the opposition's ignorance. And I was even more surprised to realize that I did feel the imbalance I spoke of, the nagging from the souls, but it was more than that. The world was unhappy because it was haunted by its former inhabitants.

He sneered, his large lip curling up and a knife-like glitter in his eyes. "You a Reaper loyalist?" he asked.

I stared back at him, feeling my own light blue eyes hooded with disregard for the red and black that swirled off his aura and threatened to squash any resistance. *Adrenaline junkie at your service.* I grinned dangerously, my lips tilting up in equal disdain, and any previous feeling of fear was banished by the rocket of my pulse at his implied threat. Yeah, this was way better than cheerleading.

"And if I am?" I asked with a practiced arch of a slanted brow.

"We kill loyalists," he spat.

I laughed, the solid derision that laced my amusement evident to both of us as I flexed my fingers. I suddenly felt like I could drop him, and I'd never been in a physical fight in my life.

"Who did you say your deity parent was again?" he asked.

I couldn't help it; he was begging to be taunted, and I wanted to do the taunting. "The Reaper," I said softly, sliding my denim jacket off in the night and standing in the chill wearing only a black tank top. The moon highlighted the perfect ivory of my skin, just like my mom's.

He jutted his face forward, his death deity eyes seeing better in the dark, widening ever so much that I saw the glint of murder. Red seemed to already drip from his large hands, and his intent was written clearly on his face. "You're the Reaper's daughter?" he asked, still in denial.

I smiled back and winked long and slow, never having felt so proud to be my mother's daughter than I did at that moment. "The one and only Grim," I said, the words dancing off my tongue as if they'd been set free.

He was running toward me before I even knew what was happening. Instead of fleeing, I stood my ground, and then I felt nothing. My sight went dark and all that was before me was the pitchest black. The silence was so profound I wasn't sure I'd ever hear anything ever again, and all bodily sensation disappeared. I was lost in a void that had sucked away all my senses.

Just as suddenly, the mute bubble was interrupted with an explosion of colors from the nighttime sky. The lingering winter cold clung to the breeze that chilled my cheeks, reinvigorating my skin after those moments spent in the abyss of nothingness. I'd finally flickered, relocating myself a few feet away from him, enough of a distance to be safe for a moment longer.

He growled. "You think you're the only one who can flicker?"

I actually hadn't been able to flicker until the moment before, when necessity called for it, but I didn't care. I laughed in response. My imminent death by his hands was of no consequence. For a few seconds, I even wondered what was wrong with me.

Before I thought about what to do next, he flickered out and was behind me with a knife to my neck. Calm laced through me, and I silently wondered why I wasn't afraid. *Oh, that's right—Rishi.*

The pressure of his hand disappeared and I grinned, spinning around in time to see the Hades spawn go flying through the air and crack into a tree. It didn't keep him down, and immediately he was up and ready to take us both down, but he stopped when he saw what Rishi was holding.

"What do you have there, Yama's son?" the guy growled and lunged for Rishi, who flickered out. Rishi reappeared with a grin of his own, the light from a nearby cemetery lantern setting his face aglow as he began to speak, holding his spear out and keeping the Hades deity at bay.

"Get back, you crocodile of the West, who lives on the Unwearying Stars! Detestation of you is in my belly, for I have absorbed the power of Osiris, and I am Seth. Get back, you crocodile of the West! The *nau*-snake is in my belly, and I have not given myself to you, your flame will not be on me."

The guy started toward Rishi again, but took one step and then, rippling like a lost soul, winked out of existence.

"What happened to him? And what were you saying?"

"It is a spell from the Book of the Dead. It has many incantations. This one was used for keeping crocodiles from desecrating dead bodies," he said evenly, his voice strained as he set the spear down and met my gaze.

"And how did that get rid of him, then?"

"It can be used to send deities with ill intentions back into the underworld. But the spear is necessary. Good thing I keep one in my car for just such situations," he said darkly.

His dark gaze was more penetrating than usual, and I had to look away, shifting my weight under the intensity of his gaze.

"What were you thinking?" he said calmly. Too calmly. I could hear the rage beneath the surface, boiling but unable to escape from his mouth because he was so tightly controlled.

"About what? The dude freakin' attacked me," I said.

"I mean telling him who you are. Do you even know what that has cost us? Possibly everything!"

Ah, now that was more like it, I thought as his voice went up two octaves. Although to be honest, I still felt that his anger was a bit underwhelming. Only when I looked into his eyes and nearly drowned in the disappointment I saw there did I understand how badly I'd messed up.

"I'm sorry," I sighed, glancing away and seeing the lost souls start to slither back toward me. "If you could have heard what he was saying, how he talked about my mother and about punishing innocent souls … I couldn't help myself, I wanted him to know who I was and that he was going to be stopped. That they're all going to be stopped."

Rishi stared at me for several moments, his eyes lighting up with shock, and something else. Possibly hope?

All at once the angry tension holding his features rigid relaxed. He walked toward me and lifted a large hand to my face, tilting my chin up before I could protest and staring into my eyes in a way that made my stomach flip and my heart beat a drum in my chest. I wasn't over Geoff, but Rishi made me feel—he made me dislike him with such intensity one moment, and in the next I could find myself staring at his mouth.

"We have to be on the same page, Blake," he said softly, and his breath beat against my lips, smelling like chocolate. Rishi had an obsession with Snickers bars. I'd seen the stash in his car.

I nodded, not knowing how else to respond, my eyes finally flittering back to his. I wished they hadn't because once he'd captured me with his gaze, I couldn't seem to get away.

"We're going to have to act fast, before they send out the alert that Grim has a daughter who's able to pass souls over. I'm surprised they didn't notice until now, but maybe that's why he was lurking in Specter in the first place. We need to get in and out of Abbadon before they organize an attack on you. Because they're coming for you, Blake. There's no doubt about that."

I stared back at him and finally nodded. He released me and I was almost sad from the absence of his touch, but I pushed the feeling aside.

"Let's go see my mom, then," I said. And that's when I inadvertently flickered out.

CHAPTER ELEVEN

MY MOTHER WASN'T THERE when I appeared in her room, so I sat down to wait seconds before Rishi showed up behind me.

"So, you're flickering now?" He glanced at me with an arch of his dark eyebrows.

I grinned and rose casually. "When lupine guy back there attacked me, it just happened. I don't seem to have too much control over it though," I said, thinking about using the bathroom and then feeling the void snatch my sensory awareness away before I could formulate more than the initial thought. Suddenly I found my gaze set on the toilet. Hmmm, yeah, this was going to be a problem. I needed to get control of this fast.

Rishi's head appeared in the bathroom doorway, a disarming grin filling his face as if I'd singlehandedly made his day with my flickering antics.

"I just wanted to make sure you made it okay," he said, covering his laugh with a serious furrow of his brow.

I rolled my eyes and pushed the door closed in his face without a word before turning to the toilet. I might as well go.

A few minutes later I emerged, shooting him a playful glare when I encountered his full lips pulled up into a smirk. "I'd put away your smugness if I were you, unless you want me to inadvertently flicker into your brain."

I almost laughed out loud when his smile instantly disappeared. Was that even possible? Maybe if you were Grim. No, that was just silly. Still, I was entertained with the idea of being able to manually mess with his memories and moods.

I strutted to the couch and sat down, flipping one leg over the other and glancing back at Rishi. He was staring at a piece of paper, his dark brows furrowed in consternation and his black hair pulled back in his customary ponytail, so silky and dark I wanted to run my fingers through those satin strands. He seemed to realize I was staring at him, because he looked up and glanced at me with a furtive expression flashing across his face, as if he'd forgotten to wipe away the emotion before meeting my gaze. The smile he'd been sporting only moments before was gone.

"What's happened?" I demanded, knowing the moment I saw his face that Mission: Scythe had already begun.

If he meant to hide it, it was too late now, and he crammed the note into his coat pocket and then looked at me. "It was from Grim."

"Yeah, that I figured. So, what's the deal?"

"She says it's time, that we need to go for the scythe now—"

"Now?" I interrupted him. There was no way I was ready to go to Abbadon and deal with all those death deities. I knew I could never pass as one. Look at how miserably I'd failed just today.

Angrily shaking his head, he slapped his hand on the kitchen countertop. "Yes, now! Grim wants us to meet her in three days in New Mexico. There's a doorway there that we can get through."

"But you and I are both death deities, why can't we just make our own doorway?" I asked as calmly as possible. "Isn't that how deities do it?"

"Deities can't enter through themselves, it doesn't work that way. And they can't just flicker to anywhere in the underworld, because the void doesn't exist within Abbadon. The void opens up in only one place, and that's where it converges with the River Styx. The river exists in both planes for but a moment, and it is there where we end up when we flicker. And guarding the entry into Abbadon is Styx herself, a death deity who also happens to be Hades's sister. We cannot cross that way, it is impossible. The only way to get in undetected is through Death's Doorway."

"Death's Doorway?" I asked, setting down one of the B&B's pamphlets on the glories of upstate New York that I had been idly flipping through.

"Yeah, not many know of its existence, but it has allowed mortals access to Abbadon."

"Seriously? Okay, so where is this Death's Doorway?" I asked, casually dropping one leg over the other while inside my body thrummed anxiously with the thought of going there.

"Santa Fe," he said, his eyes meeting mine. "There's a flight in a couple of hours. It's already booked."

"Couldn't we just flicker there?" I asked.

Rishi chuckled. "We can't flicker through with full humans; we're not sure how it might affect them. I've heard it's been only done once before and it wasn't pretty. You've experienced what the void feels like as a hybrid deity. So I wouldn't want to put Shelby at risk."

"Shelby?" I asked, a quizzical note in my voice.

He nodded, averting his gaze from mine.

"Why does Shelby need to come with us? She could get hurt in all of this," I said.

Rishi shook his head vehemently and held up the crumpled letter as if I could read the words from across the room. "Grim insisted that Shelby come with us."

Of course she did. I should have known.

"Why do you always listen to everything she says?" I demanded, annoyed by his blind insistence that we do everything my mother told us to do.

"Because she's the Grim Reaper, Blake. And she raised me," he said, so simply I almost couldn't believe I'd asked the question. She was more his mother than mine. "Grim is calling the shots here. Not you, Blake." Rishi glowered at me, his voice laced with an edge I'd never heard before. Defending my own mother against me, I thought with a sick feeling in my stomach.

Rising from the couch I marched toward him. "Oh, yeah? Then you go get the scythe. What do you need me for anyway? You're a death deity. You've probably been swinging under the radar. You go. I don't need this in my life anyway," I said, my pale blue eyes leveled with his dark ones that were now glowing fiercely.

Rocking back so that he put some distance between us, he held my gaze before finally looking away. "Because ... only the true Reaper can wrest it back from the grips of Hades," he said, reluctance ringing in his voice as he refused to meet my eyes.

"Come again?" I said, staring hard at his tensed jawline, wondering what he meant. "Are you telling me that only the Grim Reaper can get it back? Because if you are, well, hey, I am not her." I could hear the panic rise in my voice.

Finally, after a long moment he glanced back up at me. "Well, our theory is that you can, too, because you're her daughter."

"Theory?" I suppressed an urge to roll my eyes and instead arched my brows tolerantly.

"Listen, it's a good theory. Right now, no one can wield it but your mother, and no one can touch it but its true owner unless it was given away voluntarily," he said, averting his eyes from mine.

"Wait, so if Hades has it right now, it stands to reason he couldn't have taken it from her like you've led me to believe. She must have given it to him," I said as more of a statement than a question. I could tell from Rishi's expression that I was right. "Why would she do that? What could they have possibly had on her to make her give up the scythe, her power, and her ability to pass over souls? You said it's eating at her humanity as it is!"

Nodding, he took a step closer to me so that our gazes were that much more locked. "Hades threatened her sister. They can't kill a death deity without the scythe, but they were torturing her. Your mother could not bear to hear her sister's screams and so she relented, always with the plan to come and steal it later along with her sister. She never realized that Hades would convince the council to ban her altogether."

"Her sister? Santa Muerte, right?" I asked.

Rishi nodded in response. "She goes by Sebastiana, or Seba for short."

"But where is she now?"

"In Abbadon."

"But why doesn't she help Grim?" I said with a frustrated shake of my head, trying to piece it all together.

For a long, drawn-out second, a pained look passed over his face. Then he spoke. "They've never let her go."

"What? And the other death deities aren't doing anything?"

"No," he said with a quick shake of his head.

"How do you even know all of this?"

"We have intel."

"Intel?"

"Insiders."

"Yeah, I know what it means, Rishi," I said. "I mean, who is on the inside? And who is passing over my aunt's souls—unless—are they wandering around lost as well?"

"No, nothing like that," he said, walking around the bar counter to the tiny kitchen where the standard hotel coffeemaker sat. Swinging the coffee filter open, he opened a can of coffee and started scooping. "Sebastiana has several children. Hybrids like us who have been doing what they can. But even they have a hard time keeping up. They've been talking to your mother for some years now, trying to figure out a way to save Abbadon."

"So Hades has the scythe, but he can't use it. What's the point?"

Rishi sighed. "There are two scythes, you see. Hades initially took Sebastiana for leverage, but he kept her because he wants her scythe. Separated, the scythes are useless to anyone but their true owners."

"Okay, well, that's good news. I'm assuming my aunt hasn't told him where it is," I said.

Rishi shook his head and went on. "No, of course not. Because the true power of the scythes comes when they are together. And any deity possessing both would be able to use them then. Grim said it's like there's a lock and when the two scythes are brought together they magically unleash the powers of life and death.

"Where is it?" I asked, leaning against the counter and dropping my chin into my hand.

"Only Sebastiana knows, and that's why she's being contained— because she has refused to tell him. If Hades could get his hands on you, I'm sure he'd use you to gain some more leverage."

"Great," I said with a sigh. "And I'm sure my mother is oh-so-worried about sending me into the lion's den. Oh, wait, she's not, since it was her idea to send me there in the first place. Her motherly concern is overwhelming."

For the first time since I'd met Rishi and my mother, he seemed to be on my side. Maybe it was the flash of agreement I saw in his eyes, or the way he looked at me, a pained expression crossing his face. His hand came down to rest on mine, and he squeezed it, his warm, rich voice gentle when he spoke. "Blake, she has no choice right now. You're the only one who can save us from this disaster. And if she seems uncaring, well, I explained to you about how passing souls over makes them—"

"Experience the lovely range of human emotion," I interrupted with a sigh. "Right, I remember, her humanity is null and void at the moment." I slipped my hand from underneath his and avoided his look of sympathy. Although I knew the reason for her cold indifference, it didn't stop the hurt from rising in my chest. She'd reportedly still had "feelings" when she'd abandoned me and chosen to raise Rishi instead.

I grabbed the coffee pot, picked up the travel mug I carried with me everywhere, and poured the black liquid into it. "We might as well get a move on," I said.

"Shelby," Rishi said.

I turned to him and nodded. "Okay, but only if she says yes. This isn't really up to Grim, it's up to Shelby. If she says she doesn't want to go, then you need to respect that. Grim can deal."

"Go where?" A familiar voice said from behind me. I heaved a breath as I saw Shelby pop her red head in the door and close it behind her.

"What's up?" she asked, clutching her own travel coffee cup in her hand.

"I'll let Rishi tell you," I said, my gaze steady on Rishi, a sardonic smile lifting the corners of my lips.

He glanced at me, and I saw him blow out a short burst of air. He knew I was right; he couldn't force Shelby to go if she didn't want to. But he also didn't want to fail Grim.

"We're going to New Mexico. The other death deities know about Blake, and Grim says we have to go now to get the scythe."

"Yeah, and we have to leave in like the next hour," I said, exchanging my denim jacket for my hoodie and zipping it up, glancing at Rishi expectantly.

He flashed me a dark look, annoyed by my evident amusement. "You've got to get ready too, Shelby. You're coming."

I glanced at Shelby and saw her eyes widen. "Is this a request or a demand?" she said without missing a beat, tilting her head and pinning Rishi with her bright green gaze. Rishi wouldn't have seen it, but I could tell she was barely able to contain her delight. Her eyes were sparkling and a flush of excitement was creeping into her cheeks, and I knew her answer would be yes. But she was also Shelby, and no one demanded she do anything. I hid my chuckle behind a cough, watching Rishi shift uncomfortably from one foot to the other, shuffling loose change in his pants pocket with one hand.

He seemed to be struggling with his answer, and I almost felt bad for him. Almost. Finally, he glanced at her. "A request?" he said, a question ringing in his voice.

I glanced at Shelby and she dropped one eye-shadow-dusted lid at me, and I laughed. "And we've got a winner," I said, throwing my voice like a game host.

Rishi glanced between the two of us, a tentative smile touching his lips, his brows arched. "Yeah?"

Shelby nodded. "Yes, I'll come, but only because you asked so politely," she smiled perkily, quite enjoying herself.

Rishi expelled a breath of air and seemed to relax. "Thank you. It was Grim's request you come," he said, finally glancing at me.

I shook my head, still confused as to why she'd specifically ask for a human to accompany us on our trip to break into the underworld. "But why?" I asked, wondering if he'd even know.

Shelby grabbed my arm and shook it so I'd look at her. A keen glimmer flickered in her eyes and she smiled faintly. "Come on, Blake. Can't you guess why she wants me to come?"

I shook my head. "Can you?"

My best friend since we were babies looked at me and smiled and shook her head tolerantly. "She's looking out for you, Blake. I keep you anchored to this world. She doesn't want to lose you to the next," she said softly. "You told her you needed me, and she's respecting that wish."

I opened my mouth to respond, but I couldn't say anything. Did my mother actually care?

I glanced over to Rishi, who was also staring at Shelby with his mouth hanging slightly open. He glanced at me, his brow furrowed in concentration, and then his eyes slowly widened with sudden awareness. He gave a short nod to himself, and then he smiled at me. It was a smile I'd never seen. Lost were the gentle sad edges and the snarky pulled grin. Instead, it was sweet and happy, like the world had been righted for only a moment. He was happy there was a possibility my mother hadn't gone completely cold. Happy that she was looking out for her daughter. Happy for me. I could see it in the way his eyes crinkled with the smile, the soft light that lit itself there when he glanced my way.

The depth of his caring for me, for my mother, made my chest hurt and my throat swell. I shivered with something, and I wasn't sure what it was at first—until I looked at him again and thought about falling into his arms and feeling the gentle protectiveness of his embrace. It was longing.

Oh, no. Not Rishi.

CHAPTER TWELVE

INSTEAD OF GOING BACK to our houses where our parents would have asked questions, we hit up our dorms. Everything was pretty much within walking distance in Specter, anyway.

Rishi was waiting for us in his car, a black Caliber he and my mother had rented when they'd blown into town. I'd called him out on the clichéd black, but he'd just pointed out that at least they hadn't gotten a hearse. I had to give them credit where it was due.

We each threw in a backpack and tightly tied sleeping bags since Rishi had mentioned that Death's Doorway was in the woods. Who knew whether we'd end up sleeping in the wild for a night.

We got to the airport with a little less than an hour to spare before boarding. Thankfully, the security line wasn't too long. I was nervous as we stood in line, worrying more than once that Rishi had somehow smuggled a spear in his luggage.

I grabbed my duffel bag off the conveyer belt, slung it over my shoulder, and caught up to Rishi and Shelby, who was struggling to put on her tight rubber boots. I glanced behind me briefly and felt irritation bubble up that she couldn't have worn more practical footwear. I'd pointed out to her that the boots were hard to get on, but she hadn't listened when we'd been at the store.

Then I saw the familiar tilt of almond-shaped eyes and a large, wolfish sneer. It was the death deity from the cemetery, and he was staring right at me, a dark smile curling his lips as he pointed at me from behind security lines.

"Rishi, look," I said sharply. "Shelby, get up! We have to go. Now!"

Rishi glanced over and met my eyes with understanding, and we both grabbed Shelby's arms and pulled her into a run. Thankfully, she'd gotten her shoe on. I shot a look over my shoulder and saw two guys and a girl come rushing after us, with lupine guy still stuck in security.

We barely paused at the airport signs, taking a hard right and heading to Gate B28. I glanced behind me and saw that Lupine was now running with the other three, although I didn't have a chance to get a good look at their faces.

As we tore through the airport, I only hoped those that we ran by figured we were late or trying to make a connecting flight.

"This way," Rishi said, pointing toward our gate, which was thankfully boarding.

"We are now boarding rows five through ten for flight B980. If you are in rows five through ten, please join the line, five through ten."

We shuffled into line, but when I glanced back, Rishi was gone. I turned sharply to look at Shelby, but she hadn't noticed yet.

"How is getting in line going to help us?" Shelby panted, her eyes wide as she popped her head around to see where the death deities had gone. But when I glanced around and spotted them, security was leading away our four pursuers.

"What? How?" I turned just as Rishi sidled up to us as casually as if he'd merely gone to the bathroom. That was possibly what he'd done—it just didn't seem likely, given the circumstances.

His lips quirked up into a half grin, pride evident from the way his face eased into the smile. "Apparently they were so hot on your trail, Blake, they jumped past TSA. Security was already after them. I just told the TSA guy that Lupine's part of a gang and that he's been stalking you, just to reinforce that there was some major shadiness going on. If we're lucky, they'll be detained and won't be able to flicker for a while."

"Why not?" Shelby asked.

"No flickering in front of humans unless they're dying," I quickly explained. "So basically, I'd be breaking the rules if I let Shelby see me flicker," I added, glancing at Rishi with a quick smile.

Rishi leveled me with his deep, brown gaze. "You're breaking all the rules, Blake," he said softly, his grin sliding from his face. He turned to show the flight attendant his boarding pass before I could ask him what he meant. I showed my pass as well, followed by Shelby, and the three of us boarded the plane and found our seats.

I sat by the window, with Rishi beside me because Shelby refused to sit in the middle and he had graciously offered her the aisle seat. When I took my seat, I also took a breath. Mainly because I'd been running and hadn't had time to really breathe since we'd gotten on the plane. But as I leaned back and glanced out the window at the gray tarmac in the dark of the night, I realized that I wasn't scared. I wasn't even the least bit nervous. My heart rate was completely quiet now that I was sitting, and it had never been beating fast from fear. *God, what does it even take to scare me anymore?* All I felt was a rush from the chase, a flood of energy that coursed through my veins and made me want more. Why did I find getting chased by an evil death deity and his posse exhilarating? There was something seriously wrong with me.

Rishi drummed his fingers on the armrest next to me, and I sighed and pulled my arms in closer to my body. *Armrest hog.*

"So why do those guys want us?" Shelby whispered to us over the flight attendant's attempt at making the monotonous passenger safety rules sound exciting.

"They want Blake. They didn't know she existed until Miss Smooth over here told them who she was, and so now she's basically a fugitive from the Council of Death Deities. Her mother is a banished exile and her souls wander the world lost without the ability to cross over. Each death deity is required to register any children they conceive so that the council can keep track of who is reaping and where. Then here comes Blake. The daughter who isn't supposed to exist, cleaning up the mess left by Hades, who doesn't want it cleaned up. She poses an obvious threat."

"How can we even hope to get the scythe now that they know to be watching for us?" I asked, realizing the depth of my folly.

Rishi turned his fathomless dark eyes to me and smiled. "For one, the existence of Death's Doorway isn't common knowledge. They'd expect us to come in the way everyone else does and get past Styx. Plus, Hades may still not know. You see, our friend you keep referring to as Lupine is Hades's second son. He lives in the shadow of his older brother, so he may want to drag you back kicking and screaming to Hades before telling his father you exist. That way, he gets all the credit," he said, jerking his head to the right.

Puckering my brows at him, I frowned, confused. *Rishi knows him?* "What?" I said before noticing the flight attendant standing in the aisle staring at us.

I looked up at her, expecting to be asked what I'd like to drink or something, but then I stopped and stared into her opalescent, dead eyes. She was lost. The pale of her irises and the bitter twist of her lips told me she'd been haunting this plane for a while. And yet, her hope-lit face seemed more lucid than those of other lost souls I'd seen.

"Can you help me?" she whispered. Her gaze fell so intently on me, I felt glued to her eyes.

I started to nod, but Rishi put his hand on mine to stop me, and I was able to break the gaze and glance at him, the warmth of his hand on mine barely noticeable. Or so I told myself.

"She can help you," he said softly, turning to the soul.

The soul's gaze dragged away from my face to Rishi's and she gazed at him quizzically, the potential for going full-out lost whirling in the insanity of her eyes. "Yes, please ..." she whispered, hope continuing to light up her features.

He nodded, his gaze slightly directed at Shelby so as to not alert the passengers to our conversation with an invisible entity. I imagined we probably would have been booted from the plane since we hadn't even taken off yet.

She turned back to me. "You'll cross me?" she asked, desperation catching in her voice. Her uniform looked as if it was from the 1960s. It made my heart clutch, the years she'd had to endure slowly going crazy, stuck in between life and death with no one to offer any sort of release. It's not the way death should be. It's not the way life should end. I nodded.

"Yes, I can cross you over," I whispered, the depth of her sadness weighing heavily in the lines of her face. Shelby, who was staring at us, tilted forward in her seat just a bit, trying to shield us from the view of other passengers. All the same, we must have looked suspicious.

"Is everything all right?" A living blond flight attendant stepped into the space the lost soul occupied and made me cringe. *I wonder what that feels like?* Apparently it felt like something, because she shivered and stepped to the side, her expression tightening, annoyance flashing in her eyes. It was the sickness, I thought, seeping into those around the lost.

"Yes, I'm fine, thank you. Just a bit of a nervous flyer," I lied, but I figured it was a good cover since the plane had started to slowly roll forward.

The flight attendant managed a tight smile. "Well, let me know if you need anything, and please, buckle your seatbelt. We're about to take off." She nodded and moved on, leaving me staring up at the lost soul. Shelby and Rishi turned to me and I glanced at them.

"How do I do this without looking insane?" I asked. Usually, I held hands with the spirit and then they'd cross over, but not without infusing me with an energy that usually had me rarin' to go do one of those crazy 5ks featuring an obstacle course. Okay, maybe not that intense. But I had enjoyed some pretty vibrant moments after crossing over lost souls. I needed to be able to take in that energy without looking as if I was having convulsions.

Rishi smiled softly at the lost soul. "Come find us once we're in the air and able to move around the cabin. I'll head to the bathroom and you can just sit next to Blake and comfortably find your way to the next world," he said in a soothing, low voice.

The soul measured us with her gaze and then she dipped her head down with a nod. "The sooner the better," she said and then slipped away.

"This seems more complicated than it should be," muttered Shelby.

"Well, eventually Blake will be able to go places without being seen and pass over souls from anywhere. But she's not there yet."

"She will?" Shelby asked. "Like, she'll be invisible?"

Rishi nodded to her and then turned to me with a smile lifting his lips. "It's pretty cool."

Being invisible definitely sounded better than "elevating to a different existential level," which is how he had initially explained it to me during our deity-in-training lessons.

"Wait, does that mean you could have been spying on Blake before you met her?" Shelby asked wide-eyed.

I frowned. What was she getting at?

"No, she would have always been able to see me since she's also a death deity and we all exist on the same multiple levels of existence. We can all see each other. Besides, it's one of the council's rules: no perverting our abilities."

I sighed. It was good to know no death deities had been spying on me without my knowledge. We each sat back quietly, waiting for the plane to take off. Shelby opened a copy of *Vogue* and slipped in her earbuds, scrolling through her music collection on her iPod.

Rishi also slipped on a pair of earbuds, plugged them into the screen that was built into the back of the chair in front of him, and started flipping through the channels. I sighed and turned to look out my window, remembering I had yet to tell my father that I was going out of town for "spring break." He knew me well, and being a spring-breaker wasn't really my style. But I could always claim that since it was my first year in college, I was giving it a try.

The plane started to move faster and one of the attendants, a guy this time, announced we were readying for takeoff. I leaned back and closed my eyes. Takeoff was my favorite part of flying because it felt a little bit like riding a roller coaster. I'd also heard it was the most dangerous part of flying, and knowing that always made it a little more exciting.

A few minutes later, as we were ascending higher into the sky, I wondered to myself whether Lupine had managed to get away from airport security yet. A thought occurred to me. "Hey," I said and poked Rishi, who gave me a sideways glance as he slipped his earbuds out.

"What's up?" he asked.

"Can a death deity flicker onto an airborne plane?"

"Sure."

"So what's to stop Lupine from flickering here all invisible-style?"

Rishi grinned. "While I love this whole 'Lupine' thing you've got going on, his real name is Marx."

"So you know him?" I had meant to ask him about his apparent familiarity with my new nemesis before, but I'd been distracted when the lost soul had shown up. I was surprised that he knew Lupine's real name. I had just assumed Rishi had been flying below the radar, being my mother's sidekick and all. "Sure, I've run into him before ..." Rishi paused mid-sentence and cocked his head as if listening to something. Turning quickly to me he winked. "Listen, I have to go. I'll be back in a few," he said, and looking around quickly to make sure no one was paying attention, he flickered out.

Shelby was bent over the little table in front of her, trying to read something without the glasses she said she didn't need, only to see the flash beside her and give a startled cry when Rishi suddenly disappeared. I was sure he had just broken the rules by flickering out so publicly. But, of course, I was a deity rule breaker myself, so I just chuckled and shrugged when she glanced over at me.

A heavy man wearing a scarf and a fedora turned an eyeball to her and then, seemingly disinterested, went back to whatever he was looking at on his tablet, swiping the screen with one large, hairy finger.

"Shhh," I said sharply to Shelby. "He was called to a job most likely. He'll be back. But it might be a good time to call the lost flight attendant soul over," I murmured. And then the plane dropped.

My gasp and Shelby's startled cry were drowned out by the commotion of the people around us, and even scarf guy seemed to react, the disinterest of his fleshy features vanishing and leaving behind a facial tick that caused his eyelid to close every few seconds.

"Probably just turbul—" The plane dipped again and then the lights went out. Shelby reached across Rishi's empty seat and grabbed my arm, her fingers digging into my bicep uncomfortably, but I hardly noticed. The lost soul flight attendant's last words suddenly made sense. She went whizzing by, her opalescent eyes a swirling cyclone of madness and her lips pulled back so far her skin seemed to be wrapped around the last remnants of a corpse about to turn full-on skeleton, making her countenance a garish mix of comical and ghoulish.

"She said 'the sooner the better' before," I whispered fiercely to Shelby, who was squinting as she peered around the dimly lit cabin, as if she could have seen the lost soul, as if she could have made out any shape at all.

But I can see. Hmmm, I didn't realize I had super eyesight. Cool. I realized I probably shouldn't be thinking about my new superpowers when we were dropping another hundred feet in the air and passengers were disintegrating into hysteria. I, of course, stifled a laugh as we dropped again, like I always laughed as I flew all the way down the steepest crest on the highest roller coaster. But I didn't really want to die, despite my supposed death wish. I was fairly certain I could just flicker out before impact. All the other people on the plane, however, couldn't, and I fumbled about in my mind for a way to draw the lost soul to me without looking like a total lunatic.

"So? What does that even mean?" Shelby whispered back, her voice laced with panic.

"It means she's going full-on lost. She's been stuck here for a while, waiting and going madder and madder. I'm honestly surprised she was able to get it together so well earlier to have the conversation we had. Geoff ..." I stumbled over his name and paused before going on again. "Geoff started to lose it within a few hours," I said, hearing the weight of his loss still heavy in my voice.

The lights went back on, but people were in a panic and the captain had yet to go on the loudspeaker to reassure passengers there was nothing to worry about. I could feel the waves of fear emitting from the lost soul, but I found that I had begun to adapt to the lost soul sickness and was able to keep it from affecting me too much. My heart picked up only a pace with the urgency of the situation. But any worry I felt was more for the people on the plane than myself. I didn't need the lost soul causing outright panic.

I leaned over Shelby, who made an annoyed sound—which was better than sounding terrified—and I looked down the aisle. I was met by the wide, licentious grin of Hades's lupine son sitting three rows back. Marx, Rishi had said. *Great time to disappear, Rishi.* So much for the theory that Marx wouldn't flicker here. He was probably doing that thing Rishi had mentioned before—elevating on another existential level and invisible to everyone but me and the lost soul. I hoped the effort was seriously draining him.

He winked at me, and the compartments above our heads dropped open as oxygen masks bounced out. Hissing a curse, I grabbed mine, put the band around my head, and looked to Shelby to make sure she had her mask on. Her eyes were wide, and despite my own lack of fear, I felt guilt clench within my chest that she'd been dragged on this crazy trip. She'd gotten the short straw the day best friends had been assigned. Now she was stuck with a total freak of nature who had to reap souls or go slowly mad from the need to cross them over.

"Don't worry!" I yelled through the mask. "Switch places with me."

She nodded and we quickly removed our masks, and then she crept out into the aisle, clutching the seat in front of her for stability and then skirting in around me so I could take the aisle seat. We quickly snapped our masks back on as the speaker buzzed and the captain's voice finally boomed throughout the cabin, reassuring us that we'd just hit some turbulence and we'd all be fine.

Turbulence, my ass. Hades's snide, Gestapo-like heel of a son was doing something to make the lost soul act so crazy. But what, I wasn't sure. My death deity tour guide had stepped out for the moment, and I was left floundering in a situation where I could end up reaping a whole lot more souls than just the dead flight attendant's.

I wanted to yell at the guy and ask him why he felt it was necessary to take a whole plane out just to get to me. Maybe because he thought I'd be easy pickings when I had to cross over the majority of a plane. But I didn't want to scare the passengers any more than they already were by talking to someone they couldn't see, so I stayed silent, staring him down as he continued to grin at me, his almond-shaped eyes hooded, shining with nothing more than nasty glee that did nothing to hide the lifelessness of his gaze. Whatever he was doing had to be breaking so many rules within the death deity society. But I would have bet my life and Shelby's too that he didn't follow the rules much and was only here to do his father's bidding. Or, like Rishi had said, to impress his daddy.

I narrowed my gaze at him, knowing the strangeness of my blue eyes could be just as disconcerting, but he wasn't too concerned with my reaction. The lost soul flew by again and the lights dimmed once more.

I didn't know how he was making her so agitated. He wasn't doing anything that I could tell, aside from staring at me and leering. Neither my mother nor Rishi had ever mentioned souls using their sickness to affect anything but emotions, but I felt the energy emanating from her as an almost physical force, which was what I surmised was messing with the plane.

I needed to stop her before she blew an engine or did something else to make the plane go down. And that's when I saw it: a shadow against the low glow of the dampened overhead lights, a human shape that was no more than a silhouette. If the cabin had been darker, the figure would have probably been indiscernible from its surroundings. But there it was, following the crazed soul around with a face I couldn't see. It wavered out of reach, down the aisle from Marx. I narrowed my eyes at the shape, a memory clicking in the back of my mind. I'd seen this shadow-thing before, but only so briefly I'd thought my eyes were playing tricks on me.

It clawed the air with its sharp shadow fingers when the flight attendant's soul got close. I glanced quickly to Marx, who was still eerily smiling at me as if waiting for a reaction. I looked away from him, shuddering from the feel of his stalker eyes on me.

When I looked back to the shadow figure, I recoiled because it now had a face. It had thinly boned features, tight skin over a high forehead and wiry nose, wearing a stewardess outfit from the 1960s. The shadow looked exactly like the dead flight attendant now, only this version of her had grayed-out eyes and was somehow sharper.

I dragged in a breath, missing the warmth of Rishi's presence and his gentle strength and biting tongue. He truly was my guide in all of this, and I felt lost, pitching through the air as the plane dropped again, falling without him to catch me. My head slammed into the overhead compartment, and I realized too late that I hadn't refastened my seatbelt when I'd switched places with Shelby.

The pain lanced through my head, and I managed to look over at Shelby, who was staring at me with her face scrunched in horror. "Blake, oh my god, are you okay?" she gasped through her mask, looking quickly around as if anyone could help me in that moment.

I nodded, gingerly feeling the top of my head and cringing when my fingers pressed lightly down on the spot that had hit. Yeah, I was going to have a bump. Hopefully no concussion. I knew I should put my seatbelt back on, but I had to do something. "God, this is just the worst time that Rishi could get called away," I growled, rolling my eyes and in doing so, reassuring Shelby I was okay with my acerbic complaining.

She only looked mildly relieved. "Do you want some ice?" she asked. I had no idea where she'd get any, since the flight attendants were buckled into their seats at the moment, nor did I have the time to sit back and tend to my wound. I shook my head and put my hand to my head as the motion brought about a rush of wooziness. *Not now.*

I turned back to the aisle and saw that my injury had Marx grinning even wider. I smiled widely back at him and was satisfied when I saw a flicker of doubt make his expression waver. When I glanced back at the shadow figure, I saw that it still looked like the lost soul. *What is that thing?*

Seeming to answer my thought, Lupine said, "We call them shadow souls." Since he was "elevating" and no one else knew he was there, he spoke loudly enough so that I could hear him.

I snapped my head back to him and gritted my teeth.

His perpetual sneer hadn't faded. I didn't respond, aware even amidst the turmoil that I would only panic the passengers more if they saw me talking to an empty seat.

His chuckle, loud only to me, reverberated through my skull, wracking my body with cold chills. Glancing around quickly to make sure no one was watching, I mouthed to him, "What are you doing to it?"

He shrugged. "I don't have to do much. It's already pretty angry. All the shadows are. But it sure gets agitated when I tell it about all the souls living worry-free in the underworld. It really hates it here." He chuckled again, the sound pitched high and setting my nerves on edge.

Shelby put her hand on my shoulder and I flung it off with a jerk of my arm, the anger within me igniting a fire that eradicated the frigid temps from my body.

"Well, then maybe it needs to be sent on its way," I whispered. I rose, not caring who was looking at me. Most of the people were too lost in their own bubbles of fear that it didn't matter anyway.

I was sick of playing by his rules. The sharp sting of fear had never held me back before. And it wasn't going to now. Rishi wasn't here to guide me? Fine. I would just have to do things my way, which was the reckless way, but it had worked for me in the past.

Without even thinking about what I was doing, I marched down the aisle past Marx and grabbed the shadow soul, my fingers curling around the essence that dripped on me like tar. I ignored it, and just as the lost soul slid swiftly above me, I grabbed it in thin air and slapped the two souls together until only one was left. "Haunt that," I said to no one in particular, not even caring what people thought anymore.

Marx's mouth twisted out of its smile into a puckered mask of surprise, his heavy brows like two heavy slants across his face as rage bubbled up in his eerily tilted almond eyes.

"Do you know what you've done?" he growled.

"She made me whole," the dead flight attendant said with a vibrant smile and clear eyes. She took my outstretched hand without pause, and I set her free. Her exhilaration at being liberated from this realm flowed through me like a spring breeze and filled me with a smile, which I directed at Lupine the moment the rush died down.

"You've actually been quite helpful today," I told him with a laugh lifting my voice.

"I'll see you soon," he growled before he flickered out of visibility as well. I glanced around and noticed that the cabin lights had returned to normal and the plane had stopped its wild dipping.

"Miss, you shouldn't be up yet," the blond attendant said next to me. I startled at her voice and nodded, then headed back to my seat.

I eased back into my chair and looked over at Shelby, who was sitting wide-eyed, staring at me. "What just happened?" she asked, her shoulders riding up to her ears. I knew she'd be complaining about neck pain the next day.

I shook my head, feeling the ache from where I'd hit it earlier. I was in dire need of some time on a beach, preferably on a desert island with no lost souls, dying people, or other death deities, least of all my mother. "I don't know," I said. "I really have no idea."

Rishi took that moment to come sauntering down the aisle from the bathroom and climbed over me easily with his long legs. He eased down into his seat and grinned. "Sorry 'bout that. I was called to Maui, and they have the most awesome mai tais. I don't usually get to go there since there's a couple of deities working the Hindu scene, so I thought I'd take advantage."

I stared at him, giving him the best glowering look I could manage.

"What's up?" he asked, the lightness in his voice and his jovial mood making my fingers itch for his neck. "Did you two switch places?" His brow furrowed as he looked between Shelby and me.

Shelby shot him a dark look and slunk down into her seat. Pushing her earbuds back into her ears, she said, "I am never flying with either of you ever again. We're driving home." Then she dialed her iPod music up and set about ignoring us.

Rishi looked at me again, his brows arched. "What's her deal? Something happen?"

I just glanced at him. "Mai tais? Really? Go have another." Then I stuck my earbuds in as well, closed my eyes, and luxuriated in the peace of loud music and the overwhelming comfort that had seeped through my being, from my essence to my flesh, the moment he had reappeared.

Geoff. Geoff. I reminded myself. As if I needed reminding. How could I ever stop remembering? But I also couldn't stop the throb that hit my chest every time Rishi looked at me with his deep brown eyes that crinkled up when his wide mouth would curve into a smile. I couldn't move on with the boy who was death, and I couldn't let go of the boy who was dead. And my part-time gig as a death deity had become a full-time job I wasn't sure I wanted.

The ache in my head reminded me that thinking too much could be hazardous, and I got lost on the waves of music sounding in my ears, washing away recriminations and doubts and leaving me with one lingering thought.

What have I done?

CHAPTER THIRTEEN

MY WARM FEELINGS toward Rishi had all but disappeared by the time we'd collected our baggage and were making our way to the rent-a-car place, making sure to keep an eye out for death deities looking to abduct me, or whatever it was they wanted to do. I knew they couldn't kill me. Maybe they'd try exiling me too. The thought made me sick to my stomach for a moment, until I remembered that they couldn't cut my souls off from entering Abbadon unless they knew where my soul gate was located. And since I wasn't even sure where it was quite yet, I was confident that the other deities probably didn't either.

Rishi had been grilling me about the shadow and the lost soul I'd united and then sent on its merry way ever since I'd told him about it in Charlotte, North Carolina, where we'd landed to get on a connecting flight. By the time we reached New Mexico, I'd had enough.

Finally, I stopped mid-stride, causing Shelby to stumble into me. She'd kept her iPod on high as Rishi and I berated each other on the way to baggage claim and apparently wanted no part in our disagreement. She hunkered under her zip-up, her hood over her bright hair, embarrassed to even be seen with us.

"Oh get off it, Shelby. No one even knows who you are," I snapped.

She glanced up at me and shook her head, pointing to her ears plugged by the sounds of music, and mouthed, "I can't hear you." I couldn't help but give a half laugh, knowing full well that she could hear me and was just ignoring us. And she probably had the right idea. I should have plugged my own music in to drown out Rishi, who was continuously lecturing me.

I spun on him. "What was I supposed to do, Rishi? Let the plane go down? You weren't even around. You were too busy drinking your mai tais," I said, leveling him with an icy gaze.

He puffed up his chest and then glanced away, blowing out a slow breath, his broad chest rising and falling with the movement and making me forget for a moment how irate he was making me. "You're right," he finally said after a beat. "I guess I'm just mad at myself for not being there. And you're right, I should have come directly back, given the current circumstances. I honestly didn't expect him to flicker onto the plane. Killing people isn't usually a death deity practice." He spoke softly so passersby couldn't hear him, but I detected the venom seething through his tone. Rishi was taking the plane incident very seriously.

"That's ironic. We're death deities," I said, my brows arched. I noticed from the corner of my eye that Shelby seemed to have her head tilted toward us. Apparently, what we had to say was suddenly interesting.

"We reap, we don't do the killing."

I nodded. He was right. "Quite honestly, Rishi, she seemed much happier once I united her with the shadow. She was complete, whole, sane. You know, relieved ..." I pictured her before she had left me and I remembered the flash of her navy blue eyes. "And her eyes! They were ... colorful!" I said, meeting his gaze. "Marx called them shadow souls."

Rishi frowned and shifted his weight to the other side while I switched my duffel bag from my right shoulder to my left. "I'll admit, it's not something I've heard of before. I'm sorry for rushing to judgment. It was wrong of me to assume that what you had done was bad. It actually sounds like a good thing now that I'm listening to you," he said sheepishly. "You said he was controlling it?"

I shook my head and nodded in the direction of the car rental desk. Now that we weren't yelling at one another, I figured we could walk and talk at the same time. Shelby had given up on acting like she wasn't listening, and her earbuds were dangling around her neck.

"No, not controlling it. But he admitted to messing with it. He said it hated it here, on this plane. It was jealous of souls who had been able to cross over. What if—what if all the lost souls have these shadows? I think I've seen them before, but I never got a good enough look to realize what they truly were. Like, an essence of the original soul."

We got in line behind several other people waiting to rent a car and were quiet for a few moments, Rishi staring off into space as if he was trying to figure out the riddle that had just presented itself. Then Shelby spoke up. "So it's almost like this 'shadow soul,'" she lifted her fingers in bunny-ear quotations, "is a part of the original soul that's just been, like, cut off," she said softly, clipping the air with her two fingers like scissors. The only person left in front of us was too busy renting a car and signing agreements to be idly listening to our quiet chatter about lost souls and death deities.

Rishi, who hadn't appeared to hear one word Shelby had said, looked at her sharply, his head starting to bob forward in a nod of comprehension. He opened his mouth to say something that I was keenly interested in hearing, but the person behind the desk looked at us as the man in front of us moved away with two keys jingling from his hand. "Can I help you?"

* * *

"Do you even know where we're going?" Shelby asked from the backseat. I glanced back at her and felt instantly amazed that her candy-red hair was so smoothly pulled into a perfectly folded bun on top of her head. How she stayed so put together while maintaining status quo as a societal norm dissenter was beyond me.

Rishi lifted his dark eyes to the rearview mirror with a quick nod. "Yeah, I've been there before."

"You've been to Death's Doorway before?" I asked, looking over at him. "Have you tried this before?"

"Tried what?" he said, evading my eyes and keeping his gaze straight ahead on the road.

"Tried getting the scythe before?"

He didn't say anything for a moment, his hard jaw tensing. Finally, he gave me a quick look and nodded curtly.

"Well, obviously the mission failed. Is that how you know that only Grim, or as the theory goes, her progeny, can get it?"

"I didn't go in for the scythe. We've always known that it would take Grim somehow breaking the ban, or that we'd need you to get it. I went in to gather some intel, before we had the insiders we have now. Before the deities started getting tired of Hades and his bastards running things."

"So what's with the mysteriousness?" Shelby said, echoing my thoughts. He was acting strange about the whole thing, kind of edgy. Like he was hiding something. After we'd rented the vehicle, he'd excused himself to make a phone call and he'd been moody ever since. I could put money on it that he'd been talking to my mother. She had a way of putting people off. It just surprised me she could have the same effect on Rishi.

I'd never seen him anything but self-assured, annoyingly calm, or snarky, so his anxiety was a new mood. His Adam's apple bobbed nervously, and I watched the tightening around his dark eyes and the way a flush rose to his light brown skin. I couldn't help but delight in this mood, this vulnerability. *What is wrong with me?*

I was having trouble denying that from the moment I'd met Rishi, I'd been drawn to him. We were … kindred souls. I hated myself for even thinking such a smooshy thought, but I think we understood each other.

Although I didn't understand what was making his jaw pop and pulse. "What happened, Rishi?" I asked, turning in my seat so I was facing him and could shoot a glance at Shelby, who looked equally intrigued by his strange reaction.

"Grim should be the one to tell you," he said tersely, casually glancing in the rearview mirror and pausing. His eyes didn't slide away as quickly as they should have. "Damn," he said beneath his breath, and he gunned the gas. The RPM gauge approached redline as his foot slammed the accelerator to the floor.

Shelby gave a slight yelp and double-checked her seatbelt. "What's going on, Rishi?" she said, gripping the side of her door, her knuckles white as the speedometer crept up from sixty to eighty in mere seconds.

"Who knew this thing had such torque," I said, secretly thrilling in the feel of my stomach dropping away and the world around us moving faster. I glanced past Shelby through the back window and saw headlights gaining on us at a questionable speed, and I was just able to make out the black Dodge Challenger as it grew closer. It was gray outside, the sky slowly lighting up the highway we traveled along on our way to Death's Doorway. They weren't supposed to know where we were going. How were we supposed to sneak in if they were following us?

"You think it's …?"

Rishi cut me off with a nod of his head, turning to me with a crooked grin curving up one side of his face, his cheeks showing only the slightest hint of a five-o'clock shadow despite the long flight, and his dusky eyes alight with a strange glow. "Lupine," he said.

I laughed, matching his grin with my own. The flash of the world went by us and I caught my breath, rolling down my window quickly to feel the rush of the wind beat at my face and hair.

"Look, now you've got me calling him that," he added. He grinned again, beating the accelerator and bearing down on the highway like a devil in the dwindling night. My hair swept out the window as we sped up, and I reveled in the freshness of grass and sand, the freedom that swooped in on the wind and made me feel as if I was flying, as if I could live forever.

"Hey!" Shelby's voice dampened the wildness that existed within my soul. "You guys maybe are like deities or whatever you like to call your high-and-mighty selves, but I'm human!" she shouted. "I'd like to live today," she said, softer this time, her face tight, her voice shrill with anxiety.

"Relax, Shelby," Rishi said, his eyes never moving off the road as we flew through space like a comet of metal. "We'll just put your soul back in."

I glanced back at my best friend to see her face visibly drain of whatever color had been left. "Can you do that?" she whispered, her face scrunched in mild horror.

"There's a first time for everything," Rishi said, his deep, throaty laugh snatched by the wind that still pounded in on me, making me wish I could crawl out the window and lay on the hood of the car with the open road and the late winter air cutting around me like a kiss.

But I had Shelby here. She was a normal person and she had witnessed Geoff's car accident and therefore was rightfully freaked out that a car full of hater death deities was bearing down on us.

"We'll be fine," I said, trying to reassure her.

"They have a faster car," she said as she glanced back and saw them edge closer. They were still catching up, but it wouldn't be long.

"Couldn't he just flicker into our car?" I said, turning to Rishi.

He shook his head. "He's probably drained from flickering onto the plane, invisible-style, as you like to put it. Besides, he'd have to bring all his thugs to overpower us and that could get messy in a speeding car. More likely he'll try to make us crash so he can quickly grab you." He looked as exhilarated as I felt, his dark eyes lit up as he raced down the road, a half smile cocking his face. But I knew something had to give. We didn't really want them to catch us. It was more the chase that was fun. Like when you're getting playfully chased as a little kid and you delight in the pursuit, but you run as fast as you can to get away.

"We have to lose them," I said, rolling up my window more for Shelby's sake than anything else.

"How?" Shelby said.

"Do they know where we're going? I mean what's the point, anyway, if they're already aware of what we're up to. I thought the plan was to sneak in, not go barreling in with purgatory hounds on our heels," I said.

"Like I said before, no one else really knows about Death's Doorway," Rishi said, hitting the breaks so quickly that the Challenger, which had sped up beside us in an attempt to cut us off, went flying past. Rishi slammed our Chevy Tahoe back into gear and went careening up the side of the turnoff over the grassy embankment. He didn't even pause at the red light. Behind us I heard tires squeal in the distance, but Rishi had already turned down another road, and the sky was still gray enough that the shadows enveloped us from view as we gained distance from them.

In the back, I heard Shelby let out a pent-up breath and I turned to see her face, now a white oval in the gloom, start to relax. "You think they're gone?" Shelby asked.

"For now," Rishi said.

"You okay?" I asked Shelby.

She nodded quickly. "Peaches and cream," she muttered. "I just didn't realize I'd signed up to be the stunt woman in a bad movie."

"Shelb, you can go home. I didn't want you to come in the first place."

"Gee, thanks, Blake. I'm so glad I risked my life just to be a third wheel. Remind me not to care about my best friend's welfare next time."

"That's not what I meant, Shelb," I said, feeling like I too had lost my human touch for a moment. "I never wanted to expose you to anything that could hurt you. Of course I'm glad you're here! But if you want us to drop you at the next airport, I'll understand. Hell, I'd feel relieved, if less likely to maintain a stable footing without my anchor." I breathed a sigh. I could still speak and not sound like a jerk. I really didn't want to be like my mother.

She shook her head, a stubborn glint coming to rest in the shadowed set of her chin. "No, I'm staying. I really do find this all fascinating. Just promise me one thing, okay?"

I nodded. "Sure."

"Cut it out with the whole Bonnie and Clyde adrenaline rush junky thing you two have going on. It's gross," she said and popped her earbuds back in. "Wake me when we actually get somewhere. If there's another car chase, leave me to my non-heart-attack-inducing sleep, please," she said and then closed her eyes.

I turned around in my seat, smiling to myself. She'd be fine. I, on the other hand, could feel the flush to my cheeks at her insinuation that there was something romantic going on between Rishi and me. Of course, I'd been staring at him all afternoon, but I really wasn't trying to go there. I hoped he'd been too intent on driving that he hadn't heard.

"So, Bonnie and Clyde, huh?" he asked, a slow smile starting to crawl up his face.

"Yeah, you're Bonnie and I'm Clyde. Just drive," I grumbled, thankful for the shadows so he couldn't see how he affected me.

I busied myself by slipping my phone out of my bag and glancing at the screen to see that my dad had sent a text. *You coming over for dinner tomorrow night?*

Of course, the text was from the night before. The clock on my phone informed me it was only 5:35 a.m., which meant it was 7:35 a.m. there. But still, I decided to hold off on responding. I'm sure he'd wonder what was up since my exams were over. I would never get up before 9 a.m. on a day off unless forced to, and he knew that.

I slipped my phone back in my bag, casting a sidelong glance at Rishi. "So you said no one is supposed to know about Death's Doorway. Are you sure about that? They seemed to have had a good idea of where we're headed."

"I've heard rumors that Sebastiana's scythe is in this area. Although I'm pretty sure she planted those rumors. My assumption is they made a good guess when they followed us here, or else they simply did some research to find out where we were flying."

"What makes Grim and Sebastiana so special that they both have the scythes?"

Rishi lifted his broad shoulders in a shrug. "I don't think too many people know that story, and I sure was never enlightened. You could ask Grim though, you're her daughter." He glanced at me again quickly before looking back to the road.

I laughed, although absent of any humor. "Yeah, right, because we're so close."

I glanced out at the window, the dim landscape making landmarks hard to discern, despite my heightened eyesight. "So they're looking for the other scythe to power up the first one."

Rishi grunted an affirmative before speaking intelligible words once more. "If we were to get that scythe, we'd be more powerful than them, especially since you're in the Reaper bloodline. The scythes are in tune to Grim and Sebastiana, and in theory, would be to you too."

"Theories again, I see," I said, shaking my head and tsking him with my tongue.

A light ahead cast a glow on a tired roadside motel. The building was lit up though, and a sign reading vacancy made my eyes feel blearier than they'd felt only moments before. Rishi rolled the car into a parking spot and put it in park. I was turning to wake Shelby when a warm hand slid down my arm and over my hand, tugging on it in a way that insisted I look back at him.

He was suddenly so close I felt trapped in my seat, his gaze intent, but not on my eyes—on my lips. He smiled slowly, finally raising his eyes to meet mine, a slow, golden burn igniting my blood with heat. "Yes?" I managed to say, arching my brow in that way I'd practiced.

"Do that thing again," he said, his voice low and smooth, invading my senses as I never thought a voice could. My heart lurched in a way that hadn't happened even when we were in a high-speed chase. I swallowed thickly, trying to find my voice around his desire that smelled like musk and car leather.

"What thing?" I finally managed to murmur, sipping in a deep breath of air as my breathless voice gave away my weakness for him.

His smile widened, and he knew he had me, his high cheekbones and loose, shiny black hair lending him a certain primal male beauty that made me retreat until I could feel the door handle pressing into my back. "That thing with your tongue. When you chastised me," he said, mimicking my tsking of him from only moments earlier. "I found it interesting."

I couldn't help it, my eyes fell to his own lips while I tried to wrangle my cutting wit and Artemis-like spirit. I shook my head, so lightly I was surprised he saw it.

"Let's go get rooms, we could all use the sleep," I finally managed to say, nearly choking on the words that sounded liked a sordid invitation. "I mean separate rooms," I amended, inwardly bringing back the defense he'd torn down, but only by avoiding his gaze.

He brought me back to him by clasping one hand under my chin and bringing my eyes up to meet his. "First, do that thing," he insisted, his dark eyes glowing with amusement.

I frowned at him, doing my best to ignore the warm hand that commanded my chin—and the desire in me that wanted to sneak through the parking lot with him to our own private room and forget about death, deities, and rules.

The faint sound of Shelby's music percolated through the quiet car and brought me back to myself, although with some difficulty. I slowly forced myself to tear his hand from my chin and smiled as smugly as I could, all the while missing the warmth of his steady fingers on my face. "As if," I whispered with a toss of my head, feeling the black ripples of my hair bounce. It probably didn't look as cool as it felt, given that I'd been traveling all day. I hoped I came off as ambivalent, but it was all a façade. I wanted him. Almost as if it was a memory of something that never happened, the ghost of what his kiss might have felt like whispered through me, making me blink my eyes with the strangeness of it. I shivered with a rare chill and glanced at him. He also seemed to have retreated, the suggestive grin gone from his face, replaced by confusion and what also seemed like regret.

He glanced at me and cleared his throat, but before he could say anything I licked my lips and spoke, "So, like, rooms?"

He grunted with a nod and it struck me as such a guy thing to do. He was always so business-like, so sure of himself. "I'll go see what I can do," he said and jumped out of the car before I could remind him to get two rooms. I just knew I couldn't bunk up with him and remain sane.

But that didn't appear to be a problem, because he returned five minutes later with two separate keys, a room for Shelby and me and a room for him. I nudged Shelby awake and she sleepily climbed out of the car, dragging her bag across the parking lot asphalt and stumbling into the room as soon as I unlocked it. The rooms were right next to each other, but Rishi disappeared as soon as Shelby and I were safe inside, mumbling something about needing to park the Tahoe in a more inconspicuous place.

I headed to the bathroom to change. When I'd washed up, I came back out to see Shelby blearily staring at the television screen. "Are you going to brush your teeth? I have toothpaste," I said, but she just waved her hand in reply, which meant she was seriously tired.

A low knock made my heart catch air in a palpitation, and I smoothed down the long sleeved T-shirt and yoga pants I was wearing as pajamas. I walked to the door and opened it, and found Rishi standing there, avoiding my gaze.

I was so confused by his behavior I didn't even know what to say. One moment he'd been practically seducing me, and now he couldn't even look at me. *Is it just me or are death deities a moody bunch?* I honestly didn't know which version of him I preferred, but at that moment, being in control of my faculties and not at the whim of his smile worked for me.

"Make sure you peek and see who's at the door before you open it," he chastised.

"Why bother? If they find us we're done anyway."

"This will keep them from finding us so easily," he said, gesturing to the symbol of a skull and bones that he had painted on the ground in front of the door.

"Ummm, is that blood?"

Rishi nodded. "Only the blood of a death deity can keep another death deity from sniffing us out. We should be all right for the night."

"Hopefully we don't get kicked out for satanic practices," I joked.

He laughed, finally meeting my eyes with his after being away for so long.

"This place is a dump. I'm sure they've had worse tenants than a couple of death deities," he murmured, and I knew he'd recovered from whatever had come over us while in the car.

"Too true." I glanced back at the bed with distaste, knowing I'd need a shower just from staying here.

"We'll head out early, okay? Keep on the road and hopefully avoid Hades's little gang. Call me if you need anything, okay?"

I nodded.

He paused, his fathomless dark gaze softening at it came to rest on my face. "Good night," he said, holding my eyes with his own for a moment, cradling me with their warmth.

I nodded. "Night," I whispered and watched him as he turned toward his door. I shut the door before he could catch me staring, and I turned to Shelby. The TV was quietly droning in the background and my best friend had one legging-clad leg looped outside of the blanket while she slept face down in the pillow. Of course she had fallen asleep. I sighed. It would have been nice to talk to her about how confused I was. After all that had happened in the last twenty-four hours, all I could think of was that last trip into his eyes.

I peeled the comforter off the bed, threw it on the floor, fetched one of the extra blankets from the closet, then snuggled down beneath the stiff, white sheets and recalled how annoying I'd found him only the day before. He was so much easier to deal with when I couldn't stand him.

I closed my eyes and tried to push him out of my mind, but I couldn't keep the remembrance of that ghostly kiss from making me shiver. Our lips hadn't physically touched, but it had almost felt like they had. As if our souls had kissed without us even meaning them to.

CHAPTER FOURTEEN

THE CLOCK GLOWED 9 a.m. and I sighed. Sleep remained elusive, and outside my door the local lost souls had found me. I could feel their filmy eyes peering through the uselessly translucent curtains. It was unsettling even for a death deity like myself.

Feeling the heaviness of exhaustion weigh me down as I headed toward the bathroom, I figured if anything, passing over souls would give me energy. And something to do until we left in a few hours for Death's Doorway.

I slipped into the bathroom and pulled off my shirt and grabbed my jeans and hoodie from the counter where I'd left them dangling half in the sink. I pulled a clean long-sleeved T-shirt from my bag and slipped it over my head. The sweatshirt sleeves were damp when I slid them over my arms, but while it was uncomfortable, I didn't feel any colder.

I glanced at Shelby in the dim room, only the drawn curtains keeping the sun from brightening the dull interior, but she was still softly snoring away. I stepped out into the day and closed the door on her sleeping sounds. Glancing at the two souls, I jerked my head toward the dumpster and vending machine area. Maybe it wasn't the most glamorous place to pass over into the afterlife, but at least we'd be hidden.

I didn't wait to see if they followed, knowing they would. When I was tucked out of sight, I turned to the two. It was a woman who appeared to have been in her forties when she died and a boy who couldn't have been older than twelve. God, I hated when it was kids. The boy was small, and his skinny frame was tucked in a Yankees T-shirt and mesh shorts, his legs like wobbly sticks I had trouble believing could actually support his body. He stared up at me with his milky white eyes and I could see that they had once been brown. The woman—

who I instantly assumed was his mother because of the identical way they wore their grief in the creases of their faces—was petite, auburn-haired, and probably attractive once. But now her mouth twisted in regret and her nearly opaque white eyes twitched. They both wore contemporary clothing, but I could tell she'd gone lost fast. At the moment, she seemed to be waging a war to reclaim the last vestiges of her sanity.

"Please help us," the boy whispered, his eyes meeting mine for only a split second before they went wide, sliding to the side and settling upon something that made him push back into his mother.

I glanced to the side and saw the shadows, one big and the other smaller, matching the mother and son. The shadows didn't seem to be hiding anymore, although I could feel the anger and bitterness that seeped from them.

I turned back to the boy and shook my head, offering what I hoped was a comforting smile. "You don't have to be scared anymore. I can take care of them," I said. His eyes glimmered with hope and I smiled again, and before he could react, I grabbed him by the hand while reaching up for the shadow and shoved the two essences of his soul together, accordion-style, except this had only one sound: the sound of closure.

The boy shimmered and reappeared after blinking out only momentarily. His wide, brown eyes were bright again and he grinned, resembling any American boy I'd ever seen. He should have been playing baseball and running through the grass with his friends, but instead we were standing outside a crappy motel next to a dumpster that emanated with the smell of cheap liquor and filth.

But you wouldn't have known that from staring into his small but bright little face. "Do my mom before she can run," he said with authority.

She'd barely noticed what I'd done at first, but then she'd started to circle, searching for her son.

"He's right here." I pointed to the boy, but she was too gone.

For a few moments she whizzed by, wailing into the night, her eyes going crazier. I muttered, "To Abbadon with this," and I grabbed her before she could get away, reaching into the darkness simultaneously and pulling out the shadow, the blackness sliding around my hand cold and slippery. I didn't know if I was supposed to be doing this and I didn't care. They seemed much healthier, as souls go, when they were joined, and that's all that mattered to me. I brought her and her spectral counterpart together and closed my eyes as they seemed to collapse in on themselves, one moment there, the next gone. Just like with her son, she reappeared only moments later looking as pretty as I'd guessed her to be in life, although her eyes were still lined with sadness.

"Thank you," she said, wrapping an arm around her son. Turning her gray gaze from mine, she looked down at him, her lips trembling. "And I'm so sorry. I don't know if I've said it enough times, but I am," she whispered.

His brown eyes glistened and the corners of his mouth tugged down, but I could still see the happiness that warmed his gaze. "I know you didn't mean to, Mom," he said back.

I watched them, biting my lower lip and wondering what she must have done to make her so impossibly sad. I figured since I'd so kindly reunited them with their other halves, it wouldn't be too rude if I just asked. "What did you do that you need to apologize for?" I said softly, so it didn't come out as tactless as I knew it probably was.

Tears trembled on her pale lashes as she looked back to me, and I felt guilt wash over me. I should have left it alone. "I'm sorry," I said. "I should mind my own business."

She shook her head, wiping the moisture from her eyes with the back of her hand. "No, you saved us. We've been so lost. At times together, and at other times apart. So lost, our minds awhirl, barely remembering the past, who we once were. And we couldn't stop it. Now, we get to be just us," she said, looking down at her son with a soft but pained smile.

She looked my way once more, self-loathing dripping in the weight of her words. "We were traveling to see my parents and we'd stopped for dinner. I had a few too many and then got back on the road again. I ... I'd been so tired, and the wine didn't help. When I woke up I was standing over our bodies. I'd fallen asleep at the wheel and driven straight into the motel."

Ah, so that was why the other building looked like it was about to collapse. "We've been here ever since ... waiting. I hoped for so long that we'd be able to move on, go someplace better ... or worse, for me," she stumbled on her words. "But someplace better for my son, Aiden. I killed him. I'm a murderer. I don't deserve much better than what

I've received, but he didn't deserve to be abandoned. Why did no one come?" she asked plaintively.

My chest tightened as I watched the wrath of time and guilt seep even more deeply into her features than before. I didn't know if there was a heaven or a hell. You'd think I'd get the scoop, but nope. I couldn't believe, though, that a woman who so loved her son and had made a horrible mistake would be condemned for eternity in some fiery pit.

I shook my head and felt the faint touch of a smile curve my lips. "It's a long story, but it's not because you were being punished. Not by anyone that matters anyway. And the good news is I can send you to on to the next world, where I hope you can find peace."

Aiden's eyes widened once more with joy, and I couldn't help but send out a prayer to a god I wasn't sure existed and beg for an afterlife with big ball fields, cheeseburgers, and puppies—anything I could imagine a little boy would want. And a plea that his mother got to stay with him.

But his mother shook her head, her guilt profound and heavy. It was written on her face. She didn't think she deserved peace.

"Do you want to stay?" I asked. "Souls that stay because of guilt or some misguided attempt for redemption become ghosts, or so I'm told. I won't stop you if you want to stay." I knew I probably wasn't supposed to do that, but I didn't care about rules. No one else did. Hades sure wasn't following any death deity guidelines.

She stared at me hard, her arms tight around her son and her knuckles white as she dug her nails into her other hand. But Aiden let out a cry, dismay evident in the drag of his weighted protest, his unshed tears radiating off of him and causing the chilly morning air to become heavy with humidity.

He shook his head vehemently and turned to his mother, clutching her hands and button-up blouse. "I won't go without you."

I gazed at him for a moment before turning back to her. "You can stay," I repeated myself, "or you can find forgiveness by thinking of your little boy first. He's been waiting so long to be happy again." He'd never said a word to me, but as the words left my mouth I knew them to be true. Almost as if I had a window into his mind and heart, I saw how he'd slowly gone crazy, but not as insanely lost as her, and how he'd hoped in his more lucid moments for happiness with his mother once again. He believed in Heaven. And maybe that was enough. *Geez, now I'm a freakin' philosopher.*

"So?" I asked, making sure my voice was as gentle as I could make it. Which was no small feat, given my sometimes-abrasive attitude. Must be a mother-daughter thing. "Will you stay, or will you follow your son into another life and see what it holds? The only one who needs to forgive you now is yourself. Aiden already has," I said.

Oh my lord, did I really just say that? I didn't know who I was becoming, but whoever she was, she had some good lines. But they weren't just lines, and I knew that. I felt every word that left my lips, every emotion that radiated in my chest, making me want to drop to my knees and weep for the boy, for the mother, and for the unknown of their futures.

All it took was a moment. The auburn-haired woman, her tanned skin and healthy glow back in her face as it had been in life, turned to her son and looked down at him. "You want to go?" she asked, putting both hands on his shoulders and kneeling down in front of him.

His face was as solemn as the coldest winter day for but a second, and then it lit up with the turn of his smile, brown freckles dancing on the ridge of his nose and curve of his cheeks. He didn't speak or nod. His expression needed no words.

"What's your name?" I asked her as she turned to me resolutely, a spark of steel in her eyes I hadn't noticed before.

"Diane," she said. "You didn't already know?" Her brows furrowed as she tilted her head, looking at me curiously.

I shrugged. "I'm new," I said quickly and changed the subject. "Take my hands."

They both complied and I closed my eyes, their passage through me into Abbadon infusing its usual energy into my soul. I felt their joy and fear, and it was all good, because they were moving on. The door closed within me but the transfer of power, which usually came to a halt at this point, kept rippling through me, rocking every nerve so that I felt myself violently shaking beneath the onslaught of a never-ending charge. I fell to my knees, not feeling the rocky asphalt cut into my legs, only the rush of wind, the feel of freedom, and the happy sigh of a boy who'd found peace at last.

I doubled over, drinking in lungfuls of air, but it wasn't enough to help me. I felt the world spin around me, my body not under my control as I was wracked with the thundering shudder of the last ripples of energy.

"Blake!" I heard Rishi call my name as I felt myself convulsing with the current that coursed through me with the strength of a bolt of lightning. I curled my arms over my head and put my forehead to the ground, trying to control the jerking of my limbs. And then strong arms were wrapping around me, holding me tightly, warm and secure, and the power that had electrified my being tapered off until I was left trembling, swallowing air, and gasping with each new breath. I could see I was on the ground and that my head was being cradled by rough, dark hands, the warmth of one hand coming to settle on my hair with smooth, stroking gestures that calmed the cantering beat of my heart.

"You're okay now, love," he said softly, his voice light, caressing my still-shuddering inner spirit.

I closed my eyes and basked in the feel of his strong presence and the comfort it brought me. Rishi, despite his sometimes cocky exterior, had a touch that was a warm balm, soothing and light, and I felt in that moment his capacity for gentleness and compassion.

"What happened?" I murmured, although keeping my eyes closed.

He continued to stroke my hair, not answering right away. "I think it was a combination of factors. You reunited their souls, passed two over at the same time, and we're close, close to the scythe. I felt it. The power it contains must be connecting with you, amplifying what you're feeling when you cross souls over. That's my best guess, anyway."

"I think it's right," he added. "I think you're right. Lost souls need to be united with these shadows."

I opened my eyes slowly, beginning to feel the revitalization I'd normally get from a crossover, but ten times that. I lifted my head and his hand fell away. I would have cursed myself, but I needed to figure out what was going on. "Well, I don't want the scythe if it's going to treat me like Zeus's target practice," I said, although I had to admit that after the initial buzz of electricity, I was feeling good. The world blurred around me in bright colors.

"Whooa," I heard myself say as I tipped over where I was sitting. Laughing, I rolled around in the dirt staring up into the sky as it grew brighter, the colors a hopeful mix of orange, purple, and red. "Pretty," I whispered.

I heard Rishi chuckle. "Let's get you to bed for an hour or so to sleep this off. You've got a little while before we need to get going."

*   *   *

I cracked my eyes open and was met with a vision of the yellowing, cracked ceiling of the motel room. Light flooded in beyond the sheer curtains, bathing me in its warmth and making me wish I was in my own bed, curled comfortably beneath the covers. But my ceiling was white, not desecrated by age, neglect, and cigarette smoke. I sighed. Yep, I was still Death.

I felt pressure on the edge of the bed near my feet and glanced down to see Shelby perched with one leg tucked underneath her, the other dangling off the bed. She was perfectly coiffed as usual, wearing skinny jeans, cowboy boots, and a flowing embroidered top. Her hair was carefully woven into a braid down one shoulder and she wore dangling turquoise earrings. I arched a brow. "Where's the cowboy hat?" I asked, covering a yawn with my hand.

"Whatever. We're in New Mexico, I'm assimilating with the culture," she said defensively. "Rishi wants you up. He says you've slept long enough and it's time to get on the road. He mentioned you were pretty out of it after a crossover this morning. He also said you did that thing where you put the two parts of the soul back together."

I rolled my eyes and sat up, expecting to feel sore and used up, but instead feeling energy rush through my blood like a spike of espresso. "What did Rishi *not* tell you?" I muttered, smoothing my thick hair back and running my fingers through the clumps. I probably should hit the shower before we took off. I was going to Abbadon, the netherworld, and I figured I should make a good first impression. I had a feeling we wouldn't get out unscathed.

Shelby, who was holding my travel coffee cup, stretched out her hand. "I got you this." I shook my head, my fingers pulsating with electricity still. The last thing I needed was caffeine. She shrugged and tilted the mug to her own lips.

"How many is that?" I asked.

She shrugged again. "Third. But come on, I usually take espresso. This is just regular coffee, and I'm barely feeling a thing." She grinned.

I smiled back, her wide green gaze watching me keenly over the rim of the cup as she took another sip.

"Where's Rishi?" I asked, trying to avoid her eyes. I hated when she looked at me like that. I always felt naked.

"He's trying to find another car, I believe. I'm glad it wasn't my credit card we used to rent the thing," she mumbled as an aside before continuing. "Since Hades's scaries know what we were driving, he thought securing a new ride would help us get to Death's Doorway undetected."

"Cool," I said, not really listening to what she said. I was too busy thinking about the lost souls and their penchant for being split. Something about their state of being bothered me, but I couldn't quite figure out what it was. Mainly because I knew next to nothing about being a death deity. It irked me. What business did I even have crossing people over? What business did I have being the last tie to the mortal realm, when I couldn't even give them a hint of whether there was an afterlife outside of Abbadon? I thought back to earlier this morning, when the dim gray had turned to dawn, and I remembered my last moments with the mother and son, and then I remembered Rishi's comforting hands and arms holding me ...

"Blake."

I glanced at Shelby, who was staring at me with a perfectly arched brow of her own.

"Thinking about a certain brown-eyed death deity?" she asked with a smirk tugging at her lips.

I glanced at her and puckered my lips like I'd eaten a lemon, batting away the very thought. I forced myself to meet her gaze and quelled the blush that wanted to creep up my cheeks.

"Yeah, I have to talk to him about something. Don't make it seem like something it's not," I said, rolling my eyes and climbing out of bed with a nonchalant stretch.

"Defensive much?" she laughed, tilting her head back and downing the remnants of her coffee.

I fixed my glare on her and ignored that fact that she was right. I was too confused at the moment to own up, and I didn't need her in my head.

"I've barely healed from the loss of Geoff, do you really think I'd go for the death deity who worships a woman who abandoned me?" I said as flippantly as I could manage. "I have to go take a shower."

I stalked toward the bathroom, but not before I saw Shelby flinch. She felt bad, and I immediately felt bad for making her feel bad. Mainly because she was right. But I needed my privacy at the moment, so I pushed away the guilt, trudged into the bathroom, and shut the door. The effects of the early morning crossover were starting to wane a bit, and a shower would refresh me. Then it was on to Death's Doorway, and from there, Abbadon.

* * *

Shelby and her bag were missing when I emerged from the bathroom, my wet hair hanging down my back and soaking the back of my shirt uncomfortably. I'd just put my jeans and long-sleeved T-shirt back on. I grabbed a fresh hoodie from my pack and zipped it up, pulling on a pair of sneakers before slinging my bag over my shoulder.

Rishi came around the front of the building as I stepped outside.

"Here," he said, handing me a bag that smelled heavenly. I glanced inside and thanked the powers that be that at least someone in my company ate like a normal human being.

"You are my hero," I said, heading toward Shelby, who was sitting in the bed of a black F-150 with the hatch down, her booted legs dangling as she drank a cup of coffee while munching on an organic granola bar. She must have brought that along with her, because I knew she wasn't going to find such fare in the motel's vending machine breakfast nook. I climbed up next to her so that I could dig into the sausage and egg croissant sandwich.

"I'm sure he's more than that," Shelby murmured under her breath so that only I could hear. I shot her a dark look, realizing I should have known that my earlier attempts at diverting her intuitive sensitivities hadn't deterred her. I ignored her and glanced at Rishi appreciatively.

He smiled crookedly, one side of his cheek coming up as his eyes warmed. "There's a diner up the street. Figured you'd want something more than the horse-meal Shelby eats," he said with a wink. She snorted beside me.

"You mean the whole foods I eat, as opposed to the processed, hormone-filled stuff you two eat. It's a good thing you have longevity on your side given your … legacies. I, on the other hand, don't have good genes from an immortal parent that allow me to extend my life," she retorted, sniffing disgustedly as I took a healthy bite from my breakfast sandwich.

I couldn't help but grin at Rishi as the cheesy warmth and fluffy bread melted onto my tongue, melding with the mild spice of the sausage. "Sooo good," I sighed, feeling the warmth hit my stomach and bring comfort to the dull emptiness.

"I think of it this way," I added, licking a drop of grease off my finger with a smirk. "This very well could be my last meal. I'm going down there for a scythe that can kill other death deities, so I could meet my own untimely demise."

Shelby crumpled the wrapper to her granola bar and hopped off the truck. "Yeah, but you're the only one who can supposedly wield the thing besides your mother, so I feel like you're pretty safe," she said.

I jumped off the truck bed as well. "Oh yeah," I said as I lifted the tailgate and slammed it into place. "Well, last meal or not, it was yummy either way," I laughed.

I grabbed my duffel bag from its spot on the ground, opened the small, rear backseat door, and flung my bag inside. Shelby did the same and stepped up to crawl into the tight backseat. As she situated herself, she grinned at me. "I'll let you sit with Rishi up front." Her pale green eyes glowed beneath her dark lashes, expertly coated in an even application of dark brown mascara.

I just grinned. "I get shotgun because I'm in charge." I winked and climbed into the front seat, heaving myself up by grabbing the handle on the interior door. Shelby sat back and glanced out the window with a knowing smile settling on the curve of her lips.

I sighed. Sometimes, my best friend of forever was just insufferable. Rishi opened the driver's side door and climbed in, his long legs folding gracefully. He shut the door, slid his seatbelt into place, and started the ignition with the twist of his hand. The smell of his leather jacket comforted me, although I wouldn't even admit to myself that I needed comforting. It was a smell I'd always liked, and I longed to bury my nose in the scent.

"You ready?" he asked, turning to me with a grin, his shiny black hair loose around his shoulders.

I gazed at him a moment and then glanced back at Shelby before nodding. "Let's get this done," I finally said, reaching out to crank up the tunes as he rolled us into gear. The classic rock station blasted out Tom Petty's *Free Fallin'* and I tapped my foot along to it, knowing exactly what he meant.

Rishi eased the truck onto the highway and rolled down his window. The only sounds were the music and the wind beating against the car as we sped forward. I was enjoying the abandon of it all when I suddenly remembered my question about the lost souls. I glanced back to see that Shelby was fiddling with her phone, probably playing a game.

"Hey," I said softly to Rishi.

He rolled up his window and gave me a sideways glance, turning the volume down so he could hear me. "What's up?" he asked, moving his eyes back to the road.

"Have lost souls always been this way? You know, have they always been lost?"

I watched his profile as the dark slashes of his brows furrowed, the black stubble along his usually smooth face doing nothing to deter my greedy gaze. "No," he said slowly. "We didn't start to notice the instability of the souls until about ten years ago. We just assumed that it was what happened when souls stayed past their Earthly welcome, and that it didn't occur until the ban on Grim had lasted for a long time," he said.

"But it's possible that it's a new thing. Because, I mean, ghosts make the choice to stay based on some 'profound' bond, right? But lost souls are banned from Abbadon just like my mother."

He nodded slowly, casting me another glance with arched brows as if he wasn't sure where I was going with my train of thought. I wasn't quite sure either, but I had an idea. "So lost souls are essentially an extension of Grim? Her punishment is their punishment. They're intrinsically linked."

He shrugged his broad shoulders. "I'm not really sure, Blake. What are you getting at?" He eyes met mine seriously for a moment, his gaze alternating between me and the road.

"Well, when I put the lost souls back together with their shadow selves, they virtually return to normal. Why would their essences be separating? And why have you only noticed it in the last ten years? You said this doesn't happen to ghosts, but that's because staying isn't a punishment. They are linked to the living world rather than my mother. Unlike lost souls."

He shook his head, glancing at me and remaining silent, confusion clouding his face as I babbled on.

"Well, what if this separation of their souls is a new thing because it's, like, a reflection of my mother?" I said, warming up to my general thesis of the day.

Rishi nodded quickly, recognition flickering in his dark eyes as he stared out at the road, his fingers clenching. "You're saying you think the souls that belong to your mother are separating and turning lost because it's a representation of what's happening to Grim—the loss of her compassion, her humanity, the longer she is banished from reaping?"

I nodded excitedly.

He glanced at me, a smile curving his lips, although I could see the worry flicker in his eyes. "I think you could be right, but if that's true, it's more vital than ever that we take control of the scythe and put it back in Grim's hands. Who knows what could happen if she continues to lose her connection to her souls."

I nodded, the flush of my awareness quickly dying out as I contemplated my mother devoid of humanity, and a huge number of souls without theirs. I shivered. Even though I didn't often feel afraid, I knew … this could be bad. The sickness was growing.

"Hey," I said, suddenly having a thought. "Where did you get this truck, and what happened to the other car?"

Proving that she'd been listening all along as she tapped out a text or social media post, Shelby piped up from the back. "Trust me, ignorance really is bliss for the law-abiding." Although she played off the sarcasm well, I could sense the thread of unease riding beneath her acerbic tone.

I glanced at Rishi with arched brows but he merely gave me a wink, a slight smile lingering on his lips along with the gleam in his eyes. Shelby was going to have a heart attack hanging out with the adrenaline junkies in the front seat.

CHAPTER FIFTEEN

I WATCHED a world go by that was at the same time new and old. Adobes, gleaming and pristine, were set in a landscape that made me think at any moment I'd see a cowboy ride out, lazily holding the reins of his trusty steed.

"Where's this door?" Shelby piped up from the backseat.

"Santa Fe National Forest," Rishi replied.

"Well, that sounds wholesome. You know, camping, hiking, kicking back with the fam, like we're on a happy little trip together," Shelby babbled, her nervousness now evident.

I turned to meet her gaze. "Hey, Shelb, if you want us to take you back to the motel, it's okay."

"No," said Rishi sharply.

I turned to look at him, startled by the firmness of his tone.

"I'm sorry, but I don't remember this being your decision to make," I said, feeling the old irritation bubble up inside me. "You got something you need to tell us?"

"Umm, yeah," Shelby said. "I'm no psychic but I'm getting the overwhelming feeling you're hiding something."

Rishi didn't say anything, his hard jaw tense and pulsing as I continued to stare down the side of his face. His hands gripped the steering wheel tighter, his knuckles going white as we headed deeper into the park. The sun's light disappeared behind the trees that towered above, and the ice-capped mountains reared up before us.

"I think that you need to tell us now what it is you've been hiding. Why exactly did my mother insist Shelby come along?" I asked, disappointment surging through me. I should have known the demand for my best friend's presence had nothing to do with my emotional well-being.

At first I didn't think he was going to say anything, but he finally released a pent-up breath and nodded, almost like he was reassuring himself that it would all be okay. He was deluded. The fact that he had been lying to me, or keeping something from me, when I'd been having all those swoony feelings for him made my chest ache.

"Tell me now, Rishi, or Shelby and I walk and you're on your own."

"I wanted to tell you when I got a call from Grim at the Charlotte airport, but she insisted I keep it to myself until we were here. She knew you wouldn't like it."

"What is it, Rishi?"

"Yeah, I'd really like to know why I'm so important, myself," Shelby said, a hard note in her tone.

He sighed. "We need Shelby to cross through the door."

"So, like, I'm coming with you?" she said. "Into the Abba—whatever you guys call it."

I shook my head. We were missing something. "Why does she need to come with us? That doesn't make any sense," I said.

The cab of the truck was dim under the shadow of the trees, but through the leaves I could tell that the sky had turned gray as well. A storm hovered above us, broiling thick from the look of the clouds.

"We need a soul to take us over to unlock the portal. Essentially, the soul has to cross *us* over," he said quietly, averting his gaze to the road so as to avoid my penetrating, glacial stare.

"Excuse me, what?" Shelby screeched from the back. "You want to kill me so you can get the scythe?"

I glanced at her and shook my head slightly as our eyes met. "That's definitely not happening," I said, trying to reassure her.

Turning back to Rishi, I fixed him with my stare. "Please explain," I said tightly, reining in my temper that was hitting flint and sparking, about to blaze at any moment.

Rishi glanced at me quickly and then looked away even faster after seeing my disenchanted expression.

"No, no killing. Of course not! We're not Hades and his children. We're not in the business of hurting people. But, see, the door doesn't just open. We need a soul to open it for us, like a key."

I interrupted him, nowhere near appeased. "And how do you propose Shelby be that soul if she's not dead?"

I watched him flick his eyes up to the rearview mirror at Shelby and then back to the road once more, pausing before going on. "Grim knows that Shelby can astral project, and her living essence can open the gate," he said quietly.

"Astral what?" I said.

"Astral project. It's when a person can project their soul from their body into the spiritual plane."

"No, I can't do that," Shelby said quickly. Too quickly. "Grim's wrong, no idea what you're talking about."

I turned back to face her and saw that she was avoiding my gaze. "Shelb," I said softly, managing to get her pale green eyes to focus on me for a moment. "Can you really do that? And why would you want to do that?"

She tugged at the end of her licorice-red braid and clicked off her phone, which she'd been tapping with her thumb.

"I started trying to do it a while ago," she began reluctantly. "You know I've always been into the occult, and I saw a book about it once and thought it sounded pretty cool. But I forgot about it until you told me about being a death deity, and then when you started crossing souls over I got curious. I wanted to be a part of what you were doing, and I thought maybe I could help if I could see the souls myself. But the only way to do that for a mere human like me was to be on the spiritual plane. So I ... went back and got the book. And it was like right away, I got it—I understood how to project myself. One moment I was in my body and the next I was floating above it."

I stared at her, trying to comprehend the idea that she could propel her soul out of her body at will. Even harder to wrap my head around was that she hadn't told me this. But mostly, I was touched by the extent of her loyalty. Shelby wasn't a risk-taker, not like me. And for her to risk her very soul so that she could in some way help me on this dark journey brought tears to my eyes.

"What was it like?" I said softly, watching her eyes go wide and her expression dance through a mixture of emotions before finally settling on something akin to awe.

"It was amazing. I mean, totally terrifying at first. Seeing your body below you isn't natural, and it usually means, if you watch the movies, that you're dead. But when I got the hang of it, I found I could see other souls, and I could travel to really far places. Like one night I stood on Niagara Falls. On the actual water! It was possibly the most amazing experience of my existence."

"How long have you been doing this?"

Shelby shook her head lightly, her eyes focusing on nothing for a moment before she glanced back at me. "I only did it a few times. The first couple of times were like that, these fabulous moments. I mean, I could fly, basically. But I got scared. I saw the shadows. I didn't realize what they were until we were on the plane and you told me about sticking the two separated souls back together. They're dark, Blake. And I could feel their bitterness."

I stared at her for a couple of beats and finally turned and sat back in my seat, digesting the information. While she'd been talking, Rishi had been driving deeper into the park. I could feel the plugging and unplugging of my ears as we climbed. "How much longer?" I asked him.

"Not much," he murmured.

"Blake," Shelby said sharply, making me turn in instinctive response. "That's it? You just turn away?"

I flashed her an apologetic smile. "I'm sorry, I was just taking it in. So much in our lives has changed. I'm just overwhelmed that you did this seemingly impossible thing so you could be a part of this new world I've found myself in. Astral projection sounds badass... and scary—even for me," I said with a quick grin. "Why didn't you tell me?"

Her features brightened and her gloss-covered lips parted as she sighed, her eyes sparkling with a teary mist. "I didn't want you to worry. I knew you had enough going on, what with learning your deity duties— not to mention that you're about to go risk your life for the sake of the greater good." She reached out her ring-clad hand and touched mine, which was folded over the side of the seat.

"I'm not going to argue, I've definitely had some major changes in my life," I said. "But next time, please tell me. This is all pretty crazy stuff, and no matter what happens, you'll always be a major part of my life. It's not all about me," I said with a mock sigh, and Shelby laughed.

"But seriously, I'm here for your stuff too," I added. "You're my best friend, Shelb, which is why I think you should consider this carefully. You know I don't care about what Grim says. This is your choice and yours alone." I turned to set my wintry blue gaze on Rishi's.

Rishi seemed startled that the conversation had turned back to him, his gaze intent on the steep road ahead of us.

"Listen, all she'd need to do is astral project her soul and open the gate. We go in with her, locate the scythe while she waits for us, and we come back out. She goes back into her body, and we all win."

"While that all sounds dandy, you're forgetting that I'm on a time limit here. I don't know how long I can project before it becomes dangerous to my body. And what if going through Death's Doorway cuts my cord?" Shelby said, a rancorous note working its way into her voice.

"It won't," Rishi said, shaking his head.

"How can you know for sure?" she responded back.

"Because you're crossing us over, not vice-versa. You can walk through the door and, as a soul, you will open it for a period of time. I'm not worried about how long you can astral project. I've met people who could do it for hours on end and they weren't half as spiritually evolved as you."

I was looking between the two of them, fairly lost, but I didn't miss Shelby's small smile of pleasure at his mention of her soul being more enlightened than most.

"I don't care if she's the next freakin' messiah, Shelby needs to be made aware of the dangers that *do* exist, not just the ones that don't. We're going into the underworld, which was overtaken by a power-obsessed death deity who, for the record, had a pretty horrible reputation even before all this scythe business."

I expected a tirade from Rishi, but both he and Shelby were quiet. I turned to look out the window and found we were parked at a footpath.

"We have to hike from here," he said.

"Lovely," I said, thankful I'd had the good fortune to bring sneakers. But I'd only seen Shelby wearing boots meant more for style than trekking through the woods to become a sacrifice for a greater good.

I clenched my fingers, digging my nails into my palms and feeling a tidal wave of anger wash over me like a hot fire—anger at my mother for leaving me out of the loop, for showing such little regard to anyone else's wishes but her own. Asking my best friend instead of just demanding she put herself at risk would have been a nice step in the way of building a relationship with me.

But I was even more upset with Rishi, whom I'd nearly found myself liking, for leading me here and springing this on us, this newest order from my mother. She always came first. "I need some air," I said with a quick glance at Shelby, who nodded with understanding.

I didn't look at Rishi as I ripped off my seatbelt and flung the door open. I dropped down to the ground and walked quickly off into the trees so that the truck was out of sight. A light rain was coming down, although the trees caught most of the water before it could drop on me. Only the mist hit me, but instead of adding to the damp chill that hung in the mountainous air, it felt refreshing against the heat of my skin, which sweated from the rage that rippled molten in my blood. Who did Grim think she was? How did she think she could waltz into my life after all these years, hit me with the news that I'm literally Death, and then presume to make demands on not only me but also my best friend that could very well get us both killed?

I closed my eyes and leaned back against a tree that reached tall to the sky and shielded me in its embrace. I took comfort for a moment from its strength, its life force that went on for hundreds of years, instead of the momentary blip we humans spent on this earth. Although I guess I wasn't completely human. I was more like the tree, an observer through time. We were each a doorway in our own right, me to the underworld, the tree to the wild, to solitude.

My breathing slowed and the heat from my skin sizzled and began to dissipate as the misty forest air coated and soothed my soul with each inhale. I jerked when I opened my eyes and Rishi was standing in front of me, his broad shoulders slightly bowed beneath the brown of his leather jacket. His dark eyes were beseeching, nervous that he'd lost something. He had.

I was well-aware Rishi had unfairly received the brunt of my child abandonment issues, mainly because I felt like my mother had chosen him over me. But I'd thought we'd grown closer over the last six months, closer over the last few days. A spark had been growing between us. But that had just been doused. I couldn't chase away the hurt I felt that he hadn't thought he could tell me the truth about Shelby's involvement. I had believed we'd begun to form a bond, but I realized now that his bond with my mother was stronger than ours could ever be.

"Blake," he said softly, his voice tender and smooth. "I'm sorry," he began, but despite the serenity of the trees, I still felt my spirit raging.

I glanced at him, my voice quieter than I imagined it would be, edged with hurt I wished I could hide. "I've spent all this time with you, and I thought we could be open with one another. I thought we were on the same team." My skin started to steam beneath the rain again, and this time the chill did nothing to quench the smoking fire within. "But it always comes down to what Grim wants. Neither one of you even considers that Shelby has a choice in all of this. Or that I do."

He stepped forward, his dark eyes sad within the perfect planes of his sculpted face. But my chest felt no lurch. "I never would have gone along with it, Blake, if it wasn't the only way."

"But you could have told me. And you definitely should have told Shelby way before now."

He glanced away, shame written in the sagging slope of his shoulders, before he looked back at me with renewed intensity. "You're right, I should have told both of you. But you know this is not just for Grim. This is to right the balance that was tipped when Hades banned her from reaping. You've seen what's happening. This is just the beginning, you must realize that."

"Whether I do or not, I refuse to disregard the lives of others, as my mother and Hades both have done, to win this little deity war. Why can't we just find a soul who needs reaping and have them take us through?"

"Because ...," he sighed heavily, glancing away. The mist settled little droplets on his black hair and made tendrils twist and curl around his face beneath the dampness. "If it were that easy, souls would be coming in and out at whim. No, it can't be opened unless a soul still has one foot in the living world."

"A soul with one foot in the living world?"

"Yes, a living person's soul roaming free can open the door."

"So someone like Shelby, who can project her soul? How does this door even exist?"

Rishi glanced at me quickly, his face lighting up in response to my interest. I could see him warming to the topic as he began to explain. "According to Grim, there was this professor of the occult in the 1800s who focused on studying people who claimed to be able to astral project. He was scorned by much of the scientific community, but his findings were quite magnificent and he became quite adept at astral projection himself. When his wife was struck with influenza and died, he went a bit mad. He did all he could to find her on the spiritual plane, but she had crossed over almost as soon as she died, so he could not get to her."

"How sad," I whispered, seeing Geoff's face in my mind, my chest constricting with empathy for the man who'd lost his love.

Rishi nodded. "Yeah, he was more than just sad. He was fanatical about bridging the gap between life and death. Several times, he projected himself and begged Grim to take him, as well, just for a while—but she said it wasn't possible. But he remained obsessed. So eventually he created Death's Doorway."

"How?" I asked, so rapt with the story that I forgot my anger for the moment.

"He scouted in astral form for many years for a place he had heard rumors about, where the veil between this world and the next was thin. It was haunted by spirits, ghosts who had resolved their issues but were still clinging to this world. The undecided. He hung out there a lot until he convinced one of the souls it was time to cross over. The spirit's need drew Grim to this place, and just as the spirit was about to be crossed over, the professor body-snatched him—that is to say, he merged his essence with the ghost. When Grim opened the doorway within herself, it echoed back out and created a rift in the fabric of death and life, opening a doorway into Abbadon outside of herself. But not just anyone could cross through—she quickly found that only an astral body could trigger the gate into opening, which the professor did for many years, visiting his wife every Sunday until he died. When Grim finally crossed him over, he went happily because he didn't want to be late to escort his wife to their final afterlife. Grim kept quiet about the door all these years because she was unable to close it. And once she was banned, we realized it was possibly our only way back in to reclaim what is rightfully hers."

I shook my head, my brain whirling as I pondered the mind of a man who could conceive of such a thing. "But how did he know the door would be created?" I asked.

"He didn't. His goal was merely to hitch a ride down under and see his wife one last time. But with the door created, he never had to live without her. She remained in Abbadon until he was truly crossed over, and they took the next road of their journey together."

"Well, that's a love story if I've ever heard one," came Shelby's dry, sardonic voice as she joined us amid the weeping trees. But despite her tone, I could see the glisten in her green eyes. Her cynicism was mostly show—she was a huge softy inside. "So if he did it for all those years, I should be able to do it too," she said, turning to me. "Let's do this. I said I wanted to help, and I'm not going to back down from the opportunity now that it's here."

"You'll be going in there with death deities, a number of whom are not nice, as we've been told, and as we've seen with lupine guy and his crew," I said, gazing evenly into her eyes and trying to impress on her the gravity of our mission.

"Yeah, but they can't reap her," Rishi said. "She's Grim's ... and yours."

I shivered at his words and glanced at him. "Who is to say they won't start reaping other deities' souls?"

Rishi's eyes widened at the very idea. "They can't. It's the number one death deity rule. It goes against the natural order of society, of the way cultures and religions are built."

I laughed at his optimism. "Do you really believe that? They banned Grim from reaping. Her souls wander, lost and alone, turning into wraiths and eventually who knows what if left to linger longer. They're keeping my aunt hostage. Why wouldn't they start reaping other deities' souls?"

"I don't even know if it's possible or why they'd want to. They like keeping Grim's souls lost, remember?" he said fiercely. "Plus, the council would never stand for it."

I shook my head. "Just like they didn't stand for the banishment of the queen bee Reaper and the detainment of another?" I refused to admit he was probably partially right. Passing wayward souls over didn't seem to fit into Hades's grand plan.

He paused, his mouth opening and only releasing air. Finally, he seemed to gather himself, running a hand through his now soaking black hair. He pierced me with his gaze and my emotions were once again a traitor to my good sense, because I felt my throat thicken and my heart frolic and miss a beat beneath his stare. "I would never let something happen to her, Blake. Ever."

I just shook my head again, breaking the hold he had on me for the moment. I'd seen his soul shine through his eyes a few times, and I knew that Rishi had the capacity to feel very deeply. I realized in that moment that I was more like my mother—practical, and able to deny my heart and spirit the mate they so desired. But Rishi led with his heart. I had done that once, and it hadn't worked out for me. For a moment, Geoff's lanky good looks brought my unresolved grief to the surface before I quelled it.

"You don't understand, Blake. If Grim doesn't get the scythe back soon it will lead to utter chaos. Abbadon will collapse. The spiritual plane, the afterlife, all of that will be in danger," he stopped, heaving a breath, the very thought seeming to send panic lancing through his being. "This is the only plan I can conceive of right now," he finished softly.

I sighed. Shelby was well-informed of the risks at this point. "If it was up to me I'd say let's find someone a little more practiced at projecting. But—"

Rishi opened his mouth to argue before I had even completed my thought, but a shrill, piercing noise amid the quiet of the trees made me curse under my breath and almost lose my bladder.

"What the—" Rishi turned to stare at Shelby, whose eyes were sparkling like crystal, hard and uncut.

"Rape whistle," she said, batting her lashes at us, a silver whistle dangling from her fingertips. Shelby often depressed me with her stories about the atrocities committed in the world. Hence, she tended to carry around a weapons chest of sorts in her purse, including several containers of pepper spray and obviously, her whistle. She'd also once had an alarm that could be triggered by pulling a piece of string, but she'd accidentally set it off one too many times and had retired it.

"You two can finish your little philosophical argument about the death deity apocalypse another time. I think we have a bigger problem on our hands."

I tucked a smile away. Shelby usually took charge at just about the time she got sick of everyone else making bad decisions. Her shining moments were often during group projects when everyone was down to the last hour and nothing had been accomplished. She'd pull everyone together and then get an A.

"What do you mean?" Rishi asked, his body rigid.

"Where's Grim?" Shelby asked, spreading her hands. "Isn't she supposed to have met us here by now?"

Rishi's eyes widened and I glanced at him. "Yeah," he said, a frown puckering his already troubled expression. "But I haven't heard from her since Charlotte. She hasn't been answering my phone calls or text messages. It's unlike her, but I assumed she would have contacted me if anything important had happened."

"Well, since she's not here, what are the chances that something *has* happened … to her?" Shelby asked.

Rishi frowned, running his fingers through his wet hair. "That seems implausible."

I had to hold myself back from scoffing at his undying belief in her infallibility. I was happy when Shelby was the one who responded. "I think you need to be a little more realistic. There's a good possibility we're on our own here."

I felt a flicker of unease but finally forced myself to meet Rishi's eyes. "Then it's just us," I said softly.

"Are we sure we want to do this without her?" Shelby asked.

Rishi hesitated only briefly before nodding. "We need to do this."

They both looked at me and I didn't falter. As much as I hated to admit it, Rishi was right. "I agree. We can't wait any longer. We're losing time, losing any chance that Hades still doesn't know I exist. We need to strike now."

Shelby met my gaze. "I figured you'd both say that. You two can kiss and make up while I start gathering our stuff together." I snorted at her comment and watched as she started up the hill, cutting a path through the trees and roots in her fashionable boots like she was a seasoned hiker in gear properly fitted for the elements.

I glanced once at Rishi and turned to follow her. I knew I'd have to talk to him to iron out our plan, but I needed space from him if only for a moment or two.

"Blake," his voice was deep and grainy, yet so soft he made me breathe in the moist air for some clarity. So we were back to this. Despite his dishonesty, I apparently still responded to him in this way. "Are we okay?" he asked.

I stared at him for a moment, setting my features into stone. But when I shook my head it was half-heartedly.

"I don't know. I just need some time, Rishi," I said.

I saw hurt flicker in his eyes, but I didn't care. Or so I told myself as I turned and walked, quite a bit less gracefully than Shelby, up the hill to the truck. We needed to grab provisions if we were going on a hike.

I met Shelby up at the car and she cast me a sidelong glance. "Don't even tell me to be nicer to him or forgive him or any of that. You got it?" I said.

"Yes, sir!" she said, standing at attention and giving me a mock salute. I couldn't help but laugh.

As she reached into the truck to get a sweatshirt and pulled a cadet-style black cap over her head, she eyed me a bit more seriously.

"I wasn't going to tell you to forgive him, Blake," she said, holding my gaze seriously. "I'm angry too. For him to keep that information from us was wrong, no matter what your mother said. But, okay, don't be mad … That doesn't make him a bad guy. I've seen you two together. And you fit. He's into you, it's so obvious from the way his eyes follow you around like you're the second coming. And I think he's good for you. He understands you … he can help you through this transition in your life. Plus, you're both crazy. If I never was in a car chase again for the rest of my life, I'd be thrilled. But you two, you guys delight in it. While it's a bit disturbing, it only makes me think you're more perfect for one another."

But I was in no mood to hear that the man who had betrayed my trust was my soul mate—a concept I thought was silly, anyway. "Shelb, I love you, but cut it on the matchmaker stuff. It's not going to happen. Not anymore," I said, the last part of my sentence coming out under my breath.

I glanced away from her as I heard Rishi joining us. I stuffed a few bottles of water into my bag and slung it over my shoulders. Rishi was quiet as he also grabbed a backpack. I twisted my hair into a low bun as I waited for the others to gather their supplies for the trek, which Rishi had assured us was fairly short.

The three of us slammed our car doors one after the other and stared at each other for a quick moment. Rishi tried to capture my gaze, but I ducked my head under the hood of my zip-up.

"So, up the hill?" Shelby said, directing her question at Rishi.

He nodded, clearing his throat before speaking. "The climb is relatively quick. It's located near an overlook."

I merely nodded my head. We headed toward the trail, walking single file with Rishi first, Shelby second, and me bringing up the rear. I bowed my head under the dampness of the soggy air and focused on climbing.

We didn't pass anyone on our way up. The trail grew more arid and dry, the landscape opening up to reveal less green and more brown. We stopped when we got to the overlook. Rishi glanced about, and seeing no one, jerked his head to a spot off in the distance that I could already see was haunted by souls. As we approached, I saw them eye me with their white eyes, and I searched the dusty, green landscape for their shadows. What had Rishi called them? The undecided. Ghosts whose bonds with the living had dissolved, so they had become lost souls.

We approached them, and I didn't need Rishi to tell me that this was the place. The energy surrounding me felt different—displaced. Something in the atmosphere had been moved and hadn't been put back in exactly the right spot.

The souls eyed me warily, seeming to sense I wanted to make them better. I didn't wait for a word from Rishi, I merely sidled up to the first soul I saw, a gaunt little man whose ragged clothes hung off him as much as they probably had in life. I smiled reassuringly as I dug into the dark areas looking for his shadow. I caught hold of it after seeing it slink by out of the corner of my eye. Then I grabbed his hand before he could do anything about it and shoved the two pieces of soul together. The air seemed to disappear for a moment, and then it came back with a whoosh as he stood before me, his eyes a gently laced dark brown. His toothless smile curved up with a singular sweetness, despite his craggy, wrinkled face that led me to believe he'd experienced hard times in his life. He held out his hand without a word, his resolution chasing away the indecision that had only moments before haunted the recesses of his previously opaque eyes.

The rush flooded me as I felt the energy within me open to give him entry into Abbadon, where I felt him join the ranks of souls waiting to find the ultimate fate of their afterlife. When I had recovered from the crackling of my skin, I glanced over at Rishi, whose mouth was set into a crooked scowl, his brow furrowed and his lips pursed.

"Just to be clear here, sending souls over that aren't supposed to be going over probably isn't the best idea right now, so let's put a stopper on this, okay?" he growled, batting at a soul drifting by as if it were a fly in his way. I frowned. He was right. I was being careless. No one looked in danger of turning full-on dark in the next hour, although I was probably naïve in hoping we'd make it out of Abbadon in that time or less.

But I wasn't going to admit that he was right, at least not to his face. "So, let's get this done then," I said. "How do we start?"

Shelby, who had been carrying a tightly tucked sleeping bag under her arm, pulled it out and flipped her wrists so that it unraveled in the air before landing in the dust on the ground. "You're going to just lay there, out in the open?" I asked.

She shook her head. "The guardians will protect my body until I return," she said cryptically, averting her eyes from me like she always did when she thought I was going to tease her.

At this point, teasing was the last thing on my mind, but I was curious—guardians? I dismissed it, chewing my lip as I worried about her leaving herself so vulnerable to wild animals, vagrants, and creepy lost shadows.

Shelby paid me no mind, tugged the hood of her jacket over her head, and slipped into the sleeping bag, heedless of the misting rain that had followed us. She closed her eyes and then we waited. I thought it would look like she was falling asleep, but instead one moment she was laying on the ground and the next there were two of her, with one figure standing over the other. Somehow, the Shelby standing in front of me was wholly different from the one I'd known since we were little kids. And yet, she was the same. Her pretty face seemed more arresting, and her pale green eyes, always one of her best features, looked large and luminous, the green sparkling and vivid. Her licorice-red hair curled and flipped more perfectly than I'd ever seen her style it. But it wasn't just her appearance. She was just … more.

"Shelb," I said softly. "You look … different." She glanced at me and smiled, her cheeks catching a blush and igniting the twin dancing seaborne flames of her eyes.

"It's her essence. Shelby is a beautiful soul, kind, generous, true," Rishi said from behind her wavering spirit. "The notion that beauty is only skin deep is true when you're on the astral plane, in the sense that your physical appearance in reality makes little difference. Beautiful people with nasty personalities or dark intent will look ugly there, reflecting the true inner person."

Shelby merely laughed and snapped her wrist in a quick wave. "Oh, stop," she said, rolling her eyes. The pleasure she took from Rishi's explanation and the small smile on her lips did not go unnoticed by me. But her smile was not one of pride—it was one of happiness, contentment.

Shaking my head, I glanced around. "I still don't like leaving your body out here with no one watching over you," I said. I idly tried tucking a stray strand of hair back into my bun, but I stopped short with my finger caught in my thick, black waves when a mountain lion sauntered into the clearing.

"Ummm," I backed up a couple of steps and then stopped, realizing sudden movement would probably attract his attention. The large cat prowled, sniffing the ground but paying little notice to the lost souls or us. It was heading straight for Shelby. I started forward, the large cat's looming presence doing nothing to dissuade my need to get to Shelby, but Rishi grabbed my hand. I turned to growl at him, both for having the audacity to touch me, and also because I was trying to keep my friend from becoming an overgrown cat's lunch.

"Blake," he said in a whisper, shaking his head and dropping my hand as soon as he met my eyes. "He's not going to hurt her."

"What do you mean?" I hissed. "He's a humongous, meat-eating feline. And I heard they like to eat people."

I saw him quirk his mouth in an effort not to grin, and I could feel the heat rise to my cheeks. Visions of shoving him toward the cat to become its next meal danced through my head, and yet at the same time his muffled smile still enticed me in a way I couldn't deny. I knew Rishi could burn me alive. There was a wildness in my attraction to him, one I had fully decided to forsake the moment I'd found out about his deceptions. But the call hadn't dampened. It was loud, clear, and it sang through my body in a mixture of ice and fire, creating a steam so dense within my soul that I could barely fight my way back from the fog of it. He was trouble. He made me feel cold, hot, alive, afraid. And I'd felt so little since Geoff had gone away. Maybe he hadn't sang the call of the wild to my untamed soul like Rishi did, but I'd loved him for his warmth and sweetness.

"He's one of her guardians," Rishi said.

Huh? I blinked my eyes and realized that in the midst of a wild animal creeping up on my sleeping friend, I'd totally blanked out to think about how much I liked and loathed Rishi. My head snapped around and I found Shelby's spirit form standing next to the cat, which was now sitting like a sentry next to her sleeping body. Her astral hand lay against its head, and the cat nuzzled her spirit.

"What is going on?" I whispered.

"Cats are guardians to the underworld and guardians to the astral spirit," Rishi explained just as another, smaller mountain lion threaded her way through the foliage, briefly nosing Shelby's astral form and the male mountain lion before taking her place on the other side of Shelby's body.

I gazed at the giant cats and decided fairly quickly that there was no way I'd mess with the two animals, and so I had to feel some comfort that she was being guarded well. I glanced at her astral form. "Did this happen before?"

She smiled lovingly at the cats before joining Rishi and I where we stood. He looked from her back to me and answered before she could speak.

"They came today because she is crossing into the underworld, as they are not only guardians to the underworld, but they represent transition," he said. "In this case, Shelby's transition from the mortal plane to the astral plane to the underworld needs to be monitored, since there are several transitions going on. They are unbiased and remain true to their code. Although judging by the way they greeted Shelby, impartial observations can't be expected. It looks like they have little kitty crushes on her," Rishi added dryly.

I almost smiled but quelled it in time, lest he think we were friends again, and I just looked at Shelby instead. She smiled and shrugged. "I'm lovable, what can I say." Then, jerking her head to the trees, she nodded. "I see it, can you?"

I focused my gaze to where she was looking but there was nothing— just air and trees and souls hovering. For some reason I'd expected a door to yawn open black, as if the very color of death would dog us the moment we entered the place where death deities reign. Instead, there was nothing.

I shook my head, although I felt something drawing me toward the area Shelby had indicated. "It's calling us home," Rishi said, startling me, his lips brushing my ear.

Come on, do you really need to get that close to talk to me? I suppressed the ache that arose instantly.

"Home?" I said, tilting my head away from his and ignoring the regret that escaped his chest with a sigh.

"It's like DNA or something. We're genetically programmed to feel at home within the underworld. It's where our parents live, or in your mother's case, should live. We only live up here as we do because we're half human. But even Hades's children, a lot of them anyway, live below."

"You guys coming or what?" Shelby asked, heading toward the spot where she'd said the door was located. "I'd really like to get back to my body as fast as possible," she added.

We followed her silently until she stopped short, looking forward at a doorway I couldn't see. "You ready?"

I looked at Rishi and met his gaze. I was and I wasn't. The part of me that craved the rush of living on the edge was urging me forward, but there was another part of me that was still wondering what I was doing here. What brought it all together were the souls. I knew they needed me, and it was for them more than anyone else that I was doing this.

I stared into Rishi's warm, dark eyes, which were seriously set as we contemplated overthrowing the underworld together. He offered his hand and without taking my gaze from his, I took it. His strong fingers slid around mine and gave a gentle squeeze. "I'm still upset," I said softly. "But if we're gonna do this, let's do it right. As a team."

He nodded tersely, but a small smile lifted the corners of his generous mouth as we turned to Shelby. She stepped toward us, and Rishi and I broke our grip, each of us taking one of Shelby's hands. "Let's do this," she said, her glittering gaze focused solely on the doorway that only she could see.

She glanced at her body lying quietly between the two large, wild mountain cats, and then she turned forward once more. We stepped forward as three, and then all I felt was air around me, a whooshing so fast it was like every nightmare of falling I'd ever had. Just when it felt like we were going to make impact, everything went still, and I opened my eyes.

CHAPTER SIXTEEN

IT FELT WRONG before I even opened my eyes. A breeze brushed a strand of hair across my forehead, sending it to tickle my nose as it slid across my face. I smelled moist soil and heard the steady hum of water moving along a rocky bed. The air was mild and sunlight warmed my face, making my initial unease grow.

I snapped my eyes open and glanced at Shelby, who was wearing a look of surprise I was sure we shared, and then to Rishi, who appeared unworried that we'd gone to the wrong place. "Where are we?" I asked.

Rishi glanced at me, his dark brows rising. "Just outside the main estate," he said nonchalantly.

"Estate?" Shelby beat me to it, staring at the idyllic scene around us with wide, disbelieving eyes.

"Um, yeah, I second that. Estate?"

"Yes ..." Rishi said, the drag of his voice indicating he thought we were daft. "Is there something wrong?" he finally asked, confusion clouding the planes of his face, where the dark black grizzle of a beard had settled on his usually smooth features. I liked him both ways. The thought entered my mind before I could even stop it, but I batted it away. I didn't like him at all, I reminded myself. It was sometimes hard to remember.

"We're, like, in a cute little forest," I finally said. "And who lives in an estate?"

"Yeah, and what's with the bubbling stream?" Shelby asked. "Is this Heaven or Abbadon?"

Realization flickered in his eyes and the serious lines of his face broke away, his features lit with the smile that spread across his face, his chuckle low and soft. "You were expecting rock walls and dank alleys? A literal 'underworld,'" he said with another chuckle.

"Well, it does seem rather comfy for an in-between state of affairs," I said, gesturing around me.

"Yes, but it's not meant to be hellish," Rishi said softly, catching my gaze with his once again. "The death deities don't wish to live in a sunless world any more than you or I. It is a resting place for souls to gather strength before moving onto their next destination, or possibly to stay."

"What's the next destination?" Shelby asked, her breath catching in her throat. She'd always been after the mysteries of life and death, and her pale green eyes sparkled with a momentary fervor.

"We do not know. Or at least, I do not. Grim has never been too clear on what happens after death, although I do know that some souls stay here for a time. I personally believe that souls wait here for rebirth. But I can only go on what my faith tells me."

"So basically the underworld is a pretty cool place, and Hades lives in a mansion," I said.

Rishi nodded. "Pretty much. But Hades makes it not such a 'cool' place, so let's get a move on."

"And the scythe is going to be in the estate?" Shelby asked.

Rishi nodded, but I was the one who spoke. "It's in there."

Both Shelby and Rishi glanced at me sharply. "I can feel it," I breathed. It was only after I'd thought of the scythe that I'd truly been able to place what was calling to me. The scythe wanted me to find it. It had been waiting for me to find it. I could hear it—it had a voice. It told me where it was, I could see the room, the table, and the glass dome that surrounded it.

I blinked and glanced at them. "It's in a small room."

Rishi frowned. "You're sure?" he asked.

"Positive ... I can see where it is, like a map in my head opened up. It's talking to me."

I turned to see if Shelby thought I had gone nuts, but her lucid gaze was set on me thoughtfully. Rishi nodded, seeming unsurprised that an inanimate object was having a conversation with me.

"So do you know who is guarding that room?" Rishi asked.

I turned my mind back to the scythe, like a glistening presence within my head, not so much formulating a question as processing the thought. "One guard," I said, flashing a smile, although the song was so complete within me it was hard to tell if anyone was actually inside the room. "I think it's probably one of Hades's boys."

"Um, so we're going to walk into a fully fortressed mansion?" Shelby asked, her brows arching into her hair.

Rishi shook his dark head, running his fingers through his silky hair and pacing in short, jerky movements. "We have to be careful—so careful that no one detects us. We can't get caught. Not again," he said, the last part coming out so softly I wasn't sure he meant me to hear it.

"Again?" I asked.

He glanced at me, startled, confirming my suspicion. "I just meant like when Grim was first caught," he said, evading my eyes.

Still a big liar. I watched him and I knew he wasn't telling me the whole truth. Again. I opened my mouth to demand an answer, but he was already moving on.

"Shelby, you're staying here," he said.

"Hell, no, I'm not."

"That was the plan," he said, catching her gaze. "We don't need you except to take us back through. Besides, no souls can enter the estate."

"Oh, nice to know you place such value on me. I feel so used," she said, folding her arms across her chest and narrowing her eyes at Rishi. But I could tell he'd already won. She knew it made the most sense and that she'd look suspicious if any deity were to sniff her out. It was apparent to even a newbie death deity like me that she wasn't a fully passed-over soul. It was her aura, I realized after a moment. It was tinged green with life, whereas those I'd seen had turned a shiny silver after death.

"Fine, leave me while you get to have all the fun."

I laughed. "Shelb, we need someone to rescue us in case we get caught."

She started to reply with some glib comment, but Rishi pinned me with his dark stare. "We're not getting caught."

"It was a joke," I murmured, but any amusement that usually lit his eyes was absent. Instead, his gaze was grim.

I shook my head and changed the subject. "How are we getting in?"

"We're going to walk in," he said seriously. "We can easily pass ourselves off as death-deities-in-training. We just need to snag a few uniforms. It's already taken care of."

"Death-deities-in-training?" Shelby asked.

"Uniforms?" I chimed in.

"Yeah, when you're a hybrid you've got to be taught, like Blake was," he said to answer Shelby's question.

"Yeah, our girl here didn't need any training. She was crossing souls over days before you gave her the first lesson," Shelby said, a smirk lifting her lips and a flash of pride lighting her eyes.

Rishi turned to me, his eyes slightly wider. "You did? There were more after Geoff?"

I glanced away, realizing I'd never mentioned my night in the field. "Well, after I crossed over Geoff, it hardly seemed like I needed to wait for your instruction, and they were following me. I felt bad for them, so yeah, I crossed a few over after Geoff."

"How many?" he asked.

"Like fifty or so," I said.

Rishi's face only looked more expressionless, a slack-jawed blankness washing over his features as he stared at me, an unreadable thought flickering in his eyes so quickly I wasn't sure if I'd imagined it.

"That's unusual," he said softly. "Withstanding that type of energy upload usually takes years and a lot of training for hybrids. We're half human, so the mortal part of us has to be trained to take in that kind of juice. Like when you were downed only this morning," he said, nodding at me. "You were fed more energy during the crossovers because of our proximity to the door and the scythe's own energy seeping through it, and you collapsed. That's what should have happened to you after fifty souls." He paused, shaking his head, a perplexed look flashing across his face. "Maybe it's because you're Grim's daughter. She is one of the old ones."

I nodded and then shrugged my shoulders. I wasn't too concerned with the why or how, I only knew that I could do it. His little story had nothing on the call of the scythe, its glittery presence a beacon in the back of my mind.

"Whatever, so your friend is getting us uniforms and we're going to enter as deities-in-training?"

"Yes, so hold tight, we're meeting her further into the Hallowed Wood, the forest these trees connect to. She'll find us there, give us the uniforms, and then we're in," he said. All I heard in all of those words was that the person we were meeting was a girl. Had his eyes slid away at the mention? What had been their relationship? Why did I care? He had too many secrets.

"Okay, so let's do it," I said.

"Shelby, get comfortable. And if you see any death deities coming your way, go back to your body. Just make sure to come back and get us when you think you're safe. Got it?"

Without saying a word, she sullenly nodded. I walked over to her and slipped my arms around her stiff body. She tried playing stubborn but caved after a few moments and hugged me back, her smaller frame gripping me fiercely. "Don't get caught," she whispered.

"I don't plan on it," I replied. "And you, you do the same."

"I think I can manage to hide my traveling soul for an hour or so," she said dryly, pulling back and pushing me away gently, a grin tugging at her lips. "I know you're probably excited to put yourself in the hands of danger. This crazy stuff is right up your alley."

I laughed, shaking my head for a moment. "I thought it would be, but I'm actually nervous. And that's good, because there've been times when I was worried that wasn't possible."

She nodded sagely, her expression growing more intense. "It means you care ... about yourself."

I nodded and glanced at Rishi, who had walked away a few paces but seemed anxious, one foot wiggling into an almost full-out tap.

"I'd better go. We need to get our uniforms," I chuckled, still wrapping my head around the idea of formalized death deity training. I lifted my hand in one last wave and joined Rishi.

"So what does a death-deity-in-training wear?"

"It's pretty basic: black," he said.

"So why not bring it over with us—why did we need to get it from your friend?"

"It's a special uniform. The death insignia of the crow is stitched into every shirt, but it's impossible to replicate since the Fates are the ones who stitch them. Each crow is different in some way, so no deity is mistaken for another."

"So won't these uniforms be missed then?" I pointedly ignored his mention of the Fates. I just didn't want to know. The fact that my mother was Death— and so was I—was really about as much as I could handle.

"Given time, sure, but we only need to get in and out with the scythe, so I think we'll be fine," he said, shooting me the grin I hadn't seen in a while.

Before I could stop myself, I grinned back, feeling the tug of the connection that undeniably existed between us. I glanced away quickly, looking into the trees we'd been walking within. It grew darker, the afternoon sun's rays barely peeking through and starting to fade as the day wore on. Apparently night and day worked the same way here.

As we went farther into the trees, I noticed that we were walking through an orchard. Except I couldn't remember having seen apple trees full with fruit, while also blossoming pale blue buds with petals unfurled. A *hoo* sounded above, the melodic voice of an owl rounding out and resonating in a way that was beautiful and haunting at the same time, bouncing off the trees and becoming the music of the orchard.

We came to a stop after a few moments, and I realized this was the place where we were supposed to meet her. The fact that it was a girl we were meeting bothered me in a way I wasn't too happy about.

We were at a little secluded hut in the middle of the orchard, with broken apples heaped on the wood-paneled front porch. The roof cracked as an apple struck it, falling from a tree above and rolling quickly off before hitting the ground.

And then I saw her. She had rusty blond hair, the kind with red-burnished highlights. It flowed easily over bare shoulders and thin-strapped black tank top. She also wore a black cotton skirt that fell above her knees and black flip-flops on her feet. Her skin was sun-touched, golden and brown, unlike my own pale skin that was so much like my mother's.

As we approached, I tried my best to rein in my insecurity. *Who cares? He's a big, fat liar anyway.* Or so I kept telling myself, only I couldn't seem to stop the jealousy from stinging my throat and making my heart beat like a crazy drum. That was, until I met her stare.

I didn't mean to make eye contact so quickly, but once I did I was drawn in by the depth of her large, dark gaze. We stared at each other for moment after moment, the air going still with our approach, as if we were two stags in the wood. But we weren't stags, we were …

"She looks like her," the girl said, tearing her black eyes from mine for a brief moment to meet Rishi's.

I couldn't bring myself to look away. I remembered how only a few days before, I'd stared into a mirror at similar eyes, and I'd been thankful for the difference in eye color. This girl had lots of differences—the skin, the hair, the slight upturn of her nose. But her eyes, they told tales.

"So do you," I whispered.

The delicate planes of her face, so like my mother's, turned up into a smile. Her black eyes actually were different, I noticed as she took a step toward me. They shone with something akin to joy, and that was an emotion I'd never seen in Grim's emotionless black depths.

I managed to sever my locked gaze and glanced at Rishi. He looked pale, despite the brown tone of his skin.

"I figured that since you were already pissed at me over the Shelby thing, telling you about this sooner rather than later wouldn't have bought me any brownie points," he said, almost making me feel bad for him as I heard the distinct weight to his words. "But you've probably figured it out by now. Blake, this is your older sister."

"Sister." I whispered the word, barely comprehending the meaning. What *did* it mean?

"Maeve," the girl, my sister, said in response, her hand outstretched to shake mine, but the warmth and delight in her eyes telling me she wanted to hug.

I wasn't a big emotion girl. But even though Shelby had been as much like a sister to me as anyone could be, I had been lonely. I hadn't had a mother growing up. I didn't really feel like I had one now, given the lack of warmth and humanity that existed in Grim. My father and I were close, but this was a blood sister, one who shared the same legacy, and my body urged me on without my mind's consent. It was my heart that was deciding. I stumbled toward her without thinking and then our arms were around each other. She was tall like my mother, taller than me anyway, and willow thin. Her grip went around me tightly, though, and I wrapped mine around hers just as firmly, inhaling the soft scent of lilies. I was aware that in only a moment's time, I would regain my normal aloof tendencies and she would realize I was stealing her firstborn right to the scythe, but in this moment we were sisters found.

It was seconds before we stepped back, each stiffening a degree and regaining ourselves, but still sisters with the same mother, the same legacy, and apparently the same desire for sisterhood. In that alone, I felt an instant bond. Yet, all the same, with blood there were always issues. And we'd been born into dysfunction.

"I have a sister and you didn't think it was something you should maybe tell me? And my mother? What's her excuse?" I said to Rishi, my voice dangerously quiet. I could feel the resentment that had been bubbling up in me ever since Grim had proclaimed herself my mother. "So here we are, and I want to know, what's the full story?" I gazed at him, his dark eyes only meeting mine after moments of avoidance.

"We tried to get the scythe once before, but instead of you it was Maeve. She—"

Maeve shook her head.

"First, let's get inside the hut where we're less conspicuous, and then I'll tell the story," she said, her voice spun sweet in tone, her inky pools meeting mine. We shuffled inside the modest building, but I didn't take my time to look around the dirty floors. I wanted to hear what she had to say. She was quick to settle herself on a bench before beginning, glancing only briefly at Rishi who had taken a stance against the far wall, his arms crossed over his chest, his face drawn sullenly. He nodded at her, and she smiled faintly before looking back to me. "I was five when Grim came for me and left you."

The revelation was like a shock to the system, a blow to my chest that nearly knocked the wind out of me. It took me a moment to catch my breath as I swallowed back my envy. She'd had our mother in her life, at least for a bit.

She glanced away, flicking a strand of burnished blond hair from her eyes, her bangs a feathering overlay that swooped across her forehead. A golden girl, except for her moonlit gaze.

She sighed and looked back at me.

"She didn't love my father the way she loved yours, but they were … companions, for a time. He gave her an escape from the pain of her banishment, and she gave him inspiration. He was an artist, and she was his greatest subject. He knew what she was, although I was never sure if she'd told him or if he'd just figured it out. Artists sometimes see things others don't, you know?"

I nodded my head in wonder, hearing this girl spin my mother a history that included more than death and souls.

"When she became pregnant with me, my father told me she was at her most loving, her most human. But once I was born, something changed. She became colder, more distant. And then she left without a word." Her voice, so soft and sweet, twisted sourly, her pink lips puckered as if she'd eaten something tart. "My father always insisted that something must have happened to make her leave. But I knew the truth. She'd always planned to come back, but only when I turned eighteen and had come into my death deity powers. She used me—us."

She wasn't telling me anything I didn't already know, though. I nodded. "Yeah, I have no delusions," I murmured, my glacial blue gaze keeping hers, hungry to hear the revelations still to come.

She nodded and glanced away, but not before I saw the satisfaction flicker through her eyes that I was on the same page, at least where our mother was concerned.

"My father died," she said quietly. "There was a fire, it was … Anyway, I was so young, but something was triggered and my death deity abilities flickered on the moment he died, so that his slowly deteriorating soul followed me around for days, and I followed him. The problem was I could see him, but I didn't know how to cross him over. Grim was drawn to his death because she *had* cared for him, in her own way. I remember her being upset that she couldn't cross him over herself, but she realized pretty quickly that my powers had come in. Anyway, she was able to help me cross him over, and then she took me with her and raised me and trained me to replace her. When I was ten, she came home with Rishi." She stopped, glancing at Rishi with a soft smile. "For a few years, we were like siblings. But five years ago, when I was eighteen and had fully matured into my deity abilities, Mom decided it was time to try to take the scythe back. I went in through Death's Doorway, and like you probably do, I heard its call. But I didn't get very far before I was caught. I've been here ever since."

"So you're a prisoner?" I asked, rapt by this new tidbit of family history I'd never known existed.

She looked away for a moment before shaking her head. I glanced at Rishi, who had been standing stoically, letting her tell the story of their shared past. Any jealousy I'd felt previously over her time with our mother had vanished. She'd lost her father. I still had mine, and he was the one who had loved and cared for me. Maeve finally looked back at me.

"I'm not a prisoner now in the sense that I'm kept locked in a room. But I've had to trick them, make them think I want to stay here. I'm not allowed to reap souls, so I'm confined to Abbadon for my own 'protection,'" she said, using air quotes. "But I feel the souls, their essences call to me."

She glanced between the two of us and went on. "Lately, I've noticed something different. The other deities pay no notice when new souls come in. But I know when ours come through. I wasn't sure until this morning when I met a boy and his mother, but I could tell they were different from previous lost souls that were crossed over. They seemed ... healthy. What has been going on?" she asked, glancing between Rishi and me.

I shared a look with Rishi and nodded. "We believe that souls have been going lost because they've been split off from a part of themselves."

Maeve's eyes widened, but she nodded her head quickly. "That would make so much sense. Everyone else's souls seem normal, so I couldn't understand why ours were so damaged."

I smiled sadly. The plight of the lost souls was a cause I'd gotten behind a while ago, and it was painful for me to think about their suffering. "Lost souls are haunted by shadows, only seen when you look hard enough for them. The shadow is a missing piece of a lost soul, and I believe they're losing the stable and compassionate wholeness of their souls, of their selves. They need to be unified, and once they are, they're fine. More like lingering souls as opposed to lost."

"But this is new ... I never encountered such a thing as a reaper."

I nodded, agreeing with her, but it was Rishi who spoke. "Our theory is that the longer Grim remains removed from reaping, from any semblance of humanity, it affects the souls."

Maeve's large black eyes darted between the two of us, her face unreadable although her gaze was lit with fear. "Humanity? What's going on with Mother?"

"Well, she's a bitc—"

"Blake!" Rishi snapped, gritting his teeth, his eyes sparking with disappointment.

I rolled my eyes. "Sorry," I muttered, not really feeling too bad. Glancing to Maeve, I attempted to shrug my shoulders apologetically. "Grim and I didn't really get off to a good start. Or really get to any start at all. She basically came into town, told me she was my mother, who I'd been told was dead, and then demanded I pass over my newly dead boyfriend. She didn't get any more likeable after that."

Maeve tugged on a rusty blond strand and nodded, her eyes finding mine with a yearning, and in it I saw the hunger to have someone understand her. I saw that she needed me, had been praying for the sister she knew existed somewhere to finally come save her. I knew what she was feeling because I felt the same comfort knowing that someone was there alongside me, someone who could understand this. Someone who resented our mother as much as I did.

"You don't have to explain it to me, Blake," she said softly, ignoring Rishi's hard look that bored into the side of her head.

So annoying, I thought, remembering why I'd disliked him in the beginning, before my emotions got all mushy and I saw that we shared the same spark, the same love of the thrill. When I thought *he* was the one who could possibly understand.

"Speaking of your boyfriend," Maeve said, stepping closer so that our heads nearly touched, her hand taking mine as if we'd always known each other as sisters. "I have a surprise for you," she whispered, fanning her arm out so that I could see the front door of the hut creak open.

When he stepped inside I gasped. I felt my heart sputter and jump at the sight of his lanky form sauntering up to us like he'd never died at all, his sandy blond hair as messy as always, his crinkly ocean-blue eyes finding mine immediately and locking with my pale winter blues.

"Geoff," I said, my throat dry and his name sticking in my throat and coming out as a croak. He was before me with two strides, scooping me into him so my face was stuffed into his chest. He still smelled like the cologne he used to wear, a warm musk that had always comforted me, made me feel safe. Funny that even as a soul he smelled the same.

Finally, after moments of reveling in the feel of him, I felt him pull away and look down at me, his usually cocksure grin and dancing eyes serious, his face a mix of feelings.

"When Maeve told me you were coming, I couldn't believe it," he said softly. "At first, I thought she meant you had died, but then I quickly remembered who you are now. I guess, who you've always been."

He shook his head, brushing his shaggy hair from his eyes and smiling softly, his large, rough fingers coming up to touch my cheek ever so gently. I gazed up at him and it was like he'd never died, as if I hadn't kept him in my world for days while he went more and more lost. He looked so good now. Except ...

"He is missing the rest of his soul," Maeve murmured from behind me, bringing my romantic reunion to a close. I tore my gaze from his and glanced at her, suddenly realizing how close together Geoff and I were standing. I felt Rishi's gaze on us. I didn't even have to look his way. My back felt uncomfortably warm from the heat of his stare.

I ignored him. We didn't have anything but a temporary attraction that was heading nowhere fast. Geoff had been my boyfriend for a year, and we'd been friends longer than that. All the same, I still couldn't help but feel like I'd been caught cheating on Rishi, or awkward in the same way as when you know someone likes you but you don't like them back except as a friend. At least, that's what I was telling myself.

I looked back up at Geoff and sighed heavily, feeling my heart constrict within my chest. "I'm so sorry, Geoff. I didn't mean to cross you over not whole," I said, taking his hand between mine and staring up at him.

He shook his head rapidly, pulling me into his chest once more and cradling me there as if I were the most precious object in the world. When I sighed again, it was from contentment. I missed this. I missed him. I suspected I always would. I blinked back the tears that threatened. I really rarely cried, but my reunion with him was reopening a wound not fully healed yet, and it was too much to bear, especially now with all that I had to accomplish. I shook off the pain that was creeping into my heart, old and new coming to merge and remake the hurt I'd finally been able to mute over the last six months.

"I'm the one who should be sorry, Blake. I can see how much this is costing you, seeing me here. But we've found that us souls, the ones who came over missing the other half, we're unable to move on past this point. Abbadon has become a purgatory for us, one that we are trapped in."

I pulled away and looked up at him once more. He'd changed. He was dead, and now he was talking more rigidly and less like the teenage rock-and-roll boy he had been.

"I—what can I do? I have to do something," I said, turning to look at Rishi for the first time, as well as Maeve. "I have to find a way to bring their shadows here and unify them."

Maeve was shaking her head, but I wasn't having it.

"No," I said, determination making my voice louder than I'd meant it to be. "I have to," I said more softly.

Rishi cleared his throat, his voice dry and mildly sardonic when he spoke. "As touching as this reunion is, we need to get on with this. Shelby is waiting."

I knew he was right, but I couldn't help shooting him a dark look. Turning back to Geoff, I smiled softly and ran my fingers through his hair one more time. "I'll find a way to fix this, I promise you."

He nodded, his eyes filled with faith in his ex-girlfriend, who happened to be the one who sent him over in the first place.

"If I can help in any way …" he began, but Rishi shook his head, abruptly cutting him off, although when he spoke his voice was hushed and serious, with no remnants of his earlier distaste evident.

"If they found out a soul was helping an exiled deity and her basically illegal daughters recover the scythe, a weapon of so much power it has served to bring down the realm of the dead, I fear what they would do. No, Geoff. You need to leave now, and when we're out of the dead realm again, Blake will help you move on beyond this waiting place. We have a means to escape … probably," Rishi said. "You would have no way to leave and we can't take that chance with your afterlife. Hades is insane with power and greed. There is no reasoning with him. Not while Pluto is captive …"

I could tell Geoff didn't like Rishi's words of wisdom. His eyes met mine and rebellion flared in their depths for a moment, but it died out quickly. He knew Rishi was right.

"Can I have a moment alone with you before you leave?" he asked. I glanced at Maeve, who nodded and jerked her head toward the door, a sullen-looking Rishi following behind.

I watched them leave and only turned back to Geoff when the door had closed behind Rishi, who had caught my gaze for a brief moment and sent a pang through my body, making me wonder if he'd felt as strongly as I'd felt. I turned back to Geoff, and then all I knew was the pleasure of his arms around me once more, his soft, wide lips pressing against mine so tenderly my legs trembled beneath me. When he pulled back, he brushed his lips against my forehead once more, tucked a strand of my dark hair behind my ear, and then squeezed my shoulders with both hands before stepping back and putting distance between us, replacing his warmth with a vast space I knew could never be filled. Because Geoff was dead, and I was alive and also apparently somewhat immortal. Or at least I was supposed to have a pretty long lifespan.

"I just wanted to kiss you good-bye one last time," he said softly, his blue-green eyes a fog in the midst of a storm.

I felt a pent-up breath leave my lips and nodded. What could I say? He was right. There was no future here. I loved him, I would always love him, but … I had begun to move on. I knew these moments with him would probably set my healing back, because now the feel of him, the way I'd felt when I was close to him, was so fresh. But I'd never for a moment thought there was any way we could be together again. I had to continue this fight, and he had to move on and rest in peace or be reincarnated or frolic through heaven. Whatever the end point was, I was hoping it was beautiful and had rocking tunes.

"I'll see you again," I said. "I'm going to find the other part that you're missing, and I'll make sure you get to leave this place, that you get to see the other side."

He smiled faintly, nodding. "I know," he said. "It was probably selfish of me to come here and stir up old feelings, but I'm dead so I figured I could be selfish for half an hour."

"It's not selfish, it's human," I said, smiling sadly and knowing I'd always wish he could have his life back.

He stared at me for a moment, and then he slipped down onto the bench bordering the back wall, patting the seat next to him. I obliged him and sat down, leaning my head against his shoulder and smiling when he dropped his head on top of mine.

"Life isn't fair," I said.

"Nope, it's sure not," he said softly. We both grew quiet and I savored my time with him. I knew it couldn't last.

Geoff was the one to break the silence first, clearing his throat in such a way I had no doubt what was coming. "Sooo, that Rishi guy seems to have a thing for you."

He lifted his head from mine and I lifted my own so I could look in his eyes. "It's nothing," I said.

He chuckled, taking my hand in his and running his fingers across my palm. "Liar," he said, peering into my soul.

"Geoff, I love you, you know that, right?"

He nodded his head, his hair flopping with the motion. "Of course. I'm not gonna lie. I don't love the idea of you with another guy. I actually hate it. But I'm dead."

I nodded, feeling tears prickle my eyes, but I refused to let them fall just like I refused to look away from his gaze.

"And I know you, Blake. You're stubborn, hot-headed, and you have a hard time backing down."

"Gee, thanks for the lovely compliments," I said, unable to hold back a laugh.

Geoff flashed a grin and then let it slide away, an intensity taking hold of his eyes. "You like him?"

I dragged in a sigh and nodded. "Sometimes. Other times, not so much," I said honestly.

"I gather he pissed you off a few times."

I nodded, finally looking away.

Geoff placed both his hands on the side of my face and gently directed my gaze to his once more. "Unforgiveable stuff?"

I stared up at him for a moment and finally gave him a faint smile. "No, not unforgiveable."

He dropped his hands and gathered mine in between his. "Then get over it. I feel like I might be the most selfless guy on the planet at the moment when I tell you, I want you to be happy, Blake. Even if that means, you know … Rishi," he finished, rolling his eyes heavenward before looking back at me with a grin.

I laughed softly, feeling a betrayer tear slip down my cheek. "I'd say you're being pretty generous."

He collected the tear with the pad of his thumb and leaned down to softly kiss me before breaking away. "So, you going to give him a chance?"

I started laughing, shaking my head and wiping the remnants of my tears away. "Seriously the strangest conversation ever. My dead-ex boyfriend telling me to move on with a new guy."

He laughed too, sliding his arm around me and hugging me into his side. "Hey, I know I'm first choice, so it's all good."

I leaned into him and nestled against him, savoring some of my last moments with him, loving him more because he truly was the best boyfriend a girl could have had.

"So?" he asked, squeezing me against him gently.

"Yeah, I'll try not to be so stubborn and hard-headed. I'll try to give Rishi another chance," I said. "But it might not be for a while. My heart was broken when you died. Putting the pieces back together is … hard. There will be pieces always missing." I glanced up at him and he nodded seriously.

"I know what you mean," he said softly, sadness coming to rest in the bright light of his eyes. "And I'll take it. Getting you to agree to anything is victory enough."

I laughed again but was cut off when Rishi clomped unceremoniously through the door, an expression of deep suspicion on his face as he eyed me snuggled up against Geoff. He'd apparently changed while outside and was now garbed in the deity-in-training uniform, black dress pants and a black button-down with the sleeves rolled up his forearms. If it weren't for his cowboy boots and the silver embroidery of a crow in mid-flight on his shirt, he'd have looked like a waiter about to take my order.

"I'll have fries with that," Geoff cackled, casting a smirk toward me and making me bite down on my own laugh.

I noticed the glint at Rishi's waist and took in the same image of the crow, silver cast as a belt buckle. "Do they care about fashion at all?" I asked, knowing Shelby would have said it first if she'd been here.

"The girls' uniforms are better," Maeve said, slipping in the door behind him. Our gazes connected and she arched her dark blond eyebrows, silently asking me if I'd had enough time.

I nodded, smiling to myself that in only thirty minutes we seemed to have perfected the art of the silent language. But then again, it was probably more of a girl thing than a sister thing.

Maeve looked pointedly at the boys as she handed me the uniform, and they dutifully filed out the door without looking at one another.

"Thanks," I said as I slipped off my jeans and shirt, sliding a pair of black leggings over my legs. I slipped the black V-neck shirt over my head, pulling my hair out of the shirt and noticing the melancholy look floating in Maeve's black eyes, her lashes hooded over her cheeks as she stared into nothingness. "What is it?"

She quickly glanced up, a forced smile lifting the corners of her face as she shook her head and tucked a strand of hair behind her ear. "I just miss it, you know? I haven't had a cheeseburger in five years. I'm twenty-three now too. I can even have a beer legally," she laughed softly. "It would have been fun to celebrate my birthday, even though I didn't have any friends besides Rishi." She shook her head again and glanced at me. "You probably think I sound like a brat, lamenting my lack of junk food. But down here the souls can eat what they want, or they don't really eat, but if they want to get something it's not hard because it's not really real."

"I'm not really following the not real food thing," I said, buckling my own crow belt around my waist, "but go on," I said.

She waved her hand as if it didn't matter. "And I don't think deities really have to eat, although they still do. But the hybrids, we have to eat. They feed us vegetarian crap like sprouts and beans all the time," she finished with a sigh.

"Shelby would love it here," I murmured.

"Shelby?" she asked, as I held up sneakers.

"I'm assuming these shoes aren't okay."

She nodded, sadly confirming my statement and handing me a pair of black cowboy boots. "Seriously? I thought that was just Rishi-wear."

She shrugged her slim shoulders. "Nope, it's a Hades thing here. Rishi just fits in better than he ever knew," she grinned. "Anyway, I said the girls' outfits were better, not great."

Feeling silly, I sighed and started to pull the boots on over my leggings. "My best friend," I said, responding to her question about Shelby.

"Oh," she said. I looked up and noticed her lips tighten, seeing longing flash in her eyes. I frowned to myself, but the look was gone when I blinked.

"You'll like her," I said.

"Well, I probably won't get to meet her, stuck here as I am," she said softly.

I stared at her, shaking my head in confusion. "You're coming with us when we leave ... I mean, you have to. They'll know you helped us," I said.

She glanced quickly at me. "You think I can get out of here?"

"Are you serious? Of course. I'm not leaving you now that I know I have a sister."

The tight creases of her face broke and her smile lit up her face. "We have to save Aunt Seba," she whispered urgently. "It's worse for her than me. She refuses to tell them anything about where her scythe is, so they keep her drugged constantly."

"None of my family or friends is getting left behind here," I said, meeting her eyes for a moment as I smoothed the clothes over my body. "My hair?" I asked, but she was already handing me a black ribbon to pull it up with. "Well, let's go get it."

Flipping her blond hair behind her back, she smiled warily, the corners of her mouth trembling only slightly. Doubt was written nakedly across her face. But I couldn't blame her; she'd tried once before and had been imprisoned for five years.

"It'll be okay," I said, taking her hand lightly and squeezing it, noticing that our hands were almost exactly the same size and width, only her fingernails were pretty pearlescent ovals and mine were chipped with polish and torn. "This time we're going to get it, and when we do, we'll give Grim the scythe and her humanity will be restored. Then we'll finally get to know a mother who actually cares," I said, half-believing what I was saying. Hoping that what I was saying could be true, although I knew my life would never be normal. Not when I crossed souls over in my free time.

Maeve's black eyes lit up and she nodded, making me grasp on to my words and wish for a day when they could be true.

CHAPTER SEVENTEEN

THE DAY HAD DIMMED while we'd discussed our plan inside the hut, and Rishi melded into the shadows as he walked in front of me, the deep tone of his skin and the black of his outfit and hair making him seem more like a shadow than a man. My sister walked silently beside me, and Geoff had said his good-byes and left us. I'd seen the stubborn look in his eyes when he'd gone, though, and I could only hope he wouldn't try to help us in some way. He'd been through so much already, and I couldn't imagine Hades and his reject kids getting their hands on him for helping us steal the scythe, which I intended to do no matter what. Even now I could still feel its call.

The sun had settled in the trees and the light hit me right in the eyes, making me stumble in my momentary blindness. Who would have thought I'd need sunglasses in the underworld? I caught myself as Maeve grabbed my arm to keep me from falling, and I met her dark gaze. She smiled faintly.

"Careful," she warned lightly, releasing my arm as if she'd been catching me and letting me go every day of my life.

"So the plan is to enter the house after the group of deities-in-training go in for the evening to have supper, and to tell the guards that we were too caught up in multiple soul ..." I stopped, unable to remember the last part of the deity lessons.

"Multiple soul transference," she said.

"Like doing two at the same time?" I asked.

She nodded. "It's difficult for most deities in the beginning, but I'll bet if you tried it you'd be able to do it pretty easily," she said, turning as we walked and locking eyes with me.

I hadn't tried it, I only knew that Rishi sometimes mentioned it. When I thought about it, it made sense. People die all the time, so being able to transfer multiple souls at once could be helpful in this profession—or should I say *calling*.

"We're special, Blake," she added softly.

I furrowed my brow at her, surprised by her words. "What do you mean?" I asked.

"Our mother is one of the originals, Blake. That means you and I are stronger than most hybrids, than most deities. What is difficult for others is often easy for us. We should be ruling this underworld with our mother," she said fiercely, looking away, but not before I saw the fervor light her pitch black eyes.

I couldn't help but be a little surprised. For all intents and purposes, she resented my mother as much as I did. And yet here she was telling me she wanted to be a ruler of Abbadon?

"I thought you hated it here," I said, not knowing where to start with this new information.

"I don't hate it here. I hate being a prisoner here. I would come and go as I please. Instead, I feel like I'm trapped behind bars. It's infuriating when I know I should basically be a princess here, and so should you."

I shook my head, glancing sideways at her as we crept into the shadows surrounding the small garden pathway that Rishi, Shelby, and I had followed when we first entered Abbadon. I turned toward her, catching her eyes with my own gaze so that she understood clearly what I was saying. "I don't want to be a princess. I don't even want to be a death deity, powerful or not. I can't help who I am—I feel the responsibility on my shoulders, and I will continue to do what I'm supposed to do. But only because I can't imagine refusing wandering, lost souls while knowing I could help. If I could have chosen differently, I would have decided to go on living my life as I was. I'm in college, my dad is great, I had a boyfriend I loved."

"That's right, Blake. You *had* a boyfriend. He's gone. And the fact that you're a death deity didn't cause that to happen. Knowing that, would you still say you don't want this?" she asked, tilting her head curiously. I noticed in that moment that she was strong and fragile at the same time, with her slender shoulders, narrower than my own, and her skin perfectly golden from five years under a sun that didn't burn or harm. And for a moment her eyes had been pitch granite.

I exhaled a breath, having swallowed more air than I could count at the mention of Geoff, a wound that was freshly raw. "Yes, because wading through the trenches of death isn't exactly my idea of a good time. Watching the pain on the faces of loved ones as they say good-bye, passing over the ones who didn't know they were going. It's rough. Who would want to do this?"

I saw the answer before I registered it. Maeve. She truly was my mother's protégé even if she didn't like her. She should have been the one to get the scythe back. But instead, it was me. I wondered again if she didn't resent me just a little. Of course, I hadn't retrieved anything yet, so I supposed I'd have to wait and see if sister rivalry was going to rear its ugly head. But at the moment, I was just thankful that I had found this link to my past, to my heritage.

We stopped talking as Rishi hushed us with a mere look, his dark eyes wide and alert. Even in the coming gloom, I could see the rigid way he held his shoulders back, the way he tilted his head to the side and cracked his neck. The popping noise made me cringe. We were all tense. This was the moment we'd been waiting for. This was the moment where they'd failed before.

We stumbled through the stone-lined garden pathway, the three of us huddling behind a large grouping of foliage as we observed the trainees enter the mansion single-file, their faces cloaked by the shadows.

"We wait ten minutes and then we go in. We don't want the other deities to see us and question who we are. We want to blend in," Maeve said softly, our heads all tilted together, almost touching as we furiously whispered our plans to one another, making sure we were all on the same page.

"Won't the guards know?" I asked, gazing at the large entryway and nearly blinding myself by staring at the lights that cast a blaring glow on the courtyard and the town beyond, where souls waited and deities lived.

"They barely pay attention to the trainees. Beneath their notice mostly. This should work," Maeve breathed, hope giving her voice air so that it sailed through the breeze, soft and sweet.

"It will work," I reassured her, seeing Rishi's dark eyes flicker with anxiety in the dim light that was cast our way. The two of them were really scared, and I knew Rishi liked the adrenaline rush as well as I did. But I wasn't frightened. There had been a moment, actually several moments, where I had felt the flutter of my heart. But that was gone now. The scythe's voice was like music in my head, and I knew beyond all doubt that it was mine.

We stayed in silence until finally Maeve jerked her head toward the door. "Ready? Follow my lead."

Rishi caught my gaze with his own before I could ignore it all together, his dark eyes coming to rest on mine. A swirling of emotions seemed to whirl within their depths. I wanted to break away from him, from that stare that I found so penetrating, as if he could peer within my being and know who I was.

"I'm sorry for lying to you, Blake." He whispered so softly, I heard the sigh of regret weave its way through his words. "But this is important. This matters. The living may not notice the imbalance now, but it's not long before they do. We have to take the power back before it gets any more out of control. There really is no other option."

I had started to feel bad for him. I really had. He felt so strongly about this cause. And he wasn't wrong. The world was horribly off kilter because of Hades's insanity. But I'd had enough of his martyrdom.

"Don't you think I know that, Rishi?" I shook my head, automatically smoothing my regulation deity ponytail back into place, checking the ribbon to make sure it was still in a bow. I'd done this many times before as a cheerleader, and now seemed no different. Bow in hair, adrenaline rush to come. "But the truth is always an option."

I turned to follow Maeve, who was beckoning us from a few feet away. I didn't look back, even though I heard him expel his breath before he was able to catch me with a word of defense or apology. I just didn't have time for it. I'd told Geoff I would let it go, but right now I had to prepare, play the part, and then find the quickest route out of here once my hands were on the tool that had started this mess in the first place. I was also starting to worry about Shelby being all alone.

Maeve stopped and looked back at me from where the garden opened to the pathway that led to the house. I silently nodded and she heaved a breath before turning and walking briskly up to the mansion with Rishi and I in tow. I followed her, trying to look as casual as possible while taking in the moon that had risen in the sky. The lilac wafted up and hit me with its heady aroma, a scent I'd always loathed for its sweetness. Small trees lined the pathway, each one twinkling with white lights, although I wasn't sure what was creating them.

We came to the door and Maeve made her way up the steps, her reddish-blond hair bouncing behind her down to the middle of her back. She reached out and pulled open the door, sliding in with us right behind her.

Two guards stood on either side of the door, each one dressed in black—a common color theme, I'd noticed. The first guard to catch my eye was a man, tall and an overall large brute, his brows furrowed deeply and almost joining as one over a rigid jaw and heavily set face. But when he grinned, I saw the familiar tilt of his smile and knew he must be one of Hades's hybrid children. He looked just like Lupine.

He barely looked at us except to send a leering look in Maeve's direction, which she chose to ignore. "I found these two newbies hanging out after hours, thought I'd keep them from Ambrose's wrath," she said flippantly, casting a friendly flutter of her dark golden lashes in the man's direction.

The other guard was a woman, who was perched on a stool reading a book. She lifted her eyes from behind large, horned rims, her gray irises crisp behind the lenses, her hair pulled back into a slick ponytail, and her full, red lips twisting up into a smirk. "Keeping secrets from Ambrose, are we now?" she asked, a dark brow arching from behind her glasses.

I glanced at Maeve and wondered who Ambrose was. Judging by the quick flash of color that rose to her cheeks, he was someone. But Maeve dismissed the girl just as quickly, leveling her with her obsidian gaze, a discerning smile faintly etching the right side of her mouth.

"Mmm, you'd better hope I keep some secrets, Sophie," she said, holding eye contact with the glasses girl until she glanced away, licking her lips nervously.

The guy rolled his eyes. "Girls and their drama," he said to Rishi, grinning in manly comradery. Rishi was game and nodded his head.

"Tell me about it, dude," he said, jerking his head to me. I glared at him in the name of keeping up the façade.

"At least she's hot, man," Hades's hybrid said.

I snapped my gaze to his, taking a step toward him with narrowed eyes, but before I could fire out a response, Maeve had looped her arm through mine and was leading us away with a backward smile and wave.

"Later, Nik," she said.

I met Rishi's gaze as we walked away and he shrugged apologetically, an amused smile playing on his lips. "Hey, I wasn't about to argue with the man," he laughed softly.

"Misogynist," I muttered.

"Oh, Blake," he laughed, a tenderness creeping into his voice that I fought to ignore. "You're beginning to sound like Shelby."

I couldn't help but smile. "Good," I shot back, "she apparently knows what she's talking about."

We rounded a corner and were led by Maeve to an expansive, winding staircase. "Hey," I whispered as I sidled up next to her. "Who's Ambrose?"

She sighed, glancing quickly around. "He's Hades's top dog. His firstborn. He pretty much runs things around here when Hades is off doing whatever it is Hades does."

I glanced at Rishi. "We already had a run-in with another one of his sons," I murmured. "I call him Lupine."

"Lupine?" Maeve asked, her brows arching.

"You know, tall, looks like a wolf when he grins, tilted crazy eyes, actually got into a car chase with us," I said.

Maeve laughed softly, a spark of recognition lighting in her eyes. "Ooooh, good nickname! You mean Marx, right?" she finished with a nod. "He's a bit nuts," she added softly, confirming my suspicions.

"So this is it?" I gestured to the stairs that cascaded from so far above I couldn't see the top, a polished railing looking too slippery to offer any real purchase during the coming climb.

She nodded. "You're on your own for now. You know where to go. I'll make sure the door is unguarded when you get there," she said, locking eyes with me.

She was right. I did know where to go. The scythe beat a rhythm that flowed within me, surging through my veins. It was a metallic sound, the whistle of steel on the wind. And it reverberated through me more with each step forward.

I nodded. "I'll meet you at the bridge," she said, turning and running into the chest of a tall, well-built man garbed in an expensive gray suit.

He grabbed Maeve by the elbows and pushed her out a bit from his body, making my heart finally take a flutter. I may have gotten off on situations that got my blood rushing, but that didn't mean I wanted to get caught.

I followed the lines of his suit and shoulders to the dark chisel of his jaw, covered in a dark black beard, his skin burnished a darker brown than Maeve's, his eyes a dark blue beneath the longest eyelashes I'd ever seen on a man. His gaze flickered from us to Maeve, but it was with concern that he looked down on her. "Maeve, sweetie, where have you been? I've been missing you today," he said, curling a hand around her upper arm in such a way that I felt the hairs on my arm raise. The grip, the tightness of it, the hunger in his eyes—it was possessive and it made me instantly want to slap his hand away. And … *sweetie*?

She glanced at us casually, catching herself from looking panicked and smiling wanly. "Ambrose," she said, leaning into his side and fluttering her lashes up at him. "I was just helping these new trainees find their way around, they lost the group." Turning to us, she nodded, her eyes meeting mine quickly and urgently. "Go to your rooms and clean up. Dinner should be ready by six-thirty," she said.

Was it that early? It felt like it was midnight. I could only hope the trainees' rooms were upstairs. I nodded and with a quick glance back, started up the stairs, but not before I saw Ambrose slide his hand down my sister's back and usher her away. Her gaze caught mine with a plea to understand. But just what, I wasn't sure, except that it looked like my sister and Hades's number one son were an item.

Rishi glanced at me as we mounted the stairs, looking up and behind us once to make sure there was no one around. "What do you think that was about?" he asked.

I shook my head, keeping my voice low as my hand slid along the banister, less slippery than I'd assumed. "Nothing good," I said.

"Well, hopefully she'll be able to get away from him to meet us," he said.

"She'd better, because I'm not leaving without her."

"We may not have a choice," he said as we stepped up onto the second floor and glanced down the long hallway. A row of closed doors with numbers on them lined both sides.

I ignored him. I had no intention of leaving her, come what may. She'd lived down here—wherever here was—long enough. Five years long. I was confident that in the next twenty minutes, my life would be figured out and I'd be standing on the outside where we'd entered Abbadon with my best friend, sister, and on-again, off-again, possible love/hate interest.

"Deity quarters," he said with a nod. "Trainees are on the fourth floor."

"How many floors does this place have?" I asked, wondering where the second floor even ended as the corridor seemed to go on and on.

"As many as they need. This is like the hub of Abbadon. Do you know where the scythe is?"

I stopped, closing my eyes as the silver and steel and magic reverberated through me. "Up," I whispered. "Is there another set of stairs?"

Rishi looked about quickly and nodded, jerking his head down the hallway. "Let's go."

As we deftly started down the hallway, whizzing past identical doors, all shut and keeping secrets of death, I wondered again about my sister's relationship with Ambrose and the depth of their possible union. We reached the next set of stairs without incident. A large upstairs foyer led into another set of winders.

I started the climb, two steps ahead of Rishi, urged on by a feeling I'd rarely experienced before: panic. This was taking too long. Even now, Marx and his hybrid gang could be making their way up the trail to where Shelby lay. The sense of urgency spurred me on, but I felt myself trembling as my hand reached for the bannister to help me up another step. I was losing the sound of the scythe. It felt more distant, and I stopped, glancing wildly around, expecting a hoard of Hades's hybrids to come after us at any moment. A new worry shot through me, what if now that Maeve was in Ambrose's clutches, she wouldn't be able to clear the guard for us? I stopped, gasping against the railing, only halfway up the stairs.

"Why are you stopping? We've got to keep moving," Rishi said, passing me and stopping on the stair above me. I wasn't sure what was wrong with me. My breath seemed to be choking me, my heart beating so rapidly it felt like it wanted to pound out of my chest. "Blake!" he whispered fiercely, bending forward and staring into my face.

"It's fading," I said, hearing the tremble in my voice and hating it. "I can't hear it as strongly."

"Hey, hey," he said, taking my face between his weathered palms, hands that had clasped thousands of souls, seen them on their passage from life to death, and now cradled my cheeks and jaw so gently. Hands that were aged despite his youth. "Hey," he whispered, stepping down beside me and smoothing his fingers along my scalp and neck. "You can do this, Blake. We can all take care of our own parts in this, so stop worrying."

"I've never felt this way before," I whispered, allowing his warm touch, his soulful gaze to calm me. "I don't usually get too scared. But now my sister is with the number one son and number two could be on his way to Shelby, and I just kind of lost it. And now I can't hear the scythe and—"

He gazed into my eyes, cutting me off with a mere look before speaking once more. "And if you continue to panic, then we might as well give up right now," he said.

I jerked, not expecting the blunt forcefulness of his words. He stepped back, dropping his hands from my face and taking his warmth with him. It didn't matter. My breath stalled and then took a dive, slowing with my heart. I would hate myself later for letting Rishi be the one to pull me out of my momentary loss of self, but for now, I was grateful.

"Thanks," I said.

He grinned, one side quirking up more than the other. "Saving damsels in distress is kind of my thing," he said, winking.

I took another breath and laughed as the scythe's song surged through me once more. It was still located above us, but not far. It was getting stronger and it was waiting for me.

"*Death* is your thing, my dear," I said with a grin as I sailed past him up the stairs. "Besides, I do my own saving."

From behind me I heard him chuckle breathlessly, the fast pace of our climb winding him. "I can't argue with that," he said.

We stopped, peeking around the top of the stairway wall to see if anyone was coming. "One more floor," I breathed. We walked quickly down the hall and quietly rounded up another staircase. Once we reached the top, I noticed we'd come to a hallway that was slightly different than the previous two. Instead of rows of endless doors, there were only two, and I could hear the scythe's song pour into me. "Looks like Maeve was able to call the guard away," I said softy. With the door so close and unprotected, I felt like Hades was giving me an open invitation.

Rishi nodded tersely, grabbing my hand and leading us forward stealthily toward our target. We slowed as we approached the second door. It was situated at the end of the hallway, and the steady song of the scythe reverberated through my body with increasing intensity the closer we got to it. As we passed the first door, I saw that it was slightly cracked open, but I paid little notice. By the time I reached the door guarding the scythe, my mind was blank of anything aside from my intent. So when the doorknob turned from the inside, I didn't immediately comprehend what was happening.

"Someone's coming," Rishi hissed, clamping a hand around my elbow and pulling me back, my feet quickly adjusting to follow the backward pace.

Rishi dragged me into the other room and released me, glancing around quickly, his face a mask of calm. His eyes darted left and right, finally fixating on a large gilded dressing screen. Grabbing my hand, he ushered me behind the screen, and I followed lethargically, the beat of the scythe's music draining and exhilarating me all at the same time. I knew I was useless at the moment, but it was hard to concentrate when my entire being was filled with the presence of an ancient object that clearly had more power than anyone realized. When the door slammed, I gasped, swallowing a large breath, yanked from my deep connection with the supposedly inanimate object down the hall.

Rishi put his finger to his lips, peeking out through the cracks where the folding screen bent at its hinges. "Flicker out," I mouthed to him, my voice unheard, but he read my lips.

But Rishi shook his head. "I can't," he mouthed soundlessly back.

A man had entered. I knew who it was, and yet, he wasn't at all what I'd imagined. I wasn't sure which was worse, the reality or the person I'd created in my head. I'd imagined Hades sailing around in an Armani suit with shiny black shoes clicking against stone floors, like a mob boss. But what I saw was a brute. He wore a tight black T-shirt that clung to hard biceps and large, wide shoulders, his skin olive in tone, while he sported a goatee and thigh-hugging black jeans, with steel-toed, snakeskin boots peeking out from beneath the cuffs. I had been right about one thing: clicking shoes, although the tone of steel on stone was slightly more ominous. Black tattoos of symbols and letters rippled up his arms. He turned, and I saw the crags of his heavily lined face, not from age, but just from the natural planes and downturn of his features. They were fleshy, aside from the slender Greek nose that was slightly pointy. He strutted to a mirror, his form, maybe 6'3", pausing in front of his reflection as he grunted over what looked like mustard on his black shirt. When he lifted his shirt up over his gut, I noticed the humongous tattoo that dominated his back—the three-headed dog, the middle head seeming to look right at me as it snarled. Cerberus, I thought, remembering reading about Greek mythology the previous semester. I hoped the dog didn't really exist.

All he needed was a Hells Angels T-shirt and a hog at his side. I caught a glimpse of his eyes in the mirror, the dark slide of his gaze calculating and hard, like the shiny black of uncut onyx, rough and smooth at the same time. I realized then that we were in trouble going up against this foe. The guy wasn't just a behemoth. The mobster I'd imagined lived in his eyes as well. He was badass and calculating. And it was terrifying, even for me. Because I didn't see us getting the scythe out of this place without him knowing about it. Those eyes, they saw everything.

Hades grabbed another T-shirt from a mahogany dresser, the wood's red swirls and the deeply lined brown grains the only color amid the otherwise black décor. The T-shirt was old school, and the main character from *Legend of Zelda* was easily viewed across his chest—I knew this because I'd gone through a gamer girl phase. I watched as he leaned forward in the mirror and smoothed his chin and facial hair with the fingertips of both hands, and then he flipped his shoulder-length dark hair back so that it swooped like he was in a shampoo commercial.

I stifled a giggle and was rewarded by Rishi with a glare. A moment ago I'd actually been scared, but in this moment I was amused by the Hells Angels lookalike with The Godfather living in his gaze, who had Fabio-like hair and was a total gamer geek. Then, he turned and started walking toward the folding screen we hid behind, and I felt the laugh in my throat slide back down and disappear. My eyes darted to the floor behind us to see what he might be coming for. Hopefully he hadn't realized we were in the room yet.

Rishi glanced at me quickly, a flare of fear flashing in the depths of his eyes. Hades was close enough that I stepped softly away from the cracks so he didn't see my eyeballs peeking out. I looked over at Rishi once more and he reached out his hand, taking mine within his own and sliding a large, curved scythe into my hand. I arched an eyebrow and glanced around, wondering where he'd gotten it, but then I noticed a weapons display on the wall right behind us, obscured from Hades's view by the changing screen that also hid us. One of the hooks was empty.

He smiled faintly and shook his head, letting me know it was just an average scythe. But it was fitting, and I nodded my thanks, understanding the thought behind the weapon choice.

But I never had to use it, because the door creaked open and a soft voice, honeysuckle-laced and instantly familiar despite our only recent introduction, called to him.

"Father Hades," Maeve said.

Hades paused, turning and strutting as gracefully as a muscle-bound 250-pound man can, his hair bouncing behind him.

"Maeve," I heard him murmur, his deep, hollow voice like the rumble of a motorcycle after it's been brought to life, idling with a mechanical growl.

"The council is waiting for you, and Irkalla is getting feisty."

Hades's laugh boomed, a genuine smile lifting his lips as he patted Maeve on the shoulder in fatherly fashion. "That old bat? I'll have her wrapped by the end of dinner."

Maeve's laughter danced out of the room behind her, and her reply, "You always do," was the last thing I heard before Hades shut the door behind him.

Rishi turned to me quickly. "Let's go. We don't know how much time we have. Maeve bought us a little time, but knowing the entire council is in the mansion makes me a bit uneasy. Hades is formidable enough, and I'm definitely not looking to catch dinner and a movie with the Council of Death Deities. Irkalla is one of the senior deities, and when I say that, I mean she's ancient. She's also currently Hades's ally."

I nodded, wondering what her powers, other than crossing people over, could possibly be. We slipped around the folding screen and headed toward the door. Rishi paused right before reaching it and held up his hand for me to stop. Slowly, he rolled the doorknob in his hand to the right and pulled the door away from its frame, his head bent barely around the edge as his eyes darted around the hallway. Turning to me with a jerky nod, he pulled the door open smoothly, slid out, and beckoned me to follow before he slowly closed the door behind me.

I glanced over my shoulder to make sure we were truly alone in the long hallway. The scythe's music had muted to the background when we'd been hiding from Hades, but now it was back, thundering through me as we drew closer to the second door. I stopped right in front of it, a nondescript wood-paneled door, a silver doorknob no different than any other. But inside was my mother's salvation, the soul of my heritage's release. Despite the angst, betrayal, and abandonment I ached with when I thought of my mother, this meant something to me, and I hadn't wanted to admit it until now. Until I was standing outside this door on the brink of resetting a balance that never should have been upset.

Rishi's impatient exhale of breath made my hair float past my ear, tickling it and sending a jarring rush of awareness through me. "Well? Let's get this done, Blake," he said softly against my neck, his hands coming to rest on my shoulders in a show of support and probably in an effort to get me moving. In twenty-four hours alone I had liked him, crushed on him, hated him, and been seriously annoyed with him. Now all I could feel was grateful to have him by my side—potential lover or enemy, who knew where it would go? But in that moment we were friends, and his hands and his presence lent me the knowledge that I wasn't alone.

I didn't look back at him. I didn't need to. I knew I'd see the steady set of his dark eyes shimmering hopefully for a new beginning for him, for us, for Grim. I put my hand on the door and turned it. It gave without any hitch. Apparently they really weren't scared of anyone stealing the scythe. Hades was pretty cocky to believe Maeve would never figure a way to get to it. Or to get someone else in to take it.

I stepped inside and was at once assaulted by the song of the scythe. My body shook and vibrated, my insides feeling like a steel bell was ringing inside of me. The scythe filled up my entire world with sound and motion, and it was easy to spot. Almost too easy.

As I stepped toward it, the only thing I saw was the glowing, silvery glint of the blade, the ancient, carved wood handle that gleamed an even richer nut brown. It lay on a table, a glass dome keeping it preserved. Yet I knew nothing could keep it from me. I reached to lift the dome, my hands meeting the glass knob, trembling, aching to feel the weapon within my grasp.

"You should not be here." The interruption startled my awareness of the scythe, and its call to me ebbed as I turned to my right. A woman with dark, hooded eyes gazed at me from a bed I hadn't even noticed moments before. She wore a silken black bustier top and leggings, her hair as black as my mother's, as my own, but her skin was brown and her voice rang in lilting Spanish. I knew who she was. She looked enough like my mother, although this woman was Hispanic.

"Aunt Seba?" I asked softly, my eyes traveling over her voluptuous figure down to the cuff locked around her ankle and the long chain that was bolted into the wall.

"Aunt?" Her soft brown eyes, although glassy, snapped up to my own, and she gasped. "Maeve told me she found out she had a sister, but I did not realize you would come." Her softly accented voice was melodious and yet it sounded heavy, as if it drained her to form words.

"Are you okay?" I asked, stumbling toward her, kneeling by her side, and touching the steel cuff circling her slender ankle.

"Mi sobrina," she said, lifting my face with gentle hands and bringing my gaze to hers. Although her eyes were hard put to stay on my face and her long lashes dipped low onto her cheeks, her gaze held that flicker of compassion and tenderness I'd found lacking in my mother. "Sí, but they have been keeping me tranquilized ...," she said in dragging beats, her hands trembling as they fell from my face. "I have been here too long. Hades thought to drive me loco by putting me so close to the scythe, but he does not realize that although I can hear it, it does not call to me the way it does to you or *tu madre*. I am going more crazy from the boredom." She sighed, leaning back down on her pillows in weariness.

Five years was a long time to be drugged, I thought. I hoped she wasn't going to have to kick the habit once she was free. Only one way to find out.

"I'm going to get you out of here," I said. "But I need to get the scythe first."

"You must hurry. Hades will come soon, I feel it. Nothing happens in this place that he does not know. But the scythe is sharp, it should be able to cut through these chains."

I nodded and turned back toward the scythe, pushing down the warm feelings that were threatening to make me a puddle of mush over the fact that I had a sister and an aunt who seemed human, unlike my reptilian mother.

Once again, the scythe took over my thoughts, my body, my being, and then it was within my grasp.

"So Grim managed to have another daughter. I'm so not surprised." I heard the low rumble of Hades's words catch me. The song within me dropped. Really? I sighed. The first interruption might have been welcomed, but this one certainly was not.

My hand almost fell, but I didn't turn to face him. If I grabbed the scythe now, how could he stop me? Besides physically? I'd flickered twice now, why not again? I could do it, I could do it and take the scythe with me.

I wasted no time. I felt Hades's breath gather steam to tell me what he would do if I touched the scythe, but I acted before he could speak the words. I started to turn toward him, and in one motion I flipped the glass case off the table, ignoring the shattering smash despite the shards of glass that flew up and embedded into my legs. I wrapped my hand around the scythe's handle and it slipped into my grip like it was an extension of my arm. *Mine.*

I turned toward Hades, and the song, once overwhelming, now rushed and wove through me, becoming one with my blood, my spirit. I'd never felt any different when I'd first been told I was a death deity. I'd felt like a normal girl all this time, except for the moments I crossed someone over and the energy infused me, when I was usually raw with the emotions of those passing through me. But now I felt that surge of energy without the human emotions. It crackled through me, and I wondered if my mom missed this, if it had been like a drug she'd been forced to quit, because I felt like a god.

Hades wasn't smiling when I finally met his violent gaze. But he didn't look too worried either. Which in turn, worried me. I smiled anyway. "This belongs to me," I said, hearing my calm voice waft across the room. It did belong to me. It had been waiting to be used, to be set free.

"A little presumptuous, aren't we? It belongs to your mother. But what else can I expect from your generation. So entitled. See your friend Rishi there?"

I had forgotten about him, I was ashamed to admit, and I turned my eyes to the side of the room where a huge aquarium had been built into the wall. Rishi stood beside it, two large-muscled men holding him with his arm bent unnaturally behind his back. Not good.

"And your sister?" he continued. I snapped my gaze back to Hades and saw the blue-eyed Ambrose enter, his hand squeezed around Maeve's upper arm, a grim set to his bearded jaw. "Is this who you saw your wife with earlier, Son?"

Wife? But I couldn't pause to think, because Ambrose looked at me and then to Rishi, his gaze narrowing and his knuckles whitening as he squeezed Maeve tighter so that she let out a cry. "You're hurting me," she hissed at him. He turned to look at her and I shuddered inwardly for my sister. His unforgiving eyes were distant frost-capped mountains, lacking compassion or rational thought.

"You lied to me," he said furiously through gritted teeth.

She looked at him pleadingly. "Ambrose, you must see that this is wrong. The world is unbal—"

"Enough!" boomed Hades, his deep set eyes drawn sadly. "My heart is broken, Maeve. I've treated you well these last five years. I approved and applauded your marriage to my son. I made you my family," he finished, his rumbly voice the growing growl of thunder. "And now you've let the betrayer's kin in. Let her take what is precious to us."

"That so-called 'betrayer' is my mother! Have you forgotten that?" Maeve spat at him, clawing at Ambrose's grip unsuccessfully. "And you kept me prisoner here!" Ambrose shook her, but I saw his grip relax a bit.

"You've been looking to escape since the moment you got here, and I guess I was just a part of your façade," Ambrose said coldly.

"I'm sorry, Son. But like mother, like daughter," Hades said, pressing his hand down on his son's shoulder and looking over at me with a serpentine smile flickering in his eyes. "You have the scythe, my dear, but how do you think you'll manage to get out of here? It's impossible to flicker. The void doesn't exist here, as I'm sure you well know."

I was stuck, holding the scythe as its song reverberated through me, with nowhere to go. We'd failed. I felt my heart slam into my chest with the thought, and my grief for all the lost and fading souls made me feel weak.

My gaze flickered to Rishi, whose dark eyes already seemed defeated. He'd been down this road before. I couldn't let this happen. I couldn't let Maeve spend another moment here, married to the overlord's son, whose eyes held the potential to be just as cruel as his father's. Then I glanced at my aunt, who must have been using whatever energy she had to watch us, sitting upright, her heavily hooded eyes strained wide as she struggled to stay clear of the drugs and observe the action. No one took any notice of her, it seemed.

From the corner of my eye I saw her pull a hairpin from her long dark hair, previously piled up in a luxury of curls atop her head. Her hair fell down to spill across her shoulders, and she casually slid the pick into the cuff at her ankle. I wondered if this was the first time she'd even tried that. The click was inaudible to everyone but me, since all focus was on me holding the scythe. She looked up at me, meeting my gaze with such intensity I knew she wanted me to remember something, and yet I couldn't decipher her mute message. Shaking her head in exasperation, she called out to me, "The scythe, *mi sobrina.*"

"Shut her up," Hades commanded, and I realized the deity who headed toward my aunt was Sophie, the guard with the horned rims. She shot my sister a smug look as she moved to follow Hades's orders. I knew who we had to blame for outing us, I thought grimly. That's why it had been so easy to get into the room. Hades had been trying to trap us.

I felt a panic start to seize me like it had on the stairs, but I slammed it back down. The scythe, what were its powers again? As if I'd directed the question to the scythe itself, I began to feel the answer in its song, except I could almost hear words, my mother's voice saying that it could kill deities and it could cut through space and time …

I glanced over at Rishi and he slowly smiled, the fear I'd seen before absent from his dark gaze, replaced by a blazing faith that I'd never seen before.

I set my gaze on Maeve again and her dark eyes met mine, and they told me to go, even though I knew it cost her, that she longed to be free of her prison. She wanted me to fix what was wrong with the world. Or at least, she wanted me to find the one person who could: our mother. The worst would be to leave her, this girl who had become my sister in a day. I lifted a hand and wrapped it around the owl pendant that still hung from my neck, trying to draw strength from the Grim who had once maybe acted like a mother.

But did I have to leave them? I felt a renewed strength whisper through me as I wrapped both hands firmly around the scythe, a warmth kissing my palms and seeping into my skin and blood. It was a rush of energy unlike any other I'd ever felt, filling my soul with a silvery burst of light and a sweeping and burning desire to use the power I held within my hands and wipe the smug smile from Hades's craggy face.

"Come now, Blake. Put the scythe down and we can all be friends. Most of your family is here anyway. We can work something out. I'll lift the ban of souls, although I'm sorry, your mother is just not welcome here, not after she killed my poor brother," he said in a low, growly voice, and yet he couldn't hide the amusement that threaded through it and filled my head with his condescending laughter.

The scythe felt light in my hands, an extension of myself. "Maybe I'll just kill you instead," I said softly, hearing the words leave my lips as darkly as they sounded and feeling my desire stoked by the scythe. We both wanted his life.

"You're not a killer," he said with a shake of his shampoo-commercial hair, but the bounce of it was anything but funny this time around. It just served to accentuate the calculating glimmer of his eyes. "You're a gateway."

"I can be both," I assured him, and in those moments I felt it was true. I could slice him with the scythe and feel no remorse over the years he'd cost people, keeping them prisoner. I would do it for the souls abandoned, displaced, and crazed, and for my mother, who even now was probably growing more distant. Would I never know who she could be with humanity running through her essence?

A shadow danced across his expression and any glimmer of patience vanished with my words. "I'll kill your sister before you even take a step," he growled, the deep set of his gaze meeting mine. His brows furrowed heavily over his eyes and his lip puckered out in an expression of such menace I smelled rubber burning against tar.

"Father," Ambrose said in protest. Although his face had been set impassively, at the mention of losing his wife his cold exterior thawed for a moment, his gaze softening. Hope flashed across Maeve's face.

Hades glanced at his son and said, "She betrayed you. She is as bad as her mother."

Ambrose seemed to stare his father down for a moment, the hard line of his bearded jaw tightening before dropping slack, his gaze dropping in kind. "You know best, Father," he said.

All hope disappeared from Maeve's face, and she jerked her arm from Ambrose's before he could react, spitting in his face. "You're a sheep," she hissed. "I can't believe I ever thought you cared about me."

Ambrose's lip curled as he grabbed her arm again, clutching it more roughly this time with one hand as he wiped away the saliva dripping down his thin, Greek nose with the other. "And I you, Maeve," he said, his voice grumbling as deep as his father's for a moment.

"What'll it be, Blake?" Hades asked, paying little notice to the glare Maeve was shooting him or the blank expression I could tell it was costing Ambrose to keep.

"Hmmm, I think I'll take door number three," I said, and not waiting to see his expression, I whipped the scythe back and with all my strength sliced it through the air. The whistle of steel was all I heard as the world vanished, and I cut my way through an empty space unoccupied by people or things, by pathways or voids, existing somewhere between Abbadon and nowhere. Innately I sensed the essence of Rishi and my newfound family where this new realm mingled with Abbadon, and I reappeared next to Seba moments before Sophie could reach her.

I barely glanced Hades's way, but he roared when he saw me reappear. "Impossible! The void does not exist here!" And in that moment, I saw Maeve just as she slammed a steel-tipped toe into Ambrose's shin. He howled, doubling over and losing his grip on his wife, who came running toward me, slamming into Sophie and knocking her to the ground.

My aunt didn't need instructions but grabbed on to my waist as Maeve did the same to her. I arced the scythe once more, disappearing and forging my way to Rishi. When we reappeared near him, I lifted the scythe and menacingly stepped toward the henchmen holding him. The glacial ice of my eyes must have convinced them, because they dropped his arms and stepped back before Hades could gather his wits.

It had all happened in mere seconds, and I flashed Rishi a triumphant smile as I turned to Hades, who was barreling toward us, a hulking figure gathering speed. Rishi grabbed on to Maeve, and I didn't waste a moment, arcing the scythe through the air once more and leaving Hades with the image of me, the scythe, his leverage, and his pride disappearing as I told him what he already knew: "You lose." And then we vanished from his view, heading to the doorway, to Shelby.

CHAPTER EIGHTEEN

WE REAPPEARED in the wooded spot where we'd first entered Abbadon. "This thing is so cool," I whispered, glancing down at the scythe I gripped tightly in my hand.

"Finally!" Shelby's astral body looked faint, her lips pursed. "Did you get it?" Her eyes darted to my hand, and she nodded, relief dousing her worry. "Then let's go! Lupine is almost there!"

Her voice was shrill, and I couldn't blame her. She'd been waiting a while and it was her body lying on the grassy side of a cliff. I glanced around, making sure everyone was there.

"Where's Rishi?" I asked, unable to find him.

"I'm here," he said, stepping out from behind two trees. "I got thrown a little when we came back through." A smug smile curved his lips.

I held up my hand. "Don't you even—"

"I told you so," he said, a hysterical, jubilant laugh leaving his lips.

I couldn't hold back a smile as my body thrummed with the energy of the scythe coursing through me. "You were right ... I can also wield the scythe," I said. "It was a good theory."

"Obviously," he said, his smile growing wider.

"Listen, you two, we've still got to get out of here. Let's go," Maeve said urgently, rushing toward Shelby. "How do we leave?"

Shelby glanced at her with arched brows. "Who's she?" I shook my head. "Them?" she amended, her eyes flickering toward Seba.

"Later, let's get out of here. They'll be coming for us." I could hear Hades's hybrids at that moment, voices shouting from the big house.

"*Sí*, we must go," Seba said.

I nodded to Shelby. "Lead the way."

Just like before, we followed her until I felt the air rush around me, and we were through the doorway.

As we stepped out into the dusty terrain we'd left behind only several hours before, the stars twinkling above us brightly, I nearly dropped the scythe when I saw one of Hades's boys dancing around the mountain lions, who were hissing at him in warning. I turned to tell Shelby, but she glanced at me and then she was gone.

My gaze darted back to where she lay, and I saw her body come alive once more, her breath swelling as she slowly sat up, at once alert. The smaller, female guardian licked her face while the larger male continued to growl menacingly.

"If it isn't the Reaper's daughters ..."

"Lupine," I said.

He glanced at me, brows arching so quizzically for a moment that it nearly made me laugh. "What?"

"Marx," Maeve said. "I am just so sick of your family at this moment."

He turned to Maeve, his wide, wolfish grin turning up. "But sis, we're family!"

"She's his sister?" Shelby asked from where she sat guarded by her overgrown feline friends.

Marx laughed. "Sis-in-law," he said, zeroing his almond-shaped eyes on Shelby. "She's also your BFF's sister."

Shelby's head snapped to me before swiveling back to Maeve once and then back to me. "Sister?"

I nodded. "I'll tell you later. Other things to worry about right now," I said, rolling my eyes toward Lupine.

"Right, right," she said, petting the large mountain lion absentmindedly, ignoring Hades's goonish children surrounding us.

"So, what were you up to out here? I can't imagine anything good ..." Marx's eyes trailed off as he caught the gleam of the moonlight on the scythe. I smiled.

"You're not seeing things, it is what you think it is. And it's got power. It's humming through me, telling me all the things I can do with it. Like how hybrids are harder to kill than humans, but not as hard as full deities, and how it can kill both just as easily, like a knife through butter," I said, feeling the dark cloak of death settle around my shoulders. It was enough to see his smile vanish.

"My father will be coming for you," he said, his eyelids lowering as he shot me a scathing look. He jerked his head to the girl and the guy that flanked us. They'd never said a word and mattered little to me, but I caught the girl's gaze as they turned to go. It was seething with bitter hate. I clucked my tongue at her.

"Don't take your 'daddy loves your brothers more' issues out on me. The scythe and I say it's not a good idea."

She looked startled that I'd even noticed her. And scared. Hades seemed to rank his children by importance based on their order of birth. I wondered which one she was. To be the fourth or fifth or tenth child in Hades's world probably wasn't ideal. I sensed that once Hades found out they'd known about my existence two days ago, they'd all be falling heavily from grace. I'd be scared too, especially if I was the daughter out of the bunch. I'd sensed a bit of chauvinistic pig in him.

Her gaze slid away and she followed Marx out. He knew he was outnumbered, especially with the scythe. I wasn't sure how he communicated with Hades, but apparently not so fast and easy that he could call him here right away. Or he was avoiding him, which was probably a smart move.

"We should get going," I said, looking around at everyone.

Rishi nodded, picking up his pack and throwing it over his shoulders. "Shelb, say good-bye to your friends." She glanced up at him, a pout turning down her lips, but she sighed and nodded. She wrapped her arms around each of their necks and whispered, "I release you." The two cats licked her, rose, and then sauntered away from Death's Doorway.

"I wish I could take them home," she sighed.

I laughed. "Let's talk about it in the car."

"Yeah, before Hades gets his GPS on," Rishi agreed.

"I may need some assistance," Seba said, swaying on her feet where she stood with no shoes to speak of.

"What's wrong with her?" Shelby said as Maeve and Rishi each wrapped an arm around her shoulder and headed toward the trail. I started to follow, watching my aunt with concern.

"Hades has been drugging her. She was his prisoner."

"Who is she?" Shelby whispered.

"My aunt," I said.

"So you have like a whole family now."

"It appears so, although my mother is currently MIA and not the nicest women, as you may remember."

Shelby was quiet a moment as we traipsed down the trail as quickly as we could, given my aunt's state. I kept the scythe clutched in my hand.

As we neared the bottom of the trail and the car, still parked on the side of the road like a beacon to our location, Shelby glanced over at me. "So what's next?"

"Find my mother," I said. "But first I'd like to sleep."

We all piled into the truck, letting my aunt take the front seat while Shelby, Maeve, and I squeezed into the back.

"Where to?" I asked.

"Let's find a motel where we can get some rest," Rishi said, meeting my eyes in the rearview mirror to confirm with me, his voice dragging and laced with the sigh of the weary.

"Sounds like a plan," I said.

CHAPTER NINETEEN

"**SO MAEVE** is actually married to Hades's son?" Shelby asked me. Her pale green eyes, devoid of eyeliner or any other makeup, widened with all that she had learned. We were sitting cross-legged on top of the motel bed. Maeve had taken our aunt into another room to let her sleep off the effects of the narcotics, or herbs, or whatever it was that deities drugged each other with. I was rooming with Shelby and finally had been able to tell her just what had happened in Abbadon.

"So a big family reunion, sans your mother," she said.

"Yeah, pretty much," I said, wondering where Grim could be. We'd returned to find that she still was unreachable. "I always thought my dad was enough, you know? But having met my mother and witnessed her lack of personable attributes, I realized I've been feeling the absence of her all along. But she's not anyone I can own. I don't like her, like, at all. But I like my sister, at least what I know of her. There's obviously a story there that needs telling … And my aunt. I've known her for all of ten seconds. But I think she's worth knowing too. And despite my current feelings for my mother, my biggest hope is that we can actually find her, wherever she is. I want to know, Shelb. I want to know if she could be someone I could like when balance is restored, when the spark of her humanity is relit. Maybe I could have a mother and a father, and a sister and an aunt … and a best friend."

Shelby had been looking down, but she glanced up quickly at my mention of her and smiled. "I have a feeling that your mother will be a lot different with her humanity intact," she said softly.

"I really hope so," I said back.

"So what's next?" she asked as she twisted her damp hair into a bun on top of her head.

"We have to find my mother. The scythe is rightfully hers," I said, almost stumbling over the words as I turned my gaze to the weapon propped in the far corner of the room. It sure didn't feel like hers. "She can lift the ban from her soul gate and restore the balance of death back to the world. We just don't know what has happened to her."

"And what about me?" Shelby asked, making me turn my eyes back to hers, the scythe's pull moving into the background if only for a moment.

"We'll take you home before we get going," I said, adding, "if that's what you want."

She stared at me, the eyes and face I'd known so well for most of my life a mystery to me in that moment, as shadows danced along her delicate features. There was a resoluteness in the set of her expression, and I knew before she even spoke what her decision was.

She shook her head, a dried tendril of faded cherry bomb hair falling into her face. "I may not be a death deity, but you're my best friend, *my* sister. And even though you have an actual sister now, that doesn't change our relationship, or what we've been through together, or even the fact that if you ever need to pass through Death's Doorway again, I'm your only chance. I don't want to go home. I want in. I know I'm not nearly invincible like you deities are, but I'm pretty sure I keep you sane. And I want to help."

I stared at her a few long moments, hiding the smile that wanted to stretch across my lips. She'd changed. She was braver somehow. And I was a bit more cautious, I thought. We'd both changed. For the better.

"You're sure? I don't know if we'll make it back to classes in time, and I've begun to accept that this is my life now. I can't allow things to stay the way they are, not when I can feel the lost souls' sadness, and when I know how their state of being can affect the living."

She nodded firmly. "I'm not ditching my college education, but I want to see this through. Hey, some people decide to take a semester off to backpack through Europe. I'm going to go on a road trip to find the Grim Reaper. Same diff."

I laughed, shaking my head. "A little different, but I'm down with the analogy."

"Hey, you never know, we could still make it back in time to finish out the semester."

I smiled, nodding, but I had a feeling it would be a while before I was done cleaning up this mess.

I heard a soft knock at our door, and I unfolded my legs and rose. I opened the door to find Rishi and Maeve. My gaze connected first with Rishi, whose eyes glittered urgently, and then I turned to Maeve, whose serious expression made me realize that resting in this motel was but a brief reprieve. For a moment, the cheap motel with the rough, suspect comforter and its stale air lingering with ash and stubbed-out cigarettes had felt like a sanctuary. I was weary to my bones, and even a good night's sleep wasn't going to fix that. But we had a mission, as silly as that sounded. And my dad thought I was on a mini-break with Shelby. How would I explain my coming absence from Specter? Thank god spring break hadn't even officially started yet. We could ride on that for the next week.

"What's up?" I asked, stepping back so they could slip past me.

Rishi didn't move far from the door, pulling out a chair from the desk, dropping his broad form into it, and folding his arms behind his head. Maeve perched on the edge of the other bed, nervously picking at her nails. I followed Rishi's lead and pulled out the other chair in the room, dropping down into it and staring at my friends, my family. "What's up?" I asked again.

Maeve glanced up. "So, apparently, according to Aunt Seba, we have to find the other scythe, like, *now*. She says that Hades will be more determined now to get it than ever before."

"Seriously? And what about Grim?"

"Yeah," Rishi murmured, running his fingers through his loose hair. I swallowed, avoiding his gaze when he looked up. I didn't know where we stood at the moment. I couldn't find it in myself to be angry at him anymore, but take away the adrenaline and things were awkward at best.

"Listen, Seba wants to go find your mother. She wants us to retrieve the second scythe," he continued, and like a fool I looked up, caught unwittingly and unable to look away once he had me.

I shook my head almost imperceptibly. "Alone? Doesn't she, like, need detox or something?"

"No, I don't need detox," my aunt said, suddenly flickering into the room like a candle flame coming alive.

She turned, smiling softly. "A couple days of rest and I should be fine. Deities don't get addicted the way humans do. The other scythe needs you and your sister to go get it," she told me. "You need to go back."

"Back where?" I asked, already knowing the answer.

"Abbadon," she said quietly. "You must use Death's Doorway once more."

"They could be waiting for us when we cross through," Rishi said, his jaw tense.

"They have no way to know where you came through, or how you came through. All Marx knows is that he saw us come through thin air. But you will have to move fast and put as much distance between you and the estate as possible. You will be journeying deep into Abbadon," Seba said.

"The scythe is in Abbadon? I thought it was out here somewhere—isn't that why Lupine and his crew were out this way, aside from chasing us?" I asked.

Seba chuckled, low and deep. "I sent them on goose chases often. How else was I to stay entertained?"

I glanced at Maeve and she caught my gaze with a sparkle in her own. "So where is it exactly, then?" I asked.

"Yeah," Maeve said after me. "Abbadon is huge."

"I am not quite sure. I last left it with a soul, and he's been moving it around for me, but I believe him to have gone west."

"So basically, he could be anywhere?" Shelby chimed in.

"Do you know where he might be at all?" I asked hopefully.

"Or do you have any way to contact him?" Maeve asked.

My aunt sighed and shook her head. "I'm sorry, sobrinas, I do not. I do not even know the name he goes by now. That way, he could not be easily found by Hades."

"Why would you ever have trusted this man, this soul with the scythe?" I asked.

My aunt glanced over at me, her dark eyes the most lucid I'd seen them thus far. "We were in love once, but he was not mine to take. When it became apparent Hades was trying to destroy my sister and claim the twin scythes, I sought my former lover out and asked him to take it. He had died many, many years before but had chosen to stay in Abbadon. He knows the realm better than most deities. Anyway, he promised to protect it as long as I needed him to. Shortly after, I was taken by Hades, so that was the last I saw of him."

"And you don't know his name?" Shelby said, her brows arched in question. I couldn't help but inwardly echo her expression.

"Yes, how could you trust someone with the scythe and not know his name?" Rishi asked as politely as he could, although I could see the storm crashing beneath the surface of his calm exterior.

My aunt turned and one by one caught us all with her deep, mesmerizing gaze, which held an eon of knowledge. Who were we to question her? Who were we to know anything of love?

She smiled finally, her lush, full lips turning up like the Cheshire cat, and I saw my mother in the smile and I understood that we were silly young children in Seba's mind. "Love does not need a name, it only needs honor," she said cryptically, not offering to explain and telling us with her gaze not to bother asking more. "But I will tell you this. The name from his former life is one I think you will recognize, although I don't think it will help much. You would know him as Plato."

"Plato?" Maeve glanced at us cluelessly, and I realized she'd been out of school so long she'd probably never studied him. If she'd even ever been in school.

"Are you joking?" Rishi exhaled, stomping a foot down and rising from his chair. "He's one of Hades's souls. And he has this other scythe?"

Seba did not react to Rishi's anger but merely smiled and nodded. "Yes, that is why I gave it to him. He would never be suspected."

"So why do you think we can find him?" I asked.

"Because you have to, and I cannot. He does not wish to ever see me again, and I made him the promise that I would not come for him."

"Why?" Maeve gasped, seemingly enraptured by the story.

But Seba merely shook her head, refusing to tell us why a long-dead Greek philosopher would never want to see her again. "Begin in Ancient Greece, it is a city within the underworld. Search out Aristotle. He may be able to help you. But go soon."

She was right. This was urgent. Hades could easily get this scythe back, being a full deity with a legion of children at his bidding, versus me, a hybrid with a misfit band of hybrid deities plus one full human.

And that could be bad, although I wasn't sure exactly what his endgame was.

"What does Hades want?" Shelby asked, simplifying the question to its barest bones. "What is the final frontier for him? Does anyone really know?"

Seba nodded to herself, but she didn't look at Shelby, instead glancing first at Maeve and finally at me. "The two scythes together have the power to open the gateways between life and death—to bring the dead back to life. That means souls released from Abbadon, and possibly the other realms, could be revived, made alive. The power is the destroyer of life."

"How in the world could that destroy life?" I asked, bewildered.

But Shelby spoke up once more. "With the knowing comes the fall," she said, glancing at me, her eyes bright with realization. "I can only imagine that the very knowledge of death itself would have some pretty heavy ramifications. Like in the story of Adam and Eve, all evil was brought into the world when Eve ate an apple from the Tree of Knowledge. Of course I don't actually believe that's what happened, but it's a lesson: with knowledge comes consequences. Death is supposed to be an unknown. If that barrier broke down ... not to mention the elimination of all boundaries between life and death, it just would be—"

"*Muy mal.* Very bad," Seba said and turned to me. "We do not know if he means to tear down the barriers. Perhaps merely having the power would be enough for him. But I do not think so."

"So we need to get the other scythe."

"Yes," she nodded. "I believe it will call to Maeve, since you have your mother's."

Maeve nodded, a light coming to her eyes like a click. "I noticed this one's call had ceased to be so strong. It doesn't bother me anymore, it's more like a soundtrack in the background of my life."

Seba nodded. "Yes, that is because Blake claimed it as hers. The same will be true for Blake with the second scythe. It will not call to her as much as the one she carries. And the scythes will also call to each other, and that is something you will both recognize, being tuned in as you are."

"But what about your children, Aunt Seba?" Maeve asked, her brows furrowed in concern.

"The scythes are meant for sisters," Seba said softly.

"So where do we go from here? We have to find Grim," I said, thinking I could revisit the whole sister-scythe ideology later.

My aunt shook her head. "I'll find my sister. You four head to Death's Doorway."

It was the best we were going to get at the moment, and we had to find the scythe. There was so much more at stake than I'd ever realized.

"And you think you can find Gri—our mother?" I asked.

"We are sisters. I will feel her spirit call to me when I am close."

"When do we leave then?" Shelby asked quietly.

"Tomorrow," I said, glancing at Shelby. "We'll go tomorrow. Now to think of a story to tell our parents ..."

"That will be the toughest mission yet," Shelby laughed.

"But first, let's sleep," Seba said softly.

"I'll second that," Rishi said, rising and stretching his limbs.

*   *   *

Day dawned early for me. I'd been exhausted the night before, but somehow sleep hadn't come easy or stayed long. I woke when light was only a sliver in the sky, and I quietly dressed and gathered my belongings so as not to wake Shelby, who was flopped halfway under her covers with her mouth hanging open. I slipped out into the coming day and shut the door with care. I made my way to the truck and threw my bag inside, shutting the door and thinking about coffee. But when I turned to make my way to the motel office, Rishi was walking over with a steaming cup in each hand. He smiled as he joined me where I leaned against the truck, watching the sun make its daily climb. Its rays were already warm and the air was mild and fresh. Spring was finally turning the corner.

"I figured you'd be the first one up," he said, handing me a cup. I peered down into the cup and glanced up at him.

"Three sugars and two creamers." He flashed a quick grin, his eyes holding mine.

I took a sip to confirm and swallowed, grateful for the warm liquid that eased down my throat and brought an almost instant alertness to my wearied mind. "I'm slightly impressed you paid so much attention," I said, taking another sip.

"Only slightly?" He raised his dark brows, his hands wrapped around his own Styrofoam cup.

I turned and opened the car door, reaching into my bag and pulling out a plastic travel coffee mug and holding it up. "I'd have been more impressed if you'd remembered I always use this. It's Shelby's rule: 'We must be green in all we do.' The consequences of not using it aren't worth the argument, so I carry it with me. But too late now," I said, shrugging and tossing the mug back in the car and shutting the door. "If she sees this, though, I'm throwing you under the bus."

Rishi chuckled, shaking his head. "I knew I was missing something. Impressing the best friend." He didn't let go of my gaze and I found it hard to break it, but I did it anyway.

Looking down I sighed. "Rishi, I …"

He snorted, making me look back up at him. "I get it, Blake. You don't trust me, and seeing Geoff back there probably made you realize you're not over him."

I tried to interrupt him and tell him that it wasn't about Geoff, but he kept talking. "But I'm just going to say this up front so it's on the table, since it looks like you've decided not to ditch me at the first chance. I like you, Blake. Traveling with your mother, living the life I've led, I haven't had much time for dating. I honestly don't have time for it now. But … I don't need to have gone on a million dates to know that you and I are alike. I've seen the way you get. You're like me—we share a love for the thrill, for life, even when we're facing death in every moment. And we understand each other, in a way I haven't ever shared with someone else. I think we could be good together," he said, finishing softly.

I had been looking down, unable to meet his eyes, but now I looked up and faced the issue head on. "But I don't trust you, Rishi. You've shown time and again that my mother comes first. That when it comes down to it, if my mother says jump, you'd do it without consulting me at all."

"We're trying to restore life and death to its natural order," he protested, with a hard twitch in his tense jaw. "Sometimes she knows best."

I shook my head, cutting off any further words. "And that's just it. I don't care what she thinks. We, us, me. *Me*. I'm the one who has the scythe, we're the ones who are going on this mission to find the other scythe, we're the ones in danger. She's not even in her right mind, you've seen it yourself. Order needs to be restored, but I'm not taking orders from her, and as long as you are, I can't trust you. Rishi, she's got the sickness too, no matter what you want to believe."

"Your mother basically raised me, and I believe in what we're doing and why we're doing it. But I want to be up front about everything from now on. No more secrets. Can that be enough for now?"

I stared at him for a moment, unable to deny how drawn to him I was even now. He was right when he said we were of the same cloth. I felt a kindred flame in him. I sighed. "I don't know. I don't even know what I have to give at this moment."

"Hey!" Shelby sauntered out, a bag cast over her shoulder casually. Her candy-red hair was pulled up into a bun on top of her head and she looked as well rested as was possible, given everything we'd been through the last several days. "I've got the perfect story to tell our parents," she said as she opened the car door and threw her bag in the back. "I'll tell you on the way."

"It'd better be a good one," I grinned.

"I need coffee," she said, eyeing mine with hunger and sliding her eyes between Rishi and me. "Be right back. We'll talk about the coffee mug upon my return," she said, shooting my cup a pointed look as she headed toward the motel lobby.

I glanced over at Rishi, who hadn't seemed to have taken his eyes off me during the whole exchange.

"I'm not giving up on this ... this thing we have between us," he said, making my chest clench as blood rushed to my face. I didn't know what to say, and I couldn't look away as he held my gaze. A door swung shut, and I was finally able to break his hold. I saw my sister and aunt exit their motel room, dark sunglasses pulled over my aunt's eyes as she walked toward us. It looked like Shelby had lent Maeve some clothes, as she was now sporting leggings and a long ribbed tank covered by a denim jacket. I felt guilty that I hadn't been the one to think of it. I glanced down at my sneakers, jeans, and hoodie and felt fashionably inadequate for a moment, until I remembered I was the one more aptly dressed for what we had ahead of us.

"We have got to get those girls some actual hiking shoes," Rishi murmured.

I laughed under my breath, thankful I wasn't the only one who seemed to think in terms of logic. I sighed, watching my aunt and Maeve saunter off toward the coffee with a wave of acknowledgement, and then I looked back at Rishi. "Just tell me the truth, okay?"

He locked eyes with me once more and slowly nodded. "No more secrets," he murmured gruffly, taking my hand in his rough one before I could pull it away. He traced a line back and forth down the center of my palm with his fingers while he held it with the other hand. I knew he was trying to draw me back in, and it was working. Out of the corner of my eye I saw Shelby coming back and I slid my hand from his, ignoring the curve of his lips and glitter of hope in his eyes as I shook my hand out, trying to make the tingles he'd left behind dissipate, and hopefully with them, the red-hot heat running through my veins.

"And keep your hands to yourself," I finally muttered, which only made him laugh.

"Something funny?" Shelby asked as she joined us, looking noticeably perkier from the caffeine she'd just consumed. I could stake my life on it that she'd downed an energy drink before she'd even poured the coffee. She liked clean living, except when it came to her caffeine. Then she'd take it any way she could.

"Just Blake at a loss for words," he said. Shelby glanced at me, her forehead wrinkling as she arched her brows before she glanced back at Rishi.

"Well, that is something to smile about. Our friend here is pretty stubborn, but often won over by truth and justice." Shelby winked at me and then turned to Rishi, fluttering her lashes to his sheepish smile. She plugged her earbuds into her ears and climbed into the back of the truck. She popped her head out. "If I fall asleep, only wake me when something interesting happens. Except if there's any car chases. Then just let me sleep so I can avoid the probable heart attack." Then she closed the door and I knew she'd probably be out for the next several hours.

"She's pretty quick on the uptake," Rishi observed.

"That's why I keep her around," I said, flashing him a smile.

"Didn't she just drink a gallon of coffee? How can she sleep?"

"It doesn't have that much of an effect on her, I'm afraid."

Maeve and Seba approached, each clutching their own favored beverage. "I haven't had a diet soda in five years. Do you know how long that is to go without one?" Maeve asked me, cracking open her drink and gulping it for a few long seconds, her eyes closed and her taste buds delighted. "So, we're ready?" She glanced between Rishi and me, her dark eyes much too observant for my comfort, especially since I already had Shelby for that.

"We should probably pick up some clothes for you guys," Rishi nodded at Maeve's ballet flats.

She glanced down at them and smiled. "Shelby lent me these. My boots are in my bag, but I wouldn't mind a couple of things, including a toothbrush."

I nodded and glanced at my aunt, who had removed the top of her cup and was inhaling the smell of her coffee. "Don't they have coffee in Abbadon?" I asked.

"Why would they need to? Souls do not eat real food and deities that are not prisoners can leave and get one anytime they please," she said, putting the drink to her lips and sighing at the end of each swallow. "I don't really need such sustenance, but oh, I do love it." Her full lips had been painted red and I noted she was wearing new clothes.

"Where'd you get your clothes?" I asked, not recognizing them from Shelby's wardrobe and doubting Shelby's clothes would have fit my curvy, voluptuous aunt.

"I went out this morning and got some," she said, tilting her head and smiling softly at me.

I smiled back, although I wondered if she'd actually paid for her new clothes. Unless she had flickered to a hidden stash of money somewhere. That was actually highly probable.

"Well, unfortunately I'm not staying. I'm off to find my sister," she added.

"Don't you need a car?" I asked.

She shook her head with a chuckle. "*Sobrina*, I only need myself and the call of her blood. I have Rishi's phone, and he has tutored me in the ways of the super smartphone," she said, laughing.

"It'll also help you in case Grim calls or texts. Although we haven't heard from her," Rishi said.

"So," I sighed, looking at my aunt. "This is it."

She nodded with another soft smile, tilting her head and pulling me toward her in a warm, fragrant hug. She was soft, and I wished for a moment that it was she who was my mother. When she pulled back, she touched my cheek gently with her hand. "Rishi has told me how bad *mi hermana* has gotten, how far removed from her humanity she has gone. You should know, she loves both you and Maeve."

I looked away, wishing it were true but unable to believe it could be.

"Do not dismiss me, Blake," she said in her lilting accented voice. "Do not believe you know her motives, for the safety of you and *tu hermana* has always been a priority."

I smiled softly. "With all due respect, Aunt Seba, she has shown me little if no respect or affection, and the only recognition I have gotten from her has been because she needed the scythe. She didn't even tell me I had a sister. Like I told Rishi earlier, I'm doing this to regain order, for the souls who got caught in the crossfire."

"Just give her a chance when you see her again. That is all I ask," she said, leaning in and kissing my forehead.

I nodded reluctantly, not wanting to argue with a woman I'd just met and was saddened to see leave so quickly. She turned to embrace Maeve, who wiped away a few errant tears and clutched her tightly for several moments.

"Aunt Seba?" I said after she and my sister had finished their good-bye, a nagging question coursing through me.

My aunt met my gaze once more, her brows arched in question as she reached over to warmly squeeze Shelby's hand. It was a nurturing gesture and unlike any emotion I'd seen come from Grim.

"You were stuck in Abbadon for as many years as my mother's been banned, right?"

"*Sí, sobrina*," she said softly.

"Then how is it you still have humanity?"

Smiling gently, although a certain melancholy lingered in her expression, she nodded. "I was chaperoned, of course, but I have crossed over many souls through the years. A deity without humanity does not care for threats to loved ones, nor does she give up the location of her scythe when tortured, so Hades wanted to keep me softer in hopes of eventually bending me to his will. If he had not grown so fond of Maeve, I fear he would have used her against me. But his own humanity has been his downfall."

I nodded, filing her comment about Hades and his humanity away for later analysis. If there was some way to use it against him, perhaps we could solve all of this without casualties.

Rishi stepped forward to embrace Seba and then we waved good-bye. She lifted one delicate hand like a dancer through the air, pressing her fingers to her lips and blowing us a kiss, and then she was gone.

"Well." Rishi turned to us. "We'd best get on the road," he said, turning to the driver's side door and climbing inside. Maeve reached to open the passenger-side backseat door, but I stopped her.

"Hey, we didn't really get to talk last night. You going to tell me about Ambrose?"

She arched a delicate brow and jerked her head toward Rishi's profile. "You going to tell me about Rishi?" A smile remained on her face, and her eyes danced with mine.

"I guess we could both share," I finally said. "Although there's not much to tell where I'm concerned."

She chuckled with a knowing look. "Don't lie to your big sister, I can see right through you." And then she climbed into the backseat and winked.

I narrowed my eyes at her, which only made her laugh behind the glass of her window. Ignoring her already annoying big-sister attitude, I climbed into the front and locked my seatbelt in place.

"So, you ready for this?" Rishi said, glancing over at me.

"We'll need provisions."

"And to take a little detour about twenty minutes out—lost souls galore. You need to show me that shadow thing you were talking about, Blake," Maeve said.

I turned in my seat and glanced at her as Rishi started the engine, and she turned the screen of her phone to show me a map with a mass of red dots moving around.

"Does your phone actually show lost souls?"

She smiled gleefully and nodded. "It's a little piece of technology created and honed in Abbadon. I helped myself to it before we left. Full deities are black. Original ones, right? And hybrids are gray."

"How does it work?" I asked, unable to grasp that my sister's smartphone could actually show us where dead people's souls were hanging out.

"It somehow taps into the electromagnetic field through satellite and pings it back to the phone. The deity who designed this actually works for the military as a scientist. See, some hybrids do keep their day jobs."

I laughed at the sheer genius of it and how much easier it would be to find the lost souls now. I'd yet to attempt the art of multiple-soul transference, or passing over souls en masse. But I knew that wouldn't help the lost souls. They needed to be repaired, healed, before they could be sent on their way, and the job seemed less daunting now with Maeve and her seriously amazing lost soul phone app.

"What's the name of the town?"

"Glorieta," she said.

I glanced at Rishi. "You down?"

He nodded. "As long as it doesn't take too long. I should probably take some time out for an hour and do my own collecting and passing, and I can't do that when I'm driving."

"Then to Glorieta it is," I said, leaning back and closing my eyes. The car grew silent, with the only sound being the faint, muffled noise from Shelby's music ringing in her deaf ears as she snored softly, and the drone of the tires hitting the road. I was starting to drift off, the surge of the scythe in the back still singing through me but at a manageable level, when my phone vibrated.

I opened my eyes and pulled it out of my pocket, noticing I'd gotten a text message. *Where are you?!! I'm calling the cops and reporting you as a missing person if I don't hear back from you in fifteen!*

Damn. Like I said before, living a double life was harder than it looked on TV. I didn't ask for this. But there was nothing to do except embrace my new life and try not to worry my dad too much along the way. The road lay out before us, winding and long, but the sun was shining and the song of the scythe and a rush of adrenaline surged through my veins. Rishi glanced at me and turned the dial knob on the radio, smiling at me and holding my gaze for a moment, a light of hope shining within his dark eyes.

I nodded, and he turned his eyes back to the road. I couldn't be angry with him any longer. He'd done what he had to do because he believed in something greater, and in that moment I did too.

I'm the Reaper's daughter, and I'm going to take back what's ours.

The End of Book I

ACKNOWLEDGMENTS

As I release my second book into the world, I have many people to thank for being a part of my writing journey. I'm especially excited for this book because I feel as if I have cast in my anchor to become a permanent fixture in the publishing world. I hope so, anyway.

First off, I'd like to thank my husband, Ron, and my son, Bryson. Sometimes I get lost in the digital world, neurotically checking Amazon and searching for reviews, but they always bring me back to reality. To them. My true loves.

My sister, Sheilah Randall, my first reader, critic, and fan. Her advice is invaluable, even when I might not like it. She continues to be my sounding board for my stories in fiction and in life.

To my mother, Jeanne Randall, who has always believed I'd be a published author someday, even if it took forever, and who offers free babysitting and much love and support to my entire family. Thank you for loving words and language and for passing that down to me.

Thank you to my father, Bill Randall, a fellow fantasy lover, for taking the time to work on my home office and helping to turn this room of my own into a space where creativity can be sparked and nurtured.

For Jen Pedrick, who is the inspiration behind Shelby's many different hair shades, and who has always been just as loyal of a friend.

To my sister-in-law Megan Mendolera. She's been a constant cheerleader, supporter, and friend. A true sister.

To all my family and friends who have supported me on my writing journey, thank you, thank you, thank you. It means the world to me every time I hear that one of you took the time to read my book. Much love.

Many thanks to Erin Latimer, who recently stepped into the role as my marketing manager. We rock business chats with side discussions on books and fandoms, and her enthusiasm, ideas, and direction already have me excited for the year to come.

For my editor, Bethany Root. We became best girls in grad school, and although we live many states apart, we have managed to stay in touch and share this writing journey together. Her editorial guidance, honesty, insights, and continued friendship are deeply appreciated.

To Shari Ryan, my cover designer and fellow author, who not only created and visualized the concept for my cover, but who also became my friend along the way.

I'd also like to thank Kristina Elliott, a longtime colleague and friend. She's been a cheerleader, fellow fantasy geek, and a trusted source of editorial support. Thank you for wanting to be a part of my characters' continued adventures.

Of course, I wouldn't be here without Jesse James Freeman, Katherine Sears, and Kenneth Shear, who all welcomed me in to the Booktrope family and agreed to publish my books, helping me to see a lifelong dream realized. Also, to Adam Bodendieck and other members on the production team. They are always willing to answer questions and are attentive to authors' needs despite our growing family. In a phrase, they rock.

This book was inspired by various influences, one of which was the flocks of crows that tend to hop around my yard and settle eerily into the tree outside my home office window, and the other was a short story I was editing by fellow Booktrope author Alex Kimmell. His story was about an incarnation of Death who decides to try online dating. So when the crows settled outside my window, the idea of Death personified was already in my head. Thank you for adding to the inspiration, Alex.

Finally, thank you to my readers. I still marvel that I'm finally able to say I have actual readers and fans. I write for all of you in hopes that I can truly offer you magic and adventure in new worlds.

www.ingramcontent.com/pod-product-compliance
Lightning Source LLC
Chambersburg PA
CBHW050512260626
47157CB00004B/1289